CONQUEST

Robbie Dorman

Conquest by Robbie Dorman

www.robbiedorman.com

ISBN-13: 978-1-7336388-0-7

Cover design by Bukovero

For Mom, Dad, and Kim.
This wouldn't exist without you.

July 1st

1

They needed to feed. Their burden demanded it.

The cattle were unsuspecting as the shapes moved, shadows at the edge of their vision. Their big, soft eyes caught only a glimpse of what was about to slaughter them.

They died fast. Ragged claws cut their throats as the shapes descended, ripping and tearing. The cows crumpled. The shapes gathered around, feasting on the warm meat.

One shape stood away from the rest. His distended form sat at peace, his breathing calm and fluid. The hunger was there, but controlled, pushed away and down. He watched as his brothers fed. No trucks, no glints of flashlights, no ranch hands tonight. They ate in peace.

In due time, one of his brothers would replace him and allow him to feed. A shape would come, their muzzle covered in drying blood, their distended torso heaving with the exertion of the kill, of the hunt, of the feast. They would take the watch, and return his courtesy. But not yet.

He pushed the hunger down and watched. Deep inside, it demanded to be fed, to be exercised. The hunter wanted to run loose. He pulled the leash with a practiced motion. It took him years to build the discipline, and he would not let it loose. Their burden demanded it.

A shape came to him, eyes and teeth glistening. They took his post, and he walked into the fray, the earth starting to grow saturated with the spilled blood. He moved in on one of the kills, the other shapes moving aside for him. He plunged into the flesh and swallowed, gulping down its mass, chewing through cartilage and connective tissue.

He gave the leash a little slack, and it took every inch he allowed. He fed.

The others were filled, their lust satiated. Their eyes followed him, watching him eat.

•

Miles away, The Pack settled into their campsite. Their bikes were lined up at the entrance of the camp, gleaming, the chrome reflecting the lantern light. The heat was heavy, the air dry and brittle, no wind to speak of. Shadow took stock. The Pack was eight strong now, and Shadow led them.

They loitered around the site. Abe, the first recruit, was reading with a penlight in his mouth. Shadow trusted Abe. He always backed Shadow's play. Tall and skinny, he had legendary endurance.

Kid, the newest member, sat by the fire while cleaning his fingernails with a pocket knife. He was handsome and charming, and his silver tongue had pulled their fat out of the fire more than a few times already.

They all had their habits, their routines. They needed them to lean on during the decades on the road.

Shadow sat in the middle, nearest the lantern. Jack sat next to him.

Shadow had pulled Jack out of the wilderness. Jack had the most in him, had come so far, grown so much. His plain white t-shirt was dirty, his hair matted, brushed back.

"I'm tired of cattle," said Jack, breaking the silence of the camp.

"There ain't much else out here," said Shadow. "Though we did pass some goats a while back. Might be able to find a bear or deer in the woods."

"That's not what I mean, and you know it," said Jack.

Shadow didn't look at Jack, but spoke to him directly, his voice hushed and gravelly.

"How many times, Jack? How many times do we have to talk about it?"

Jack looked at Shadow. Shadow's silver hair hung down his back, his gray scruff obscuring his face. He wore his riding leathers. He never wore anything else.

"Enough times for me to get a satisfactory answer," said Jack. "Look at us."

Shadow did, taking in the campsite, and his men. He gave them shelter from the world and taught them how to live.

"I see brothers," said Shadow, finally.

"We're vultures, Shadow," said Jack. He stood up. "You taught us to be scavengers. We pick at the edges. We take what won't be missed."

"It's our lot," said Shadow, his voice straining. He had

said it so many times. "It's our burden to bear."

"It doesn't have to be. We are so much *more* than them," asked Jack. "But we're *here*. Look at this. Another dirty pit."

"It's all we have, Jack," said Shadow. "I can't help how we were born." Jack had brought it up, time and time again. And in the end, he always listened to reason. Shadow made him understand. The world wasn't meant for them.

Jack stopped, and stared at Shadow. "I'm tired," he said. "It's been a long time, and I'm tired of it."

Shadow knew it, knew it had been leading to this. He'd hoped Jack would lead after he was gone. To hear that Jack didn't want to lead, wanted to quit when it got hard, made Shadow's guts ache, a stabbing hurt that came out of nowhere.

He looked to Abe, to Gunner for support. Everyone was listening, he knew. Little was said around here without someone listening. Abe would tell Jack to stay the course; Gunner would take him aside and talk him through it.

Neither moved, didn't even look in their direction. He understood it. They'd followed this path longer than Jack, with less complaints. Shadow would handle it.

"You can't just quit," said Shadow.

"I don't want to quit," said Jack. "I want you to see reason. There's room for change, Shadow."

"We will die, Jack," said Shadow. "Believe me, I know. They will hunt us down and slaughter us like those damn cows. It ain't fair, I know, but it's our life."

"You're right," said Jack. "It's not fair. And I won't do it anymore."

Goddamnit, Jack. Shadow looked at him, finally. His back was turned to him. His guts were aching. Jack would force his hand. He always challenged Shadow. It was part of why Shadow loved him. But Jack could not be allowed to leave.

There was no leaving The Pack.

"You can't leave, Jack," said Shadow, standing up. He gave the leash some slack. "You know that."

Jack turned on him, standing in front of the lantern, the haze obscuring the light. Jack was cast in shadow.

"I didn't say I was leaving," said Jack. "But you're right."

Shadow's mind turned, and he saw what was happening. He'd read everything wrong. The men turned to face him. Their silence wasn't giving Jack room to blow off steam. Their silence was agreement. He could feel Bark looming behind him without even glancing.

"We're tired of it," said Jack. "Too many years. I'm sorry."

Shadow glanced past Jack. The rest of them looked back. Smirks, grimaces, dead stares.

He met Abe's eyes last. Abe met his gaze briefly, and then dropped his vision. Shadow couldn't believe it.

"You with them?" Shadow asked.

"You can't fight the tides, friend," said Abe.

Shadow only nodded. His face contorted for a moment, but he pushed the feelings down, in control again. He looked to Jack. Abe moved back, disappeared into the darkness.

Jack looked to Bark behind him. "Hold him down."

Bark grabbed him from behind, his massive frame easily restraining Shadow's arms. He didn't struggle. He felt his will leave him. All these years. All of this, for nothing.

He felt the shape inside pull at the leash, but still he held it tight. He wouldn't let go now.

"Against the stump," said Jack. "Gunner."

Gunner had drawn a machete from a sheath on his bike,

and flipped it to Jack, who caught it out of the air with ease. It was sharp.

"It's the only way," said Jack.

"Please take care of what I built," said Shadow, Bark's frame on him from behind.

Jack brought down the machete and Shadow's head fell. Blood poured from his neck, seeping into the dirt.

"I'm going to make us better," said Jack, as he looked at the darkening soil.

2

Sheriff Heather Hill wiped the blood from her nose. The dry air was going to kill her, if the fires didn't.

She parked near the slew of fire department vehicles, and walked down the trail. The wildfires were still miles away, but the smoke obscured everything, the world turned gray. The dust of the trail floated up with every step. She reached to check her nose again. No blood.

Heather was tall, a hair over six foot, and her long strides carried her down the trail quickly. She'd run it a few times earlier in the year, before the fires reached the county. It had been beautiful, if a bit dry. So much had changed in a few short months.

She found Joe Coffey a ways down the trail, taking a quick breather and waiting for her. He was a short man, stout, and no doubt strong. He was nearing the age he'd have to retire from field duty. His face was honest, and at that moment covered in sweat and grime. He was dressed in his fireman's gear, his full helmet off and sitting next to him on top of a thermos of precious, ice-cold water. He looked miserable.

He stood up when he saw her, removing a glove to shake her hand. "Sheriff."

"Chief," Heather replied, taking his hand in hers. "How's it looking?"

"Like hell," he said. "Water?"

"You need it more than I do," said Heather.

"You're probably right," he said. He paused. "We're losing ground."

"How much?" asked Heather.

"Only a little right now," said Joe. "But we can't afford a little. The trees are fucking kindling. I've never seen it this bad."

Heather glanced at the forest. They stood tall, but with red leaves. They were dead. Work of the beetles coming from the west. Thousands of dead trees, and the hottest, driest summer on record.

"Fucking trees don't even have the common courtesy to fall down," said Joe. "Goddamn global warming."

"What's the plan?" asked Heather.

"Keep working," said Joe. "Not much else we can do. Try to cut a fireline up the way, but it hasn't fucking worked any-where else. Maybe it will here. My crew is dead tired and there's no end in sight. Fucking Happy Fourth of July. If I see someone lighting off fireworks—"

"Don't let JH hear you say that," said Heather.

"He'd have to leave his office for that," said Joe. "Good business sense won't help me out here."

"How much time do we have?" asked Heather.

Joe thought about that. He sipped his water. He looked at her.

"A week," said Joe. "At the current pace. But you know wildfires. Always predictable."

"Should we evacuate now?" asked Heather.

"I would have done it yesterday," said Joe. "There's nothing but dead trees between here and town. We gotta get those people out of there."

He looked past her, down the trail. "Goddamnit. Made a liar out of me."

"What?" she asked. A fast glance answered her question.

"Speaking of hell," said Joe, under his breath.

JH Bieter was walking down the trail, his loafers kicking up dirt with every step. His face was red, and he was starting to sweat through his suit. She hadn't told the mayor about her visit with Joe, but he'd found out anyway. JH always found out things he wanted to know. She suspected Buzz fed him information, which pissed her off royally. But Buzz was a good cop otherwise. And it was hard as hell to find good cops to work with in Conquest.

"Imagine seeing you here, Ms. Hill," said JH as he walked up to them, trying to keep his breath steady. His silver hair was already stuck to his head, rivulets running down his plump face. Heather could see his bald spot. She wondered if he realized that.

"Chief," said JH.

"Mr. Mayor," said Joe, with a curt nod.

"How's the good fight going?" asked JH.

"I was just telling the sheriff that she should probably evacuate Conquest. We probably have a week or so before the fire reaches the town, and there's only so much we can—"

"Evacuate Conquest?" asked JH, his voice cracking. "On Fourth of July weekend? I respect your opinion, Chief, but this is our biggest tourism weekend, fire or no, and kicking those people out of town just because of a little fire—"

"It's burned almost 10,000 acres. It's a miracle no has died," said Joe.

"And I'd like to keep it that way," added Heather.

"Of course, Ms. Hill, of course," said JH. "But there will be 50,000 people visiting our fine town this weekend. They will be spending lots of money. They will be paying sales tax, tax that pays our salaries, and funds our police force. I want that money in our coffers, to be clear. If they are forced to leave, they may never come back."

"They won't come back if they die inside a burning hotel, either," said Heather. "After a few dead tourists the town won't have to worry about them visiting ever again."

A look of disgust, of utter rage passed over JH's face in an instant and then disappeared, swallowed down. Heather saw it. JH looked away from her, toward Joe Coffey.

"Chief," said JH. "You said we have a week until the fire reached the town."

"Well yeah," said Joe. "But that's just an estimate—"

"A week is more than enough time. After Monday most of the people will have left, and then we can quietly announce an evacuation, one that won't disrupt most people's vacation plans," said JH, not even glancing at Heather.

"This isn't an inconvenience!" said Heather, her voice

echoing through the haze. "We could lose the damn town, and I think it'd be better if we didn't lose people along with it."

"Even more reason to not evacuate until absolutely necessary," said JH. "We need all the money we can get, in case the fire does reach us. And, unfortunately, you cannot evacuate without my consent, which you do not have." A small, polite smile grew on his face as he looked at her.

Her hands balled into fists. She swallowed her anger, forced her hands apart, and then walked away.

JH looked at Joe, the smug smile still on his face. "Women."

3

The office was dark and cold at 6 AM. James Bieter flicked on the lights.

He turned on his computer and started a pot of coffee while it booted up. The office would go through three pots a day. He'd drink one of the three.

Yesterday's receipts had been good. Business was up, year after year. Reports from the fire were on his second monitor. It was advancing. Things could never be simple.

He worked through his email, firing off replies to people's problems from yesterday. The other employees began to trickle in. The people who worked in the park checked into a separate office, so his remained quiet.

The office employees were almost all women. He made a point to hire women. He also made a point to get caught looking at them at least once or twice a day.

They didn't like him. It was necessary.

By mid-morning, his hands shook. He closed his doors and added whiskey to his coffee. His hands settled.

Marie, the office manager, delivered the mail at 11.

She handed him the normal assortment of bills and paperwork that he would look at before delegating them to the various people around the office. She also handed him a big manila envelope.

"This was in with the mail, but it didn't come from the post office," she said, shrugging.

"You look nice today," he said, a dark, flirtatious edge to his voice.

"Thanks," she said, giving a polite smile. She could never hide the discomfort in her eyes, though.

He opened the normal mail first, and quickly dispersed it. The envelope waited.

He dumped the contents on his desk. A thumb drive and a typed letter fell out. The letter was folded in half. He unfolded it.

James,

The thumb drive contains photos that show you for what you are. Clear evidence of you entering and leaving the Lion's Den, and various photos of you kissing other faggots. Even some of you getting pounded in the ass in that alleyway behind the hotel. The drive contains roughly one-third of the photos I have. In one week, I will send them to your father and post them online to all relevant news outlets, unless you wire $50,000 to #0260095-004.

One week.

James's body went cold. His heart pounded, and he could feel tears welling up in his eyes. He closed them until they receded. He was hyperventilating. Slow down, slow down. He drank the rest of the spiked coffee, and then got up to close his office door. He locked it for good measure.

He pulled the flask from his desk and took a long swig from it, the whiskey burning his throat as he swallowed. It helped. A little.

His heart was pounding, but he could control his breathing. His hands shook as he plugged the thumb drive into his computer. It auto-opened, and the screen showed row after row of preview images. He opened the first, and it was clearly him, open-mouth kissing another man in the parking lot of the Lion's Den.

The Lion's Den was a bar, attached to a hotel. It was a two-hour drive southeast, over the border in Montana. A lonely stop in the middle of nowhere, a gay bar, an open secret. The hotel served closeted men and truckers.

He'd first gone there a year ago. He'd had business in Missoula and the temptation had overridden his fear.

He stopped on the way back, and spent the night there. He met many men like himself, drank with them, and eventually had sex for the first time with a man, at age 37. Being there, with men like him—it was the first time in his life that he could breathe.

The man's name was Steven. Steven had a family in Montana. He was a farmer. He loved his wife and his children. He came to the Lion's Den four times a year, he said. James didn't know Steven's last name. None of them used their last names.

It was dangerous. They had warned James, his first time

visiting the bar. They gave him advice—about how to survive, about how to stay hidden. Most of it was easy. He had hidden his entire life. Performed for his father, for his co-workers, for his wife. Wearing a mask was second-nature.

He'd gone back twice more in the intervening year. These pictures were from his last visit.

It would destroy his life. His father would disavow him. He would lose his job, his wife. He would have nothing.

Who took them? Who sent the letter? It could be anyone. His father had plenty of enemies, most of whom would never admit to it. His mind went first to Sheriff Hill, but this wasn't like her. She kept her hands clean. It was why she clashed with his father, who never saw a pie he didn't want to stick his fingers in.

Could he trace the bank account? Maybe, but not without help, which meant revealing more than he wanted to. They would set up a dummy account, and then transfer it out. Could he find the truth in a week? Probably not, part of the reason for the deadline, he was sure.

Could he get a hold of $50,000? Yes. Between his personal and business accounts, easily. But someone would notice. If not Susan, then someone here.

If he paid, he'd just get bled dry. Whoever it was would take more and more money. It would always work. The threat would always work.

He wouldn't pay, consequences be damned.

One week.

He could run.

Or eat a bullet.

The phone rang, and he jumped. It was his father. He

took another shot from his flask and answered.

"Burns Mine Tourism Group, James Bieter speaking," he said, always his answer to the phone. It didn't mean anything anymore.

"James," said JH.

"Father," answered James.

"How's business?"

"Going well," he said. "It's up, year after year."

"Anything can be built upon a strong foundation," he said. He said it a lot. It was his go-to line whenever James even subtly intimated that he was better at business than his father.

"I'm not calling to chat," said JH. "I talked to your wife."

Christ.

"I called her, and when I asked about how you two were doing, she broke down in tears. She wouldn't discuss it with me, only said that she was trying to make it work."

Anger rose in James. *Using Susan to spy on me?*

"Would you mind explaining to me what is happening between you two, and how the fuck you're going to fix it?"

James hit his desk, hard. Everything on it shook.

"We're just going through a rough patch," he said. "We'll be okay."

"Fix it," he said. "Voters don't want divorcees as their next sheriff. If you're going to beat that cunt next November, you need a wife and a smiling baby."

"I never agreed to that," he said.

"Listen. I have gifted you with everything you've ever touched. I don't care what you have to do, but I want Susan happy and smiling the next time I see her. And make no mistake, you *will* be running for sheriff, or I will take everything back from you."

His father hung up, the dial tone heavy in James's ear.

4

"Welcome to the Burns Silver Mine! First discovered in 1871 by Charles Burns, it soon became the lifeblood of Conquest. Where you're standing was the entirety of the mine originally. The thousands of feet we'll be walking today were first dug out by Burns himself, and then the many men he hired to work the mine over the years. Please follow me," said Alice. The tour group gathered around her at the entrance of the mine. Her blond hair was almost luminescent in the stark white light of the lanterns that hung around the edges of the mine. Her fair skin completed the look, making her seem almost like a ghost.

Kyle and Kazuko Yamamoto followed Alice as she delved deeper into the mine. Her lantern lit the way as the tour group followed her closely. Kyle hung back from the group with his grandmother so he could translate.

Kyle translated Alice's initial spiel for Kazuko as they walked. The mine was musty, smelling old, and its cold, damp walls soaked any clothing that touched them. The group was happy to be inside, however, compared to the hot, smoky soup that awaited them once they left. Almost all of them had planned their vacation months in advance, and so they were forced to make due with the fires.

"<Thousands of men,>" said Kazuko. "<You mean the men who toiled for no money, broke their backs for the rich man who took everything.>"

"<Grandmother,>" said Kyle. "<Are you going to be like this everywhere we go?>"

"<I only want you to know the truth, young man,>" said Kazuko. "<These white people will lie to you.>"

"<Grandmother!>" he said sharply, under his breath.

They reached the next stop in the tour, where a small exhibit of different mining tools were set up.

"The pickaxe, the hammer, even dynamite were all tools used by the miners of the time. For the first three decades of operation, the mine was incredibly successful, with literal tons of silver pulled from the mountainside. Conquest was originally the name of the mine, but the title grew to include both the town, and the mountain that surrounds it. Charles Burns's sons took control of the mine, but dark times lay ahead for Conquest."

Alice stepped aside and let the group look over the assortment of tools. Kyle translated again for his grandmother.

"<A town called Conquest,>" said Kazuko. "<How subtle.>"

"<I don't know,>" said Kyle. "<It is quite impressive.>"

"<Yes, quite an impressive scar upon the Earth,>" said Kazuko. "<What an amazing rape of Mother Nature.>"

"Christ," he said, sighing.

Alice led them deeper.

"As the century turned, the three Burns brothers started expansion of the mine. Its location made it difficult, and just as their investment started paying off, the mine dried up. Slowly but surely, the Burns' fortune did as well. They searched for other sources nearby, but all their effort was fruitless. The town's economy faded as the silver stopped flowing. People left for greener pastures, and Conquest, for a time, was just another small mountain town—a stop for truck drivers and for mountaineers who wanted to climb all three peaks surrounding the town."

"<The tour guide is pretty,>" said Kazuko. "<You should ask her out.>"

"<I'm not going to ask out the tour guide,>" said Kyle. "<It would be incredibly rude.>"

"<She doesn't have a ring. She is well spoken,>" said Kazuko. "<You'll make a good woman out of her.>"

"<Please, Grandmother,>" said Kyle. "<Can we have one vacation where you don't accost a nice woman on my behalf?>"

"<You need a wife,>" said Kazuko. "<I want grandchildren.>"

"<I have plenty of time to provide you grandchildren,>" said Kyle.

"<But perhaps I do not,>" said Kazuko. Kyle looked at his grandmother in the light of the lanterns. Recently, she'd brought up her own mortality more and more, but she looked immortal. She was a hair more stooped than she used to be, but she was a stone, unbreakable. She carried a cane, but it was just another accessory, now acceptable at her age. She would outlive him *and* his grandchildren.

They reached the end of the tour, as deep in the mine as they would go. They walked hundreds, if not thousands, of feet into the side of the mountain. Kyle was not claustrophobic, but he couldn't help but feel uncomfortable.

"The mine continues much farther, but this is our last stop. The mine laid fallow for decades, as the town of Conquest shrunk. It changed hands multiple times, each new owner thinking they would be the ones to revitalize the mine and the town both. They all failed. Until, that is, a scant twenty years ago, when Mr. JH Bieter, a local businessman, bought the deed to the mine, and instead of trying to mine it built up the historical village around it, creating an attraction that became the center of the Conquest Revitalization Project. Mr. Bieter is now the mayor of Conquest, and the town has never been more successful."

"<No conflicts there,>" said Kazuko. "<The owner of the town's most important business also running the town.>"

Kyle did not object, because he agreed it sounded shady, but small towns worked like that. He missed Seattle.

"Now, a demonstration, one we do at the end of every tour. The mine today is well lit by electric lanterns, safe and reliable. In the mine's heyday, however, it was lit by gas lanterns, either hung on the ceiling, or carried by hand."

She opened up a small cabinet nearby, and pulled out a gas lamp. She lit it, and then hung it from the low ceiling. Finally, she pulled out the walkie talkie that was holstered on her belt.

"Mack, kill the lights," she said, and after a short pause

the electric lanterns turned off, leaving them in the dim glow of the single lantern. It was spooky.

"Now imagine, that you are miles deep in the mountain, and the gas runs out."

She opened up the front window in the lantern and blew out the flame, leaving them in darkness.

"Don't worry, for us, the lights are just a call away. But for a moment, I want you to stand here in the darkness and put yourself in the lonely miner's position. You are miles deep, and there is no light. What do you do?"

Everyone was silent, and Alice let the silence linger as the pitch-black darkness enveloped them. Kyle felt his grandmother slide her arm through his.

"If you stood in the darkness long enough, you would start to hear drums. Boom, boom, boom. There are multiple stories of lost miners and cavers who heard the drums and lost their minds. But what they were really hearing was the sound of their own heartbeat."

Alice was silent again, for a moment. Then the sound of the walkie talkie could be heard again.

"Mack, the lights," she said, and the cold, white light of the electric lanterns returned. Kyle smiled and looked at his grandmother. She smiled back.

They left the mine, the end of the tour coincidentally leading them directly into the gift shop, full of knickknacks and touristy garbage. Kazuko held on to Kyle's arm as they perused tiny statues of the town's mascot, a cute wolf puppy named Yappy. Kyle was looking at a shelf full of novelty beer coozies, his grandmother subtly tugging at his arm, when he realized they stood in front of Alice, the tour guide, who had stuck around to answer questions before her next group set out into the mine.

Kazuko touched Alice's arm and smiled, projecting all the matronly charm she could. She pulled Kyle closer to her.

"<Ask her if there are any resources in town that talk about the Japanese influence on the history and creation of the town,>" said Kazuko.

"<What?>" asked Kyle, confused.

"<Ask her, and tell her that I want to know,>" said Kazuko. Kyle, slightly befuddled, looked at Alice and smiled as wide as he could.

"Hi. My grandmother doesn't speak English, and she wanted to know if there were any resources in town about any possible Japanese influence on the history and creation of the town?" he asked.

Alice smiled at Kazuko, and then turned back to Kyle. "I'm sorry, there's not a lot, and it's an aspect of the historical village that needs more representation. The Japanese were an important part of the culture, but largely because of negative reasons. The local white population mostly ran them off and set anti-Japanese laws in place that kept the immigrants segregated. That's before we get to the largely anti-Japanese sentiment centered around World War Two and the internment camps," Alice answered.

Kyle translated for his grandmother. Kazuko nodded appropriately at the answer, smiling again at Alice.

"<Ask her if she does freelance tours of the town,>" said Kazuko.

"<What? No,>" said Kyle.

"<Do it,>" said Kazuko. "<Say that I would love a tour guide who won't whitewash history. Tell her I'll double her rate for her help.>"

Kyle's jaw tensed involuntarily, but then he regained himself, smiling again at Alice.

"I apologize, but she insisted I ask if you are available for freelance local tours of the town. Someone who is culturally sensitive is important to her. She says she'll pay double your normal salary for your time," said Kyle. He could feel himself wincing, getting ready for the discomfort he was undoubtedly causing this young woman.

Alice instead smiled at Kazuko again. "I couldn't take her money. How about this—I work the late shift tomorrow. I'll join you two for brunch tomorrow and give you the lowdown on the best things in and around town to see, and I'll answer any questions she has. Only payment I ask will be the cost of the meal."

Kyle translated for Kazuko. She smiled, no facade or projection present.

"<See, she is perfect,>" said Kazuko. "<Tell her it's a date.>"

Kyle resisted rolling his eyes. "She thinks that's a great idea."

"Awesome," said Alice. "What's your number?" Kyle gave her his number, and then she texted him. "Now you have mine. Give me a call later and we can schedule everything."

"Great," said Kyle. He extended his hand. "Kyle, by the way. This is my grandmother, Kazuko."

"Nice to meet you," said Alice. "Alice. I've got to get back to work, but I'll talk to you soon."

Alice walked back towards the queuing area for the next tour group, leaving Kyle and Kazuko in the gift shop.

"<What have you gotten us into this time?>" asked Kyle.

"<I've still got it,>" said Kazuko, cackling.

5

Arthur Stone hammered the cold silver into a scalloped shape, his heavy hammer pounding it flat with every blow.

A small crowd watched Arthur as he worked. He tapped on the piece for several more minutes, and then slid it back into the oven nearby. The oven was hot, painful to be near, but Arthur showed no effect. The crowd tended to move along, especially on summer days like today.

He turned to the crowd, removing some of the safety gear and revealing himself to them for the first time. Arthur was a big man, over six feet tall, with broad shoulders and a bald head, a thick white goatee on his face. A healthy amount of sweat covered his head, and he grabbed a nearby towel to wipe himself. He looked over the crowd.

"Any questions?" he asked, his voice loud, but not as

loud as you'd expect. He had to force himself to project to his visitors.

"You were hammering that piece of silver, and then you put it back into the oven. I thought it was the other way around," said one man.

"You shape silver cold," said Arthur. "It's not like steel or iron. You heat it afterward so that it'll soften and not crack after you work it some more."

"Were there silversmiths in Conquest back in the boom years?" asked another. Some people had already filtered out, the heat too much for them. Arthur didn't take it personally.

"There were a couple," said Arthur. "Mostly people making jewelry. Burns diversified how he sold his silver. Jewelry naturally returned more than silver bars by weight because of the work put into it."

A small boy stood up front, staring at the hammer, the oven, and the tools lying around, his eyes wide. He raised his hand.

"Yes, young man?" said Arthur, smiling. Kids were the best part of the job.

"Do you make any weapons with silver?" he asked, shy and excited at the same time.

"I get that question a lot," said Arthur. "No, no silver weapons. Silver is a relatively soft metal, like gold, so it wouldn't be very useful in combat. A steel weapon would smash right through it. The silver doesn't hold an edge."

"Then what's that?" asked the boy, pointing up near the ceiling.

"You caught me," said Arthur, feigning surprise. "That is a silver sword. But it's only for decoration."

"Can I hold it?" he asked, but his mother grabbed him

and started pulling him away.

"I'm sorry, son, *I* don't even get to hold it," he said as the boy was dragged away, the mother looking back at the big silversmith with an apologetic look on her face.

After the piece had heated thoroughly he pulled it out and let it cool while he hammered on the next. The process was firm, reliable. He lost himself in it, occasionally pausing to answer questions from his visitors whenever he took a break. He pounded the silver. The hammer was a part of him. All of his tools were, and when he used them his mind was free, clear. No worries, no loneliness, no fear. Just the tools and the metal.

He looked up after a time and the crowd was gone. This part of the historical village was closed for the day, closed for nearly an hour. He hadn't noticed. He realized he wasn't alone. Heather was there, leaning on the wall. He got up, removing the safety gear and wiping his face.

"How long have you been there?" he asked.

"Not long," said Heather. "I was beginning to worry you were going to work all night."

"I was somewhere else," he said.

"Yeah, I know," said Heather. Something was up with her. She wouldn't have stopped in unless something was wrong.

"You okay?" he asked. She needed to vent about something. He knew it.

"I'm…" she said. "I'm going to explode."

"Don't explode," he said. "I'd hate to have to clean everything."

"You're not funny," she said. "I'm gonna kill JH. That patronizing asshole."

"What is it this time?" he asked. Heather started pacing,

her fists balled.

"The same as it's been for weeks now. The damn fires. God damn JH. God damn him."

"What did he do?"

"He's stuck his damn head in the sand. This goddamn town could burn to the ground and all he'd care about is if he got his money out," said Heather. Her arms were shaking.

Her arms were shaking. There was so much blood. He couldn't fathom there being that much blood in a little girl. Her father, her brother, were dead next to her. Her arms were cratered and split, rips, tears, an imploded field of destruction. He was afraid to touch her. Her arms shook, trembled, the blood pouring out of her. Keep your eyes open, he said. Don't give in now.

She was on the verge of tears. She stopped pacing, unclenched her fists, and forced the tears back down.

Her arms had barely worked afterward. Stitches, reconstructive surgery, tendons replaced, bones reset with plates, and endless hours of physical therapy. He had been her companion through hell, after the adoption went through. She always wore long sleeves now. Even in this heat.

She sat down, breathing deep. He put his arm around her.

"Joe Coffey says we have a week. Maybe. Then the fire hits the town."

"They can't stop it?" he asked. They'd stop it. Joe was a good man, a good fireman. It wasn't the first fire, and it wouldn't be the last.

Heather was quiet. "This one feels different," she said, finally.

"And we can't evacuate the town before Fourth of July

weekend," said Arthur.

"Bingo," said Heather.

Arthur hated politics. Shaping silver made sense. You had the metal, the fire, the hammer. Simple interactions. Men weren't that easy. He stayed out of it.

"You just got to keep trying. Change the culture," said Arthur. He believed it. Lead by example. She tensed at his words, and then pulled away and stood up. *Damn, wrong answer.*

"How long will that take?" she asked. "How many years will I have to sit here and be treated like a child? How much of my life do I pour into this place?"

"I can't answer that," said Arthur.

"JH owns half the town, and the other half works for him," said Heather. "I can't fight that."

She didn't say anything else, but he could hear the implication. He'd worked for JH, for years now. She looked at him, but he didn't have an answer.

"Why are we still here?" she asked.

An easy answer didn't come to him, only a knot of dread deep inside that pulled at him, tears threatening to well up in his eyes.

"You're better than him. Leaving won't help. Staying and fighting will."

"But will it? What am I fighting for? A tourist town in the mountains? I'm the Hill girl, the girl that fought wolves to them. Always will be. I try to make a goddamn administrative decision and,they smile and they nod and they ignore me. Or they take my idea and call it theirs." She was nearly yelling now.

He wished Emilia was here. She would know what to say.

She spoke to him sometimes. Usually late at night, when he really needed her. She wasn't here now, though. *You're on your own, you big softie.*

"This is a hill I don't want to die on anymore."

She didn't say anything else, but he could hear it anyway. "I'm only here because of you." *You're keeping her here.* She could live in Missoula, or Spokane, or even Seattle or Portland. Anywhere besides a podunk mountain town that will never let a woman be more than what she is now.

"You don't have to stay on account of me," he said. It hurt to say, but he said it anyway.

She shook her head, sighing, but saying nothing. She wouldn't leave him. He knew that.

"I can't leave," he said, his voice soft.

"I know, Dad," she said. She was calm again. She never stayed angry for long. She kissed him on the forehead and left.

6

Alice Ames' shift was over, and she wanted to go home.

Instead, she was in the office. The historical village's office was tucked away, a nondescript building among a village of recreations. It housed the support staff for the village, and Mr. James Bieter had asked Alice to stop in at his office before she went home for the day.

She went home at six, and the support staff went home at five. James was alone in the office. And now she was alone with him.

Every woman who worked for James had a story.

"He called me 'girl.' We're the same age."

"He touched my shoulder every time we talked."

"He asked me out for drinks. We're both married."

Alice had never noticed anything odd about James's behavior toward her. He was her boss, and he sometimes frustrated her, but all of her bosses had frustrated her. As far as she knew, she was just another employee to him.

He had never harassed her in any way, but she believed those women. Where there's smoke, there's fire.

The women would take cigarette breaks together, or eat lunch at the small picnic tables behind the office. They'd congregate, and gossip, and whisper about how they'd avoided James's last clumsy overture. He'd walk by, and the subject would suddenly change.

Sometimes a woman would quit, tired of his behavior. He was in charge. His dad was the mayor. He didn't *have* to change, and so he didn't.

Most of them didn't quit. They soldiered through, and took it as a part of the job. They deflected, they avoided him, and they warned the other women.

Alice knew of one that had tried to report him. It was before her time, when she was still in middle school. The woman had gone to the sheriff, and reported James for sexual assault. He had pinched her ass as she left his office one day, and it was the breaking point.

Old Sheriff Cochbrin had smiled for her, and placated her, but when she'd said she meant to press charges, he suddenly questioned her, challenged her. No way James could have done that, he said. And even if he did, it was harmless. The woman had left, no charges filed.

If you asked her grandmother, who knew both James and JH Bieter, who went to church with both of them—and almost certainly voted for JH for mayor—she had never heard of such a thing. Such a ghastly, awful rumor. Why would you burden a good man with that? That girl was probably asking for it.

Alice went into the office knowing all of that, yet walked in anyway. She needed her paycheck.

She walked up to his office door, already open. She rapped on the door, poking her head through.

"You wanted to see me?" she asked.

"Yeah, Alice, come have a seat," he said. James was behind his desk. You could see the systems of order underneath all his clutter. His brown hair was thinning, and you could start to recognize his dad in him. He tried to hide the spare tire around his waist that he couldn't lose. Everyone noticed.

She sat down, smoothing out her uniform unconsciously. A kid had spilled some soda on her earlier, and the stain stood out.

"Don't worry, it's nothing bad," he said. Her face must have looked grim. Getting called into the office at the end of shift Friday was not a good sign.

"Melanie has a lot of good things to say about you," said James.

"That's very nice of her," said Alice. Melanie was a good boss, in that she mostly just left them alone and let them do their jobs. They ran tours through a mine. It wasn't rocket science.

"How do you feel about working in the office?" asked James.

"What kind of work in the office?" asked Alice.

"Melanie has too much on her plate," said James. "We've grown too much. She needs help, and she suggested you. You'd be an assistant manager, so you'd work directly below Melanie, help train new guides, plus you'd be doing logistical stuff that she doesn't have time for anymore. You might work the occasional tour when we need it, but you'd be inside 95% of the time."

"That'd be great. I'm definitely interested," said Alice. A promotion. It raised a new set of problems in Alice's mind, but she pushed them away. A promotion was a promotion.

"Will I be getting paid more?" she asked.

"The most important question," said James, smiling. "You'll be salaried, start at 38,000 a year."

She took home 27.5 last year, working full time.

"Where's the dotted line?" she asked.

"No signature necessary," said James. "After the holiday weekend, you'll start training with Melanie. Your paycheck will reflect the change the week after."

"Awesome," said Alice. All her worries had been for nothing. Out of the heat, into the air conditioning. A bigger paycheck.

"Have any more questions for me?" he asked.

"Um, can I have this week's paycheck?" she asked.

"Oh, of course," he said. He opened a desk drawer and grabbed it. He held it out to her, the envelope hanging in the air between them. "I'm glad you're taking the position, Alice. We'll all get to know you better. I was wondering—do you want to go out and celebrate?" he asked. "Tonight?"

Her stomach dropped, and she could feel her head getting hot. He stood over her, a half smile plastered on his face, his eyes wide and charmless.

"Just the two of us?" she asked.

She reached out to take her paycheck. Her thumb and finger grabbed it, and pulled. He wasn't letting go.

"It would be tonight, yes," said James. "Everyone else is

busy with their Fourth of July plans."

"I don't think that's a good idea, Mr. Bieter," said Alice.

"Please, you can call me James," he said. "And I always like to take out employees for a drink when they're promoted."

"I shouldn't," said Alice. She still held the envelope, but she'd have to yank it out of his hand if she wanted it. His eyes still staring at her, though she was unable to meet his gaze.

"Why not?" he asked. "Just a friendly drink. Nothing sinister."

"I don't want to be out too late," she said. "I've got a long shift tomorrow."

"Only one drink," he said, his voice pleading. "I promise. Just one drink, and then you can go home and rest for tomorrow."

All she wanted was the paycheck and to go home. He'd just given her a promotion. What would happen if she turned him down?

This is what they whispered about.

She jumped as the room was filled with Taylor Swift. Her phone. *Oh thank God.* She pulled it from her pocket and looked at the screen. It was the tourist with the grandma from today. It could have been Satan himself and Alice *still* would have answered with joy.

This was her chance. She flashed a quick look of apology at James and pulled the envelope out of his hand with a quick yoink. "Sorry, I have to take this. My mom. Have a good night, Mr. Bieter."

She stood up and walked out of the office without a second glance. She answered the phone. "Hi Mom, just give me one second."

As she stepped outside, the door closed behind her, the smoke embracing her. She could breathe again.

"Sorry about that," said Alice. "Kyle, right?"

"Yes," he said. "I thought I had a wrong number for a second."

"Just had to get out of a situation," she said.

"Just calling to work out the details for tomorrow."

"Right, of course."

Her heart was racing, but the tension that had been building inside of her was finally starting to ebb. She could feel an eye twitch, and suddenly she realized that she *did* want a drink. Something to take the edge off. She didn't want to be alone.

"Where do you recommend for brunch?"

"About that," she said. "What are you doing tonight?"

•

When Alice left the office, James was alone again. She didn't see James collapse into his chair, and she didn't see him suddenly rise up and slam his door shut in frustration. No one did. And no one saw him grab the flask from his desk and take a long swallow.

7

Susan Bieter worked in the kitchen. Everything would be perfect.

The oysters cooked in the oven, and the salad only needed to be dressed and topped. She took out a red wine the internet said paired beautifully with both. The pasta was ready to drop whenever James called, and it'd be out and covered with olive oil and Parmesan by the time he got home.

She had gotten a new dress in the mail and it fit like a glove, which made her very happy. She would slip into it right before he got home and surprise him. He would love it on her. Red, strapless, a retro pin up that made her blond hair pop. Showed a little too much cleavage to wear in public, but it was fine just for him at home.

Susan walked through the house a final time. She had

mopped the floors, cleaned the bathroom and kitchen, and laundered all the sheets. Neat and tidy.

James should be calling any minute.

It was nearing 7 o' clock. He was usually home by now. There were no business dinners, or getting drinks. He'd be home soon. She knew it.

They had been high school sweethearts. He was different from the other guys. He had a car, for one. A new one. A big Lincoln Navigator. It was impressive in the school parking lot. He had money, from his dad, but that wasn't the only thing. He was driven, even then. He had been class president and valedictorian. James had direction while all the other guys had been happy to smoke weed and play video games.

She hated describing high school to people. She had been a cheerleader. She was part of the popular crowd, but hadn't felt that way then. She felt watched. And hated.

James was above it all. He wasn't the cutest, or the funniest, but wasn't afraid of the future. When they started dating, he'd talked with certainty about what was going to happen to them. He would take control of the mine from his father. He would build on it, make it better, make it more successful. They would get married. They'd have a big house with a big plot of land. They'd have two boys, and their boys would go to the same schools they went to, and eventually inherit the business. They'd take his name and carry on the legacy of their grandfather and father.

He'd been mostly right. JH had run for mayor, and given up the business to James. They got married in a beautiful ceremony at Conquest's biggest church. She had cried and cried. That was 17 years ago, to the day. They'd bought a big house, with a big backyard.

He wasn't right about everything. No boys followed. No children at all.

The noise of lock-in-key could be heard from the front door. James was home. He hadn't called.

Susan scrambled to the kitchen and dropped the pasta in the boiling water. It would be out soon enough. The oysters needed just five more minutes. She walked to the front door. James came in, his eyes tired.

"Hi, sweetie," she said, hugging him hard. "How was your day?"

"Busy," he said. His breath smelled like mints. To cover up the whiskey.

"I've got a special dinner almost ready," she said. "Fifteen minutes and it will be all set."

"Okay," he said. No reaction. He walked past her, down the hall, into the bedroom. He disappeared into the dark, and then into the bathroom.

Susan watched him go for a moment, and then turned back into the kitchen. Everything would be perfect. She pulled out the oysters. She had baked them on rock salt. She removed the oysters from the salt, moved the salt over to the serving dish, and then put the oysters back on top of it. She'd never made it before, but it looked like the cheese and breadcrumbs had browned perfectly. She dressed the salad, and topped it after mixing. She pulled the pasta from the water, and plated the noodles. She coated them with the most expensive olive oil they sold in Conquest, and then grated fresh Parmesan on top.

The dining room table was set. They never got to use it, and she was excited. She lit the two candles, and then brought all the food to the table. It looked perfect. She grabbed a quick picture for Instagram.

She walked back into the bedroom. He was sitting on the edge of the bed, with his shoes off, staring at his phone. He clicked it off as she approached.

"Dinner's ready," she said. "It's on the dining room table. I just need the bedroom for a second."

"Why?" he asked.

"I want to get ready for dinner," she said, and shooed him out of the room. He rolled his eyes as he walked out. She closed the door and changed into her new dress. She even put on her black heels, long neglected.

She walked back into the dining room on her high heels, her pace deliberate so she wouldn't fall. James was at the table, looking at the food.

"Happy anniversary!" she said, smiling at him.

He looked at her, confused. "Oh, right. Happy anniversary." Nothing else. He might be slurring his words, but she wasn't sure. *Oh James, what is happening to you?*

She sat down across from him. "Dig in," she said.

"What are those?" he asked, gesturing towards the oysters.

"Oysters Rockefeller," she said. "They're oysters with spinach and melted chees—"

"I'm not eating that," he said. Her heart went cold.

"You like oysters," she said. "We ate them at the wedding."

"My dad likes oysters," he said. He was definitely slurring. "It's the only reason we had them."

"You can eat the pasta and salad, then," she said. She wrung her hands under the table. "They're okay, right?"

"Yeah, sure," he said.

They ate, the table quiet. First time eating alone together in months.

"Do you like my dress?" she asked.

"Yeah, looks nice," he said. He had finished his pasta and salad. He was looking at his phone.

"Would it kill you to talk to me?" asked Susan, finally. "To make some effort?"

He put his phone down, and grabbed and threw the plate of oysters. The rock salt spilled all over the floor. The oysters splattered, the melted cheese sticking to the floor and walls. Susan cowered in her chair. She started to cry.

"What do you want me to say?" asked James, standing, speaking loudly, but never yelling. "You want effort? How about the 60 hours of work a week I've put in for the last 15 years? How I've grown the business, far beyond what my father ever did. Hello, Susan, how are you? The big house I bought us sure is clean. Good job! I sure as hell never get a 'good job'. I still come home to goddamn oysters. My own wife doesn't even know me."

She was openly weeping now. "I wanted to make something special," she said, her voice wracked by the tears.

"Don't you dare cry," he said.

He stood, staring at her, waiting for a response. One didn't come. Susan sat at the table, her face buried in her hands. James walked into the bedroom, put on his shoes, and then left, slamming the door behind him.

Susan cried.

8

Runt was the tip of the spear and he was riding into Conquest.

At least that was what Jack had told him. "You're the scout. You're reconnaissance. You're the tip of the spear." Rah-rah bullshit to try and get him excited about working while the rest of them got to hunt. Meet the new boss, same as the old boss. Jack, Abe, Bark, Kid, Gunner, Beast, all out hunting, and he was stuck scouting. Bullshit, is what it was.

At least Shadow was dead.

He remembered when Shadow had first approached him. He'd just gotten out of prison. Eight years on assault and battery. Would have gone right back in if he hadn't run into Shadow.

Runt was short. His high school growth spurt got him all

the way to 5'5", and it was really only 5'4 1/4". He had a chip on his shoulder, and that was before the change. Runt was out of control.

Shadow had seemed real cool at the time. First time he'd met another like him, which went a long way. Shadow never did tell him how old he was, but he once talked about the Civil War, and his story sounded first-hand. Shame he had to die. The group had outgrown him.

Shadow had known how to control the change. Said he was self taught, and Runt believed him. He was an animal before he met Shadow. It bled into everything. He didn't believe in inner peace bullshit, but he knew when something worked, and what Shadow taught, worked.

When you've been out of control your whole life, someone putting you back in it is mighty charming. He had described it back then to Gunner as a miracle, and he still thought it was.

Jack came to him first. He was the second-oldest recruit. Abe was the oldest, but Jack was smart. Smarter than any of them, and he saved 'ole Abe for last.

Runt had asked him, point blank, "You want me to help you kill the man who taught me a miracle?"

Jack knew exactly what to ask. "How much time was that worth to you? A decade? Two?"

Runt had been with Shadow for nearly fifty years. "I get it."

"And with all the freedom he gave you, how much has he taken away since?"

That made him think. How many times had Shadow told him no? How many times had Shadow told him that peace is the only choice, even after some motherfucker earned himself a beating? How many cows had he had for fucking dinner?

So Shadow was dead, and Runt was scouting ahead for The Pack. He seldom got to ride alone. The wind roared past him. This goddamn smoke could fuck off, though. Fucking fires.

The road curved between peaks, rivers, and lakes. A beautiful ride if he saw any of it. It was already dark, and the smoke made everything past 20 feet invisible.

His motorcycle roared down the road, and he started seeing signs of civilization. Conquest was out in the middle of nowhere, which he guessed was some of its charm. The brochure at their last stop advertised "Disconnect in Conquest" and "Travel Back in Time." These motherfuckers loved their nostalgia vacations. Runt remembered the past. It fucking sucked.

The highway split in two, and Runt followed the road to the right, into Conquest. The lone paved road was the only way in or out of town. Runt followed it for ten minutes on his bike, a slew of people heading out. Fires chasing 'em off. The vast forest to his left stood as a barrier between the rest of the world and Conquest. He could see three peaks that surrounded the town in the distance. More natural defenses.

As hard as it was to get there, coming into town couldn't be more accomodating. The welcome sign read "Conquest: The Best of America's History," and there were signs placed everywhere in town, for parking, for a historical village, for bars and restaurants. American flags flew all over the main drag, a giant billboard advertising a fireworks show on July 4th. There was a recent addition to the billboard: "Cancelled due to risk of fire."

Still, plenty of people milled about, even with the air filled with smoke. They were on their vacation, goddamnit, and no fires were gonna stop them. A part of him admired them. Stupid motherfuckers.

He cruised all the way down the main drag, a long strip of hotels and bed and breakfasts greeting him at the end of the road before it looped back around through the side of town that hugged the base of the mountain.

He followed it around to where the locals lived. Plain apartment buildings, small houses. He eventually passed the historical village, closed for the night. The sheriff's office was right nearby, and a deputy was standing outside, smoking a cigarette. Runt gave him a gentle wave and wide smile, and the deputy just stared at him. Fucking pigs.

He finished his circuit of the town. He was starving. Resentment rose in his mind when he realized his brothers were hunting at that very moment. *Hold on, Runt.*

He had chosen the name Runt. They all chose their names, their true names, their Pack names. Shadow had sold it as a true identity, one that was at peace with their dual natures, one they used in brotherhood. Runt hated his real name. That was enough for him. A new name, a new life.

His father had called him Runt. He had been a big man. Beat the shit out of Runt, over and over again, until Runt ran away at fourteen.

Shadow had always taught peace, made it a condition of his education. As soon as Runt learned how to control the change, he'd gone home and found his father.

He died screaming.

Runt spotted a dive bar called "Sally's" at the back end

of a block and wheeled his bike over to it. Jack could wait on his report. He could get some food and a couple drinks, relax for a bit, take in the local nightlife. Reconnaissance. Tip of the spear.

Runt sat at the bar, nursing his fourth whiskey. He'd eaten two burgers, and was thinking about ordering a third. He was *still* starving. He had slowed himself down as much as he could, but eventually the taxman comes, and you gotta pay the bill.

The whiskey was actually having an effect, and that's how he knew he was hungry. It felt nice, though, and so he delayed ordering another burger. He could feel the warmth flow through him, and it was nice to be on his own for once. *Can't remember the last time I went to a bar by myself.*

This was a nice place, despite the big bartender, Tom, looking at him like he was a leper. Brought him his whiskey fast enough, and Runt tipped him well. When else did he get to spend his pocket money?

If this was a taste of life with Jack running things, Runt couldn't be happier that Shadow was dead. He drank the rest of his whiskey, and motioned to the bartender for a drink. The big fucker walked over.

"You want another? That'll be five in 90 minutes," he said.

"I can handle myself, boss," he said. And Runt surely could. Tom didn't say a word, just eyed him some more before grabbing another glass, dropping a single ice cube in it, and pouring the single malt over top of it.

Runt paid the man, and drank his drink. The bar was pretty busy, and Runt almost felt normal again. His eyes bounced around the room, scoping out every single person in it. Local. Local. Local. Tourist, tourist. Local, local, local.

Local *and* tourist. Hmm. He could see the locals' eyes glance over him and then dismiss him in the same motion. He was just another biker, his leathers giving him away.

A girl and some Asian kid on a date got up to play pool. His eyes lingered on her. Young, blonde, in a sun dress. It clung to her and he stared. She glanced at him as they walked by, but he didn't stop looking. Suppose he was starving in more ways than one.

9

"<I told you, you have charm,>" said Kazuko.

"<I don't have charm, Grandmother. I have a pushy grandma,>" he said, his back to her as he slid gel through his hair. It took a metric ton of the stuff to keep his hair down.

"<A friendly brunch tomorrow turned into a date tonight,>" she said. She was flipping through the channels on the hotel TV. "<I did not make that decision. She did.>"

"<It's not a date,>" he said. "<We're just getting a drink.>" He said that, but he wasn't sure of it. It was a strange turn. He considered himself handsome enough, and he was in good shape, but there must be something more to it than that.

"<Oh yes, just drinks,>" she said. "<That's what I told

your grandfather. And then your father popped out.>"

"<I didn't need to know that,>" he said. He finally got his hair to look okay, although his cowlick was still standing up. He squeezed out more gel.

"<I may be old, but I am not dead,>" she said.

"<That's the way I like you, Grandmother,>" he said. His hair felt plastered on, but it was all in one place.

"<If you need the room later, just give me the high sign and I can go for a long walk,>" she said.

"<First, ew. Second, no,>" he said.

"<I just want you to have some fun, Kyle,>" she said. "<You are just like your father. All work and no play…>"

"<Yes, yes, I know,>" he said. Shaved, showered, with his hair as good as it was gonna get. His green eyes looked back at him in the mirror. He wore his nicest jeans and a button down with the sleeves rolled up. He was ready. It was just drinks, no need to worry. He tried to tell that to the knot in his stomach.

"<I'm serious,>" said Kazuko. "<Come here. Sit beside me.>" He took one last look in the mirror and took the spot next to her on the bed.

"<Why do you think your father moved here?>" she asked.

"<To find opportunity in America,>" he said, delivering the same answer his father had told him so many times. Whenever Kyle slacked off in school, whenever he wanted to skip soccer practice, whenever he wanted to go out instead of study, the familiar refrain rang out. "<I came to America to find opportunity, and now my only child is squandering it.>"

"<That is what he says,>" she said. "<But it is not the

truth.>"

"<He came to America to get away from your grandfather,>" she said. Kyle had only met his grandfather once, when he was a child, on his first trip to Japan with his family. Kyle remembered sitting on his lap while he chain smoked. He remembered his closet full of suits. He remembered very little else.

"<I loved your grandfather with all my heart. I still do. But he was relentless, driven. He had to be if he wanted to succeed in Japan. It was what attracted me to him in the first place. But it was the part of him that I grew to hate. When your father was born, he was so happy.>"

"<When I saw your father, I saw a precious baby. Your grandfather, however, saw his legacy. A man to carry his name into the future. And I don't think he ever saw your father as anything but that. He loved your father, but that name was always more important. I hated it, but I didn't blame him for it. I blamed Japan,>" she said. She paused, collecting herself.

"<Grandma, you don't have to—"> he said.

"<Tut tut tut,>" she said. "<Not done yet.>"

"<When your father left us, I was deeply sad. However, I knew his only chance at shedding his father's unhealthy influence was to move far away. I was hopeful that, in America, he would develop a healthier attitude.>"

"<He didn't,>" Kyle said, finishing her statement. Kyle's father worked harder than anyone. His memories of family vacations were almost always cut short by business emergencies, or alone with his mother.

"<No. He was unable to escape it. It followed him to America, and it still persists, in you,>" she said. "<You are a

part of your grandfather's legacy. Do not allow it to control your life.>"

"<I won't, Grandmother,>" he said. His phone buzzed. Alice was outside, waiting for him. "<She's here.>"

"<Then I will stop lecturing you,>" she said. "<Have fun. And don't forget to smile. You look so much cuter when you smile.>" She winked.

Kyle stepped outside the motel room and Alice was waiting for him, wearing a simple dress and sensible shoes. Without the burden of work, she looked twice as pretty.

"Hi," he said. "You look great."

"Thanks," she said. She started walking, and he followed her to the sidewalk. A motorcycle revved by, and Kyle's ears screamed.

"Where are we going?" he asked.

"I've decided we're going to get some local flavor," she said. "Get you outside all the normal tourist spots."

"Sounds great," he said. He didn't know what else to say.

"How's your trip going so far?" Alice asked.

"Not bad," he said. "Could be better, with the fires, but I'm sure you're more worried about it than I am."

"You say that," she said. "But I haven't really thought of it. I'm sure when it's here I'll be anxious, but it seems so—I don't know—abstract right now."

"Just a fact of life?" he asked.

"Yeah, kinda," she said. "We've always been at war with Eurasia."

There was a brief silence between them.

"Is your grandmother enjoying the town?" she asked.

"As much as she can enjoy anything," he said. He paused. "That's not fair. She's enjoying spending time with me. That's really the only reason for her trip."

"That's nice, then," she said. "She's from Japan?"

"Yeah, lived there almost her whole life," he said. "Moved in with my folks in Seattle a few years ago when my grandfather died."

"Is that where you're from?" she asked. "Seattle?"

"Yeah, born and raised," he said.

"Why did you two come out here?" she asked. "It wouldn't be my first choice. Or even in my top twenty-five."

"I go to UM, and this was a 'cute little tourist hole,' as my grandmother described it, roughly translated," he said. Alice laughed.

"I've never heard a better description for Conquest," she said. "Your grandma is sharp."

"Why is it called Conquest, again?" he asked. "I've yet to see a real reason listed anywhere."

"The tourism board for the city basically made us omit that from all the tours and educational material. Charles Burns, along with being a miner and entrepreneur, was also a huge racist. He *loved* Manifest Destiny, and merged that with his love of the Crusades, and so after he found the mine he saw it as fate—as part of conquering the West."

"Jesus," he said.

"He loved Jesus, too," she said. "But not nearly as much as driving native peoples off their land."

"Conquest is kind of a big name for what just seemed like a mining town," he said.

"You just don't understand his vision," she said. "Imagine, as far as the eye can see, white people."

"I don't really need to use my imagination," he said, and Alice laughed again.

They walked past the string of hotels, about to hit the rows of bars, restaurants, and tourist shops. The foot traffic picked up. She led him through the crowds, and farther back into town, off of the main drag. There was still a slew of people, but the pair had a little room to breathe back here. They ended up at a hole in the wall place that said "Sally's" in big red neon letters over the door.

10

Heather let herself into Sam's apartment, feeling her way through the dark. Sam wasn't home yet.

Heather turned on the lights, and fed Measles, Sam's German Shepherd. He was grateful, a good dog. Heather sat down in the recliner in the living room, closing her eyes.

How much more of this could she take?

JH had railroaded her at every turn. The fire was just the latest blow. And what could she do? The town owed everything to him. He didn't just bring it back from the brink, he had brought it back to life. It had been a rotting corpse for years, and he'd given it CPR. He made the mine solvent again. He spearheaded the Conquest Revitalization Project, and brought in business.

She was sheriff because of her story. Hometown girl, victim of a terrible tragedy, here to stand for justice and order. She was young, she was strong, she was pretty, but most importantly, she was local. She had announced her candidacy before Cochbrin died of a coronary on his toilet, but not long before. Without him in the running, she'd won in a wash.

But did she stand a chance against James Bieter? Word on the street was he'd be running against her when her term was up, and he had everything she did and more. And, he was a man.

Heather had grown up here. She knew most of the people in the county by name, and vice versa. They smiled, treated her with kindness. Whenever she was out on patrol, people would wave her down and give her bread, or cookies, or even pies, in the case of Ms. Cooper who lived out on Route 217. They loved her.

She worried, though. She worried that once a competent man ran against her, they would flip in an instant. He was a Bieter, and apparently running the mine better than his father ever had. She'd heard rumors about how he treated female employees, but those same rumors didn't stop JH from winning. Bringing it up would hurt her more than help. He was smart, and JH was on his side.

Stop, Heather. Stop. Stop thinking, for once. Measles jumped up and laid in her lap. He was too big to be a lap dog, but that didn't stop him from trying. She stroked him, her hand settling into a rhythm. His head rest on her arm.

Growls filled the air as they surrounded her. Her father and brother both yelled for her to run, but that wouldn't work. They moved much too fast. And she wasn't going to abandon her family. They were all she had.

It was so dark, and the shapes circled. Her father and brother fired their shotguns into the dark as the wolves wheeled around them. She only had a flashlight. She was trying to give them targets, but they moved so fast, so many of them.

Her dad shouldered the shotgun and fired again. There was a yelp and an indistinct spray of red. Her brother was covering the other side, but he couldn't see much of anything. A shape dove between them, a bag of cement mix hitting her in the chest. She fell. The wolf's jaws came down on her. She got her forearm up, and it closed down on her arm. She screamed in pain, its fangs cutting through flesh and crushing her bone. Her brother fired. BANG.

Heather woke up, Measles tumbling off her lap with a yelp. Her heart was beating a mile a minute. She couldn't catch her breath.

"Hello? Heather?" asked Sam, as she walked in the door, a paper bag full of groceries in her arms. "Measles okay?"

She caught sight of Heather, and dropped the groceries on the couch nearby. Heather's nose was bleeding. Sam grabbed a box of tissues and yanked a succession of them out, then held them to Heather's nose. Heather was crying.

"What's wrong?" Sam asked.

"Holy shit," Heather said. "Fuck." She'd been a teenager the last time she'd had that nightmare.

"Heather, what's wrong?" asked Sam again, insistent.

"Just. Need. A second," she said, trying to slow down her breathing. She wiped the blood away from her nose. Sam backed off a few inches, but watched her like a hawk, her EMT training coming through.

"It was a nightmare. Bad," said Heather, her heart finally slowing. "Is Measles okay?"

"Yeah, he's fine," Sam said. "He's already forgotten that he fell." Sam drew her a glass of water. Heather drank.

"Are you sure you're alright?" Sam asked. "You're bleeding."

"It's from the fires. Killing my sinuses," she said. "Bled earlier too. Probably opened back up when I got startled."

"Thought you were working tonight," said Sam.

"I called Darla in," said Heather. "I was too angry to work."

"Well, lucky for you, Chinese food is imminent," said Sam, with a smile.

"I don't smell any," said Heather. "It in that bag?"

"Nooo, those are groceries," said Sam. "But I will call and they will deliver."

•

They ate Chinese until they were about to burst. There was still so much left.

"Feel better now?" asked Sam. She was shorter than Heather, but strong, hard from riding trails and living outdoors.

Heather unbuttoned her pants. "I'm going to explode."

"Don't do it in here," said Sam. "I don't want to lose my deposit."

"You're not funny. Yes, I feel better," she said. "Don't get me wrong, though, I'm still pissed."

"But just a background-level pissed," said Sam. "I get it."

"He'd rather burn a few tourists to death than lose out on any money," said Heather. "I don't understand it."

"Heather, I hate to tell you this, but most of the town would probably agree with his decision," said Sam. "They elected him because he makes money. That's the long and short of it."

"It's their homes!" said Heather.

"If and when you evacuate, some of those people will refuse to leave. They'd rather burn down with the ship."

"You miiiight be mixing metaphors," said Heather, teasing.

"All I'm saying is, this is not limited to JH," said Sam. "He's a shithead, but if he's Jim Jones, the rest of the town is happily drinking the Kool Aid. It is this place."

"That's not fair," said Heather. This was her home. "There are good people here."

"That elected JH," said Sam. "That have continually re-elected him despite all his shitty behavior."

Sam wasn't wrong. When his wife was still alive, the gossip mill had said it was a marriage of convenience. JH churned through beautiful secretaries, all under orders to wear short skirts and high heels. Rumors of reported allegations were swept under the rug, allegations that followed him into the mayor's office. He had won re-election four times. And the rumors continued, both about him and his son. But no one ever went public, and no charges were ever filed.

She was sure Sheriff Cochbrin had something to do with that. Him and JH had been friends for decades. She looked up the records, and sure as hell Cochbrin had never filed a single report about either JH or James. Those women's complaints disappeared into the wind.

"It won't get better if I leave," said Heather.

"It might not get better if you stay," said Sam. "Come with me. You're crashing against the glass ceiling, and eventually it'll break you."

"I can't leave," she said. "They elected me."

"It's a job, just like any other," said Sam. "They'll appoint a new sheriff, and life will continue in Conquest."

"The county board will appoint a new sheriff," said Heather. "And JH sits on it. He'll make sure James gets the position."

"And?" asked Sam. "You'll be far, far away, with me. You can't fight the tide, sheriff. When you live on a volcano, you can't expect it to not be hot."

Heather looked at Sam. Her light auburn hair hid one of her eyes, but Heather could see she meant what she said.

"What would I do?" asked Heather.

"You'd work with me," she said. "You sure as hell can ride a horse and work a trail. You're good with people. I've got a good reputation, and you'd have it too."

Heather didn't answer her. Instead, Heather crawled next to her on the couch and kissed her, soft at first, and then harder. Sam returned it. They moved to Sam's bed, and made love.

•

"I was serious," said Sam afterward. She held Heather, softly stroking her arm. Her fingers danced over the scars that covered it. "Earlier."

"I know you were," said Heather. She heard her phone vibrate in her pants. Her cop alarm went off. She crawled out of Sam's embrace and grabbed her phone. Her home screen was full of missed calls and texts from Darla.

"I have to go," said Heather as she pulled on her clothes.

"Do you have to?" asked Sam.

"Sorry," said Heather. "I take one night off and the town goes to hell."

11

Alice was glad she decided to go out, sitting in the packed confines of Sally's.

Sally's was a locals bar. Sure, tourists ate there, but they tended to stick to the main drag, the places that looked friendlier. It was small, but fit a lot of people. Johnny Cash bounced off the wood paneled walls. By the time they got their drinks, it was CCR.

Not that Sally's wasn't friendly, but it was one of the few places that stuck around from the truck stop days and kept going, not driven out by JH Bieter's "Revitalization Project." Tom, owner and operator, was behind the bar, and he would gladly tell you that it was extortion. He was a giant, 6'6" and broad shouldered. His ranting and raving at town meetings had eventually led to JH giving him an exemption. "It's important for us to keep some local flavor in Conquest," said JH, with a smile, at that meeting.

Alice and Kyle sat at a booth, both drinking a beer from one of the three craft breweries that had sprung up in Conquest. Tom brought them both burgers and fries from the kitchen. It was the only thing Alice ate at Sally's, and it was leagues better than the burgers you got at the fancy restaurants that cost three times as much. Tom eyed Kyle as he served them.

"I don't think that guy likes me," said Kyle. "He keeps giving me a stink eye."

"That's just Tom," she said. "You haven't lived here for twenty years, so he doesn't trust you."

"That seems," said Kyle, taking a long sip from his beer, "like a slightly too stringent metric for trust."

"It takes at least thirty for him to warm up," said Alice.

"Can I ask you something?" asked Kyle.

"You just did," she said.

"Touché," he said. "Why did you ask me out? I mean, I'm glad you did, but it was out of the blue, and I was just a random guy with a grandma."

"To be fair, you're pretty cute," said Alice, teasing him.

His cheeks flushed at that.

"Alright," she said. "My boss was being a creep and you called at the right time. I wanted some company."

"Fair enough. You like it here?" he asked, swallowing.

"It's alright," she said. "It's pretty, at least when it's not on fire." She shrugged." It's a small town, but it's always busy. Plenty of work."

"I assume you're from here," he said.

"As much as anyone," she said.

"What does that mean?"

"When you say you're from Seattle, what do you mean?"

"My parents live there. I was born there. I grew up there."

"But did you really? Or was it a suburb, and you call it Seattle because it's close enough?"

"I mean, isn't that what everyone does?" he asked. "But yes. I guess it's not Seattle proper."

"Then in that way, yes, I'm from here," she said. "But really, my parents live a half hour away, in a little tiny house on the side of a hill. But this Conquest didn't exist when I was born. It wasn't *really* here until I was in high school, which gave us a place to hang out and see movies."

"So this place isn't home," he said.

"The *area* is home," she said, finally. "Conquest is made up. Which is fine."

"Is fine enough to keep you here?" he asked.

"Good question," she said. "Are you going to move back to Seattle when you graduate?"

"I don't know," he said, shrugging.

"Same boat," she said and raised her bottle to him. He touched his bottle to hers.

They finished their food.

"You wanna play some pool?" she asked. The empty tables beckoned.

"I'm terrible," he said. "But sure."

Kyle went to the bathroom after Alice wiped the floor with him. She was racking the balls for their next game when she felt a hand slide up her skirt and squeeze. She spun, swinging her elbow as hard as she could.

"What the fuck!" she said, the biker at the bar earlier dodging her elbow, a shit-eating grin on his face.

"Hey, sweet cheeks," he said. "No need to be so feisty."

She grabbed the pool cue from the table, ready to hit him. "Why the fuck did you think you could touch me?"

"I take what I want," he said, still smiling. He was shorter than her, his dark hair cropped close. His beady eyes gleamed, like a rat. He wore leathers.

"Get the fuck away from me," she said.

"You know that Asian boy ain't gonna be able to satisfy you," he said. "I've got what it takes."

Kyle walked back from the bathroom, and immediately saw something was wrong. He hadn't noticed the biker before, but Alice looked like she was about to bash his brains in. The biker saw him as he approached.

"You have a problem, sir?" asked Kyle.

"Oh, that's cute," he said. "Leave, boy."

"He groped me," she said. Heads started to turn.

"What the fuck is wrong with you?" asked Kyle.

"Just getting what's mine," said the biker. He spit on Kyle, saliva sticking to Kyle's face. Kyle swung at him, and caught him on the jaw. It staggered Runt, and Tom's arm were around the biker. Tom pushed him outside, pulling him up into the air and throwing him out onto the sidewalk.

"Leave," said Tom. "I call the cops next time I see you."

"You motherfuckers!" yelled the biker. A few people walking up and down the street looked in his direction, and then continued on their way.

Tom just stood in the entrance, waiting. He was twice Runt's size. Runt spit on the ground, staring at him, defiantly. Tom did not move. "Leave."

The bar settled down eventually. Tom came over and talked to both Kyle and Alice. When they assured him they were okay, he went back to work, and the bar returned to relative normality.

Alice and Kyle returned to their booth, both of them flustered by the encounter. Tom brought them both drinks, on the house, and it helped take the edge off.

"Sheriff has a deputy in a squad car outside watching the place," said Tom, before heading back to the bar.

"Twice in one fucking day," she said. "Goddamnit."

"I'm sorry," said Kyle.

"It's not your fault," she said. "You didn't have to hit him."

"I probably shouldn't have, but I really wanted to. What the fuck compels people to act like that?"

"It's not complicated," she said. "He believed what he said."

"It's shameful," he said. "The way some men act."

Alice didn't say anything to that, just took a swallow of beer. Not that she was used to the harassment, because you never get used to it, but men always responded with violence. If she threw a punch every time someone harassed her, she'd be in fights all day. She didn't have the time for it. Kyle had thrown a punch, initiated violence. She was Kyle's, for the night, and he needed to protect his property. She looked at his eyes, his gentle eyes, and knew he didn't have that thought, not consciously. But she knew what men did.

Alice and Kyle left Sally's late. They got along, they discovered, and both liked IPAs. The night was finally cooling, but the ever-present smoke was still there. She leaned into him, allowing him to put his arm over her. It felt good, a welcome touch for both.

Then something pulled Kyle away.

The biker pulled Kyle real close and shoved a blade into

his guts, stabbing him over and over, covering the blade and the biker's hand in blood. He let out all his frustration in that blade, grunting with each thrust.

Kyle made no sound as everything was driven out of him. He was unconscious before the biker stopped.

Alice screamed.

It was fast, the biker finished with Kyle in seconds, letting him fall to the sidewalk, blood pouring from his abdomen. The biker looked at Alice, still holding the blade, his arm covered in blood up to the elbow. He looked like a surgeon fresh from an operation.

"This is your fault," he said, looking at Alice. "And now you get what you deserve."

"Drop the knife or I drop you," said Deputy Darla Martin, her revolver extended, pointed at the biker.

"Goddamnit," said the biker. He turned to look at her. Darla was short, the same height as him, a pear-shaped woman that the biker barely saw.

"This ain't your business," he said.

"I'm pretty sure it is," she said. "Now drop the knife." She cocked the revolver. "I won't miss from this close."

He grimaced.

Darla looked at him, waiting. The moments weighed in the air. She watched his face, as he decided if he was going to get shot or not. Then it changed. Just for a second, a shifting of his cheekbones, maybe. It was hard to tell, the streetlights and smoke obscuring everything. But then it was back, and Tom was there, in the doorway with his wait staff, leaving for the night.

"Call an ambulance, Tom," said Darla, her pistol still pointing at the biker. Something in the biker gave up at that point. He tossed his knife at Darla's feet, the blade clanging off the sidewalk.

He held his hands out to her, the right one dripping blood. "Take me away."

12

Kate and John pushed themselves down the trail. The sun was setting, and they wanted to get back to the car before it got too dark. It was going to be tight.

They had started the day early, hiking out of Conquest, and traveling the switchback trail between two of its three peaks, and then crossed into the wilderness beyond. They had seen the Drop Falls, the Five Sister Lakes, and Two Beaver Valley as they walked.

Their goal for the day was audacious, but it always was. The trail they took was rated for sixteen hours. Their goal was to do it in ten.

Kate pushed ahead of John, as they descended from Black Peak. The trail was rough, and the dry conditions made it hard to breathe. Their nostrils clogged with dust and smoke. Even Cap and Bucky, their two hounds who went everywhere with them, struggled.

Kate paused for a moment, looking down the mountain at the trail in front of them. She was lean and her auburn hair grayed at the temples. She fixed her pack's strap again. It had been bugging her the entire hike. It was time for a new one, or at least for this one to be properly mended. Cap, his lead attached to her waist, took the opportunity to sit down. They weren't going to make it back before nightfall.

John caught up with her, approaching her with his normal stealthiness. He was lean as well, his body harder and tighter than ever, even as he entered his late 40's. Early retirement was the best decision he'd ever made. His hair was gray, but not thinning. Bucky, his lead tied to John, sat next to Cap. John dropped their bowls on the ground and poured fresh water into them. The dogs slurped, their tongues lapping at it.

"We can still make it," he said, studying the sky. The fading orange of the sun bled through the haze. The damnable smoke had slowed them down.

"I don't think so," said Kate. "Still, worst comes to worst, we have the lights. Just have to keep the dogs close."

With the dogs' thirst slaked, they continued, Kate moving ahead. They moved fast, but did not speed up because of their self-imposed deadline. They kept a studied pace, with learned precision, knowing that the other would never be far. John was slow at first, and Kate had been impatient. She'd learned patience, and John had shed weight, gained speed, and they'd cut across every notable trail in North America with Bucky and Cap attached at the hip.

They walked for another hour, down beaten paths and

over dead trees, finally collapsing under their own weight. The barest glimpse of the sun still remained, but dusk had settled into the mountainous woodland, the haze obscuring any view of a true sunset. John closed his eyes, resting them.

John looked up again, making note of the time and their rough location, and then realized he should be able to see Kate. He knew exactly how far ahead she was at any time, part of the knowledge they shared with their past several years together hiking. But she was nowhere to be seen.

He didn't panic. Panic was the enemy.

"Kate," he said, just under a yell. No answer. Maybe she couldn't hear him, lost in her own thoughts or feeding Bucky.

He continued ahead, watching the trail ahead closely, listening for any noise whatsoever. He would probably hear her long before he would see her, especially in the growing darkness.

The panic was building, but he continued to push it away. It wouldn't help anyone if he lost his head. He slowed down, turning on the light attached to his pack. His eyes pored over every tree, every piece of brush, looking for a sign of her.

"Bucky," he called this time, and there was a response, a muffled bark, coming from off the trail. He moved toward it, his eyes on the ground ahead of him. Going off the trail here was risky. Other hikers might not come by for hours or days.

He called for Bucky again, and the same muffled bark came back to him. He moved toward it, stepping through and around the underbrush, underneath the mixture of dead and live trees that fueled the approaching wildfires and clouded the sky.

A crashing noise behind him. Something fell from a tree? He suddenly feared wildlife. Bears and mountain lions posed a serious threat, and the image of the vicious animal on top of Kate popped into his mind, its claws and teeth red with blood as it ripped at her throat.

He shook the image out of his mind. *She's fine. She probably hit her head, and got dazed. Bucky is right next to her. He would have barked or growled at a bear or mountain lion, and you've heard neither. Find her, get back, it'll be okay.*

He hadn't imagined the crashing noise, though. He didn't see anything, his visibility outside the cone of light effectively nothing besides vague shadow. He stepped backward, placing his feet with precision.

Something grabbed him, pulling him down and dragging him backwards. His light blinked off, and a hand covered his mouth. His arms and back crashed through brush, leaves, branches, and he felt blood well out of new scratches.

He stopped moving, now on his butt. He turned to see Kate still holding her hand over his mouth, her eyes wide and her other forefinger over her lips in the "shh" gesture.

Kate did not overreact. Something was wrong. His eyes asked the question.

Her mouth went to his ear, her whisper so quiet that half the sound vanished before it reached him. He heard her, "There are things out there."

Things. They had hiked, seen the worst nature could throw at them. Grizzlies, rattlesnakes, alligators. They had heard a mountain lion, never seeing it, and carefully retreated from the area. She didn't use the word bear, or lion, or even animal. Things.

His eyes betrayed his confusion. Another whisper. "They are hunting us." She pointed, her hand tucked up against her face. Her finger led through a narrow window past the small copse of underbrush they crouched inside. She had turned his light off as she pulled him backwards, and the hazy twilight made actually seeing anything impossible.

She continued to point, and John continued to watch where she pointed. His vision acclimated, his pupils growing wide in the darkness. Shapes appeared in the haze.

"Keep Cap quiet." Another whisper. She squatted on Bucky, his lead line wrapped around his mouth to keep it shut. He pulled Cap to him and did the same, unbuckling Cap from his belt and wrapping the lead around his muzzle.

His eyes returned to their small window. The shapes shifted in and out of view. He counted several of them, never more than two visible at a time. They were hunched, distorted shapes. Big, but no bigger than the grizzlies they had seen, once upon a time. His mind contorted, trying to make these shapes and the bear shapes overlap, but reality persisted. They couldn't be bears. Not a bear from this world.

They waited. The sun set, the last light fading through the smoke. They waited, but there was no sound from outside their hiding place. Nothing could be seen.

John's legs began to spasm painfully, and he dug his knuckles into them, trying to drive out the pain. They had no water. As he shifted his weight, Cap bolted, anxious and unsure of the situation. John started to move to recapture him, but Kate grabbed his wrist, holding him still.

Her eyes looked at him, a desperate sadness in them. She shook her head. She could fathom losing Cap. She couldn't fathom losing *him*. They waited, for anything. Cap must have shaken loose of his muzzle, as he started to bark, first farther away, and then closer as he came into view. He stood at the entrance to their spot and barked once, curious. Kate's grip loosened on John's wrist only then.

He straightened up, letting his legs flex and bend, the muscles trembling, waiting for the charley horse to hit. It didn't and he pushed out through the bramble, trying to stay as quiet as possible. It was his specialty.

When they were home, Kate would often be startled by him, without him even trying. He would surprise her while she was folding laundry, or doing dishes, brushing against her without her ever hearing him. While hiking, he was soundless. Even when he'd had an additional fifty pounds, he was light on his feet, and now, lighter, he was invisible.

He stepped out from their hiding place, his eyes casting about through the smoke and darkness. He saw nothing, with Cap at his heels, happy to be moving again. Kate was right behind him.

John didn't hear what hit him, only felt a massive, sharp impact.

John lived a sedate life. He had been lucky and smart enough to avoid any real conflict. His brother, Steven, was a veteran. Two tours of both Iraq and Afghanistan. Narrowly avoided death multiple times. He had once described seeing an IED go off, the massive pieces of distorted and deformed shrapnel that tore through men.

Kate had no point of reference for what happened to her husband. A shape was near him, *in* him, a distended arm slashing across John's torso. His intestines spilled out of him, obscene and impossible. Gore splashed her face.

She ran. She ran hard and fast, a slim volume of moonlight filtering through the smoke lighting her way. *Have to make the pass.* If she got out the other side, she had a chance.

The alpine trees and brushes scratched her, blood welling up in dozens of cuts as she stormed through the trees, charging downhill, alighting from foot to foot as obstacles popped into her eye line only a moment before she would hit them.

She could hear them behind her. Their light footfalls softly scattered dead needles and gravel as they chased her. There was no sound otherwise, her breathing getting heavier as she pushed herself harder. The pass was less than a half mile away. They were faster than her.

The shapes were big. They loped after her, but they still obeyed physics, and she darted into tight clusters of trees, cutting between them as she ran. They'd be on her soon.

She ran harder. She couldn't see where her feet landed until a moment before they hit the ground, and the terrain was rougher around the pass. She was making ground on them, as their footfalls fell farther and farther behind. She took another massive leap, and realized too late that there was no ground where it should have been.

Pain brought her to consciousness.

Her leg was on fire. One of the shapes had her slung over his shoulder, and each step jostled her leg. She couldn't see it, but even attempting to move it sent debilitating waves of torment through her body.

Most of her strength was gone. She beat at the thing's back, her fists doing nothing. It carried her back up the incline. All three of the things chasing her were here. They made a noise, a choppy gargle that reverberated deep inside of them, echoing across the peak.

It dropped her near a downed tree, pain exploding through her again. She could finally see her leg. It was catastrophic. The bone was through the skin at her shin, a compound fracture. She knew she'd never run again. She couldn't bring herself to touch it, and just let the leg hang.

The shapes surrounded her. She could make out five of them, loitering around something. One turned and looked at her, gesturing with a limb. There was a click, and then a sudden light cast shadows across the small clearing. One had John's light, and had turned it on. The something they loitered around was John's body.

The same one approached her, and as it walked through the light she got a glimpse of it. It didn't seem possible. Obscene, impossible musculature. Coarse hair, like a pig. Teeth too big for its mouth. And then it stepped out of the light.

It loomed over her. The smell of sweat and blood filled her nostrils. A massive hand palmed her head, and she waited for it to squeeze, to finally end this. It didn't.

That would have been a mercy, and these things were not in the business of mercy.

The thing instead turned her head, stepping out of her vision while making sure she was looking at John's body as the rest of them began to feed on him.

They surrounded him, burying their faces in his gore. The thing's hand held her face. She closed her eyes, but then a single claw pried open her eyelid and held itself there, threatening.

She kept her eyes open after that, tears flowing down her face. John's body was only recognizable for moments, and then it was just—just parts.

They eventually stopped. It was still night.

They ate her next.

July 2nd

13

The Pack rode into town.

Jack led them, the other five behind him in formation. It was early, the sun rising only in theory, as the smoke had thickened overnight.

Jack had been woken from a deep slumber by Runt, his lone call from the lockup. Jack had taken the news well enough, after calling Runt a "fucking idiot" three or four times. Runt gave him all the recon he could, and Jack told him to not do anything stupider than Runt already had.

Abe was the first Jack told.

"Shit," said Abe, astute as always. Abe was tall, 6'4" and lean. He looked like Abraham Lincoln. He had been Shadow's right-hand man.

"What do you think?" asked Jack. *My first fucking week*

of leadership, and Runt pulls this shit.

Abe looked at him, his big eyes open and clear. "We have two choices. Either we go get him, or we leave and hope he doesn't sell us out."

"Runt has a record, too," said Jack. "He's in their database."

"They'll run him," said Abe. "Probably already have. And he'll be somewhere in his 70s or 80s, him looking no older than 40."

"Someone will notice," said Jack. He paced. *Fuck.*

"If we can get him in the first 24 hours, before he gets charged formally, we have a chance," said Abe. "Nothing will get recorded, and we can fly the fuck away."

"We have to go get him," he said, finally. "I don't trust him."

Abe didn't ask him "then why did you send him in the first place", but Jack knew he was thinking it. He glared at Abe, but Abe was already up, packing his few things, getting dressed.

"Everyone, wake up," said Jack. "We've got ourselves a situation."

They rode and hit town just as people began to stir. The early-morning adventurers were already out to kayak, hike, or climb. Business owners pulled up shutters and unlocked doors. They saw the six bikers ride into town on the main drag, their bikes roaring at every stop light.

If Shadow had been here, this would have never happened. He would have never sent Runt alone into a town. He'd known better. He'd known that Runt was irritable, prone to outbursts, uncontrollable. Especially when he was alone.

They turned, and then turned again, pulling into the local sheriff's office. They all got off their bikes, stretching their legs.

Jack walked into the station. A man sat at the front desk, middle aged, in uniform. Balding, wearing glasses, but stocky.

"Excuse me, I'd like to talk to the sheriff, please," said Jack, mustering as much charm as he could and flashing a polite grin.

"And you are?" asked the man, looking at Jack over his glasses.

"Name's Jack," he said. "Jack Samson."

"And why exactly do you want to talk to the sheriff? She's awfully busy," said the man. "We had quite a night."

Jack smiled again. *A she, huh?* "That's why I'm here. I'm an associate of the man you arrested last night. I was his one call."

The man perked up at that, showed some kind of life, and then eyed him. Jack kept the same easy, polite smile as the deputy looked him over. "Is that right? Let me talk to the sheriff," he said, getting up and walking back into the station. He returned a few minutes later.

"She'll talk to you," he said. "Follow me." The deputy led him back into the station, where a handful of desks filled the bullpen area. Only a couple of them seemed to be occupied. It was ringed by enclosed offices, but again they all seemed empty except the sheriff's, which the deputy led him to, opening the door for him and then closing it behind him.

Sheriff Hill stood up to greet him, even going so far as to shake his hand. "Sheriff Hill," she said. She was tall, almost as tall as him. Brown hair, green eyes. Fit. He smiled at her.

"Jack Samson," he returned. As they let go, and he sat down, he smelled her. The room was filled with her scent. He knew her. They'd met, before. But when?

"You wanted to talk about a Mr. Steven Iskilbitz?" she asked, reading off the rap sheet she had in front of her.

"Is that Runt's real name?" he asked. "News to me."

"Yes, the only name he would give was just Runt," she said. "But fingerprints came back positive. And that's where my questions start. Do you ride with him?"

"Yeah, me and the crew," said Jack. "They're outside. This isn't official or anything, right? I can leave at any time."

"This is just a friendly chat," said Heather.

"Right," said Jack. "Yeah, we ride together. We started over in Minnesota and we're going across to the Pacific, and then cutting back through the country. At least that was the plan, anyway." He could feed her a bunch of lies and get the info he needed to take Runt out.

"So, you only know him as Runt?" she asked.

"Yeah, we have a riding club back home," he said. "We met him through that. It's kind of an unofficial thing, you know. Always just told us to call him Runt. Childhood nickname or something."

"Hmm. Well, if my reports are correct, Mr. Iskilbitz is 86 years old," she said.

"That's impossible," said Jack, feigning shock. "It's not like we celebrate birthdays or anything, but he always said he was in his forties. He sure as hell don't look 86." At least Jack had a hard number on his age. Runt would never tell any of the boys anything about his past. Shadow had known some, but he wasn't going to be telling anybody anything.

"He certainly does not," she said.

"Maybe your report is wrong," he said. "Got the files mixed up somewhere."

"That was my first thought, but everything else matches," she said. She shook her head. "I don't know. My other main question is, does Mr. Iskilbitz have a history of violence, or of sexual harassment?"

"No, he's as gentle as a lamb," said Jack, keeping a straight face. *Actually, Sheriff, he's either the first or second most deranged member of The Pack, depending on what kind of mood Beast is in. And we sure as hell don't leave Beast alone to his own devices.* "Why do you ask?"

"The nature of his crime—" she said, "—is quite frankly, ghastly. He assaulted a young woman, was kicked out of a bar, waited outside, and then attacked her companion, a young man. It was vicious."

"When he called me, he said it was self defense," said Jack. "Told me maybe grabbing the girl was true, but said he was just drunk. Said he was outside later on accident, wandering around drunk, and the kid attacked him for what he did earlier. Not saying it's right, but—"

"Mr. Samson, your friend stabbed the victim 14 times," she said. The man's in critical condition, hanging on by a thread. There are three witnesses, including one of my deputies."

Jack didn't have to feign surprise, because the son of a bitch hadn't told him that part. "Jesus," he said. "He didn't tell me that."

"And he has no history of violence that you're aware of?" asked Heather.

"Always quiet, always pretty laid-back kind of guy," he said. "When does he see the judge?"

"Tuesday, after the holiday," said Heather.

"I think we'll be sticking around until then, at least," he said.

"There's a fire heading this way, so be aware. If I had my way, we'd already be evacuated," she said.

"Who's against it?" asked Jack.

"I didn't tell you this," said Heather. "The mayor."

"Politicians," he said. "It's always the way. Same back home in Minnesota. I could tell you—"

"Sorry to cut you off," said Heather, "but I've got a lot of work to do. They found two hikers mauled this morning."

"Dear god," he said, smiling inside, shocked outside. When had they met? Every person had their own smell, as distinct as a fingerprint, according to Shadow. And he never encountered people twice. Couldn't have been too long ago.

"Yeah, pretty rough," she said. "Any other questions?"

"Can I see him?" he asked.

"Tomorrow," she said. "Maybe. We're understaffed, and prisoner visits require at least two of us."

"Then I'll see you tomorrow, Sheriff," he said. "Thanks for your time." He stood up and reached out his hand for another handshake.

"Have we met before? You seem awfully familiar," he said as he left.

He let her look at him, long and hard. She shook her head.

"Not that I can remember," she said. "Have a good day."

He rejoined The Pack outside.

"We have until Monday to get him out," said Jack. "Let's get to work."

14

James went into the mine production office early Saturday morning. JH was waiting for him.

"Hello, Son," JH said, sitting in his old spot behind James's desk, sipping a cup of coffee, a fresh pot brewed, reading the newspaper.

"Christ, you scared the shit out of me," said James. He was wearing the same clothes he'd worn yesterday.

"Not as much as you're scaring your poor wife," said JH, folding the newspaper in quarters and laying it down on his desk. "She woke me up at 6 AM this morning. She hadn't slept because you were gone all night. What did I tell you yesterday? Was I not clear enough?"

"You told me to sort it out," he said, trying to stay calm. "But it's not always that simple."

"Bullshit, it's not that simple," said JH. "You smile, and you say what they want to hear. And you definitely don't flee the house, never to return."

"It was better for both of us for me not to be there last night," he said. Probably because he would have ended up breaking down and telling her everything. He'd gone to the Lion's Den instead, driving through the night. He needed to be himself, if only for a few hours.

It was a spur-of-the-moment decision, and a very bad one. It wasn't fair to Susan, who he'd hurt. It wasn't healthy, either. But it was the only place he could breathe.

"No, it was better for *you*," said JH. "It was not better for her, and it definitely wasn't better for me. You're lucky our town was a complete fucking shit show last night, or people would be talking about you skating out on your goddamn wife."

"What?" asked James.

"A tourist was attacked outside Sally's by a biker. Then, two hikers were mauled to death up in the mountains, on the other side of the pass," said JH. "Fucking shitshow. You should be happy. No one is paying attention to you, the son of the mayor, the most important businessman in this whole town, the future Sheriff. Go back to Susan, apologize, and tell her you'll make everything okay."

"I don't think I can do that," said James.

"What does that mean?" asked JH, sitting up.

"I don't think I can go back to Susan and lie to her face," said James. "We're not happy, neither of us. A child isn't coming, and even if it was, why would I subject it to being raised by parents who don't love each other? We'd be happier apart." It was time for this conversation. It was long overdue. His father needed to hear this, needed to hear the truth.

JH grimaced and closed his eyes, sighing.

"I don't want to be sheriff, and I don't want to be married to Susan," said James. "This is a long time coming—I'm gay." He stood up straight, puffed out his chest, and looked at his father, whose eyes were still closed. JH stood up, opening his eyes but not meeting James's gaze. He breathed deep and walked up to James, then grabbed him by the nuts and backed him up against the wall. James was powerless.

JH stared up at James's face, his cheeks starting to redden.

"You don't think I know you're a fag? How stupid do you think I am? You've fooled the town, and you've maybe even fooled your precious, dull wife, but you haven't fooled me. I knew when you were 13 and I couldn't get you to play any sports. I knew when you were 17 and Susan had to drag you to a dance, where you kissed her like she's your sister. I knew on your wedding day, and I knew when you couldn't bring a boy into this world that will take control of my name, and I especially knew when you stopped at that hotel full of Sodomites on your business trips to get fucked in the ass by a bunch of sinners!" He breathed. He looked James in the eye.

"I'm going to tell you some things, my only son," said JH. "And I want you to take them to heart. Do you understand?" He accentuated his words with a squeeze. "Say 'yes, I understand.'"

"Yes, I understand," said James.

"Good," said JH. "What you want *doesn't fucking matter.* You are a cog in a machine, one of the tires on a car, a pawn, a peon. This is your lot in life and this is what you get. I built all this shit." He gestured to everything around them. "Do you think I *wanted* to marry your mother? Do you think I *wanted* a miserable little shit as a son? Hell no, but it was what I was dealt and I made the best of it. You're going to do the same." He squeezed again. "Say it."

"I understand," said James, withered.

"For so, so long, I thought I could just take care of you, provide for you, and that would be enough to put you on the right path. I paid for everything; I gave you a career; I bought you a house. But it didn't work. I had to use a more strict approach. So be it."

"Do you need a drink to get you through the day? So did I, for a long time. Do you need to fuck around on your wife to not go insane? Lord knows I did. Do you need to drive out to the middle of nowhere so you can get butt-fucked by a stranger? Whatever. You keep it in the shadows. You keep your fucking mouth shut, and you keep your wife happy, and you have a lovely bouncing baby boy. Got it?"

"Yes," said James.

"And you *will* be running for sheriff, and you *will* win. We'll drive Hill out, and we'll run this town the way it should be. We'll make Conquest great. And you don't say a word about being a homo to anyone. Not even on your fucking deathbed. Do you understand?"

James nodded, his face red and tears welling in his eyes. His heart was ice cold.

"Good," said JH, and then he let go of James. He went back to the desk and grabbed his newspaper. "I've got work to do," he said, and walked out of the office.

James ran to his trash can and threw up.

15

Susan wandered through the smoke and haze.

After James had stormed out, she'd cleaned. Cleaned up the oysters he'd thrown across the room, cleaned the kitchen after the dinner she'd made, and cleaned the house after all the cleaning she'd done during the day in preparation. Cleaning gave her purpose, kept her mind off things. She had done a lot of cleaning.

She tried to sleep, but couldn't. James wasn't answering his phone, and after a while it went straight to voicemail. She had put on Disney movies and laid on the couch, watching them, her eyes distant, Ariel and Simba and Belle just washing over her.

The life of a princess. She got what she'd wanted. A big house with a beautiful kitchen and a smart, successful husband who would protect and provide for her.

She had expected James to come back through the door at 3, or 4, or even 5 AM, drunk and sad. He would apologize with slurred words, and she'd accept it. They'd establish a truce, be pleasant to each other, and play act a happy marriage. That would last for a while. Then James would explode, would drink, would sulk. They would argue.

But he hadn't come back, and her general anxiety turned into real fear. What if something happened to him? What if his drunk driving had finally killed someone… or him?

She had called JH. If anyone knew where James was, JH would. JH was always nice to her, always polite and pleasant, even when he was cruel and merciless to James, which he was more and more often. James's mother had died when he was a child, before they met, and JH had been handed the reins of James's upbringing. He'd pursued it with the same relentless and punishing schedule that he pursued everything.

They'd been chatting more and more lately, JH calling her during his lunch break, letting her chew his ear for twenty minutes or so. The talk was rarely anything of substance, but—it was someone. Someone willing to listen, even for twenty minutes, even if it was just to be aware of James's behavior.

JH didn't know where James was, but JH would find him, and send him home. That was six hours ago. Susan couldn't stay in the house any more.

Did she want James back? What were they fighting for, or even against?

She dressed up, wearing the dress from last night that James hadn't noticed. It showed too much cleavage but Susan didn't care. She walked into the busy part of town, full of restaurants and bars, full already, people abuzz about the news from last night. The smoke and haze was even heavier.

She found herself in the small park in the exact center of town, full of brass plaques, town history, and the visitor center. Across the street was the massive parking lot and the train station, both full of people as they visited the town on the holiday weekend. A massive totem pole stood across the street as well, a tribute to the Native Americans who had once called the area home. She had never seen a Native person in town.

She walked around and read the plaques. She was sure she'd read them before—she must have, living here her whole life. This one about Burns' Mine, this one about the mountains, this one about the death and rebirth of the town. All of it true, all of it lies, telling a tourist everything and nothing about Conquest.

She ended up on a bench, watching the pigeons fight over crumbs from the nearby food trucks that parked there every Saturday during the summer. She heard a voice from her periphery.

"A pretty woman, sitting alone," said the voice. "That is an injustice that I cannot tolerate."

Not today, pal. She turned and saw the source: a stunning, beautiful man wearing riding gear. *Oh. Well, maybe today.*

"May I sit next to you?" he asked. He didn't wait for an answer, but she would have said yes anyway. A delicate curl dangled from his short, blond touseled hair. Light blue eyes shone out from his soft and delicate face. His facial hair was stubbled, the kind that seemed impossible to maintain, but was undoubtedly calculated. He simmered. He was a little taller than average and his pants hung low on his hips, a thin inch of skin showing between the bottom of his shirt and jacket, and above his waistline.

He sat at the other end of the bench and spread out, ensuring there wasn't enough room for someone to sit between them.

"Pardon my intrusion," he said. "Thought I'd keep you and the pigeons some company."

"Don't know if I'm in the mood for company," she said.

"You looked like you needed it," he said, then reached out a hand to her. "You can call me Kid."

"Kid?" she asked. She shook his hand. It was soft. "Come up with that yourself?"

"I did not, as a matter of fact," he said. "But it grew on me. You have a name?"

"I do, and you can have it as soon as you give me your real name," she said. "Kid."

His eyes narrowed, a playful bargain being struck between them.

"What do folks do around here for fun?" he asked.

"What are you here for?" she countered, instead of answering. This gorgeous man kept asking questions, it was about time she got some in.

"That's a great, great question," he said. "I thought I knew, but every day I'm a little more doubtful. You know the assault that happened last night? I ride with the assailant, and we all came in this morning to see what was up."

Susan had seen the news. Stabbings didn't happen in Conquest. "You're friends with that monster?" she asked.

"No, I just ride with him," said Kid. "We ain't friends."

He had a way of sticking his tongue out just a little when he wasn't talking. He licked his lips. She realized that she was gawking at him. She looked away, her eyes moving back to the pigeons. If he noticed her staring, however, he didn't show it. Maybe he was used to it.

"People do a lot of stuff here. They go to the historical village, they go on the mine tour, they hike the trails, they go down to the man-made beach at Clearwater Lake, there's a couple of golf courses if you drive further north—"

"That's what *tourists* do," he said. "You live here, right? What do you do for fun?"

"I mostly stay at home," she said, an honest answer being the easiest one.

"Cook for the hubby?" he asked.

"Well, yes," she said. "You're being mean."

"I am, sometimes," he said. "Comes out at the worst moments."

"That's what most men say," she said.

"I'm not like most men," he said, his tone serious.

"That's also what most men say," she said.

"You're not wrong, but I'm a different sort," he said. She believed him. She felt like she was being bedeviled, but the gorgeous stranger's charms were working on her. She'd probably be a little more resistant if she had slept at all last night. "You still haven't told me why you're alone."

"You're right, I haven't," she said. "My husband is at work, and my friends are busy." Neither were lies.

"So you decided to wear that astounding dress and sit in a park that you've probably seen a thousand times in your life?" he asked. She had forgotten about the dress. Everyone else was wearing khaki and dad hats. "I've traveled a lot in my life, seen a lot, and you immediately stood out in this town. You're broadcasting something."

"And you just had to check it out?" she asked.

"What else am I supposed to do? Wait for that fire to come burn us all down?" he asked. "Standing still for too long is dangerous."

"Wise words for such a young man," she said. "How old *are* you?"

"Older than I look," he said, a slight grin on his face.

"More mystery," she said. "Can't you just answer my question?"

"I can't, actually. What are you doing tonight?"

"I just told you I was married," she said. "You're still asking me out?"

"One, you're not wearing a ring," he said. "And two, yes." She'd taken her ring off when she prepared the oysters last night. She'd never put it back on.

"What's a really nice restaurant in town?" he asked.

"The Stone Buffalo is nice," she said.

"You like it?"

"Yeah, it's fantastic," she said. James had taken her there for an anniversary. Was that three, or four years ago? She couldn't remember. It was during one of their truces.

"I'll be there for a few hours tonight, at the bar, If you're interested." He extended his hand again. She took it. His hand was soft.

"Andrew," he said.

"Susan," she replied, and he walked away into the haze.

16

Arthur hadn't planned on visiting the old house, but he wanted to see it again before it burned.

He woke up early. He always did. Art missed the sleep more when he was younger.

The sun was still down, the air thicker out on the porch, the smell of smoke overwhelming. He drank his coffee. It tasted like ash.

He dressed and headed into town. He had errands to run. He was running low on groceries, but his mind kept wandering, and when he passed the parking lot of the grocery store he kept driving, heading out of town. The road was still empty this early in the morning, a few cars bound for town to get an early start on the day.

He hit the main highway then turned west, directly toward the fires. He passed signs warning about them, about the smoke. He continued on, and soon there was no traffic. The haze thickened.

It wasn't long before he was there. The house still looked exactly as he remembered it. The house wasn't his, and the gate was locked, but the Mackenzies were gone, evacuated. He parked off the short dirt road that led to the gate and bent down, climbing between the fencing. They wouldn't mind.

He walked down the long gravel trail to what used to be home. He had driven up and down the trail countless times. Every divot, every dip, every mud puddle was ingrained in his mind, the spots where he could pull his truck off and not get stuck.

The ranch-style house was back a ways, and he was sweating by the time he reached the front drive. It had been gravel, now paved. The hanging, swinging chair rocked back and forth in the slight breeze on the empty porch.

It was the same chair he'd had, a couple pieces of wood replaced, new chains and cushions. It was where he used to take his coffee. Heather had loved swinging on it. They hadn't had one next door.

He stopped, and looked out from the porch. The front yard was laid out in front of him. Past that, the trees. Past that, the fire. Smoke rose in the distance, big plumes coming up from the advancing wildfires. They were close now, and advancing faster. He knew Joe Coffey, and the men fighting alongside him. They weren't getting paid enough.

It was dark inside. No one home. He pulled out his key ring and flipped through 'til he got to the one he was look-ing for, the one no one knew he kept. He told himself it was just for nostalgia's sake, but he knew well enough that no matter what the deed said, that house was still *his*.

Unless the Mackenzies had changed the locks. Always a possibility.

They hadn't, though, and his key slipped right in. No alarm panels anywhere, and the phone didn't ring, so he figured he was safe in that regard. The house might not be here next month, he figured they'd be fine with him taking a trip down memory lane. And if they weren't, better to ask for forgiveness than permission.

He walked in and it was time travel.

He had just come back from a trip into town. He had picked up both groceries and his work supplies. Emilia was cooking dinner, smelled like macaroni and cheese. He would drop off the groceries, give her a kiss, learn how much time he had, and then get some work done while the food was in the oven.

The furniture was different now, what the Mackenzies left behind, but he saw through it. He saw his house again, their house again. They had moved out so far from town because it was quiet, and because it was cheap. He had made a name for himself with his jewelry pieces. They were tired of people.

He walked into the master bedroom, where he and Emilia had made love over the years. Tried to have children. It was him, the doctor said. He was shooting blanks. They'd talked about fertility treatments, but they both figured that if God wanted them to have a child, they would, doctors or no.

He walked into the other bedroom, where Heather had slept. Briefly.

Her first night there she'd woken up screaming, screaming so loud Art thought he was in a nightmare. A little girl couldn't make that noise. The covers were on the floor, and he had woke her. Her arms, still bandaged, still mending, shook, just like that night. They circled her, in her nightmare. And this time, there were no weapons, no defense. They still hunted, and the hunt didn't end.

They gave it a shot, but the nightmares, the screaming, didn't stop. He loved this house, him and Emilia both, but Heather wasn't getting better there. Arthur didn't believe in ghosts, or vampires, or the Loch Ness Monster, but being there was hurting her. They moved.

He walked outside. The sun was moving higher in the sky, the orange globe visible through the haze. He cut between the fence and walked next door to the former Hill residence. Their property was much larger, it being a working ranch, but the houses were quite close, and nearly identical in construction.

They had joked about that a lot. When Art and Emilia moved in, the Hills had become fast friends. John lost his wife years ago, and never remarried. His oldest son stayed with him, to help work the ranch. Little Heather was a tomboy, wanting to be just like her dad. She'd run over and watch Art work the silver, and he'd tell her all about what he was working on today.

They became close. He didn't have the key to the ranch, but it was deserted as well. The people that bought it had turned it into a vacation rental, where you could live the ranch lifestyle for a week or two. A lot of people around here made fun of those kind of people, but Art understood. It was why he moved there. Made him feel proud of their decision. They'd had the courage to go for it.

He looked inside, but he knew the place by heart, partly because it was so similar to his own old home next door. Emilia would cook for them all at John's place from time to time. She joked that it was still her kitchen. She had tried to get John dates with some of her girlfriends, but he always declined. He'd never gotten over Laura's death. There was no replacing her.

He walked out into their front yard, the parallel gravel road leading to the Hill house. He walked right to the spot. It wasn't marked, but he knew it. There was the big tree, and the few small boulders. He stopped. This was the spot.

The gunshots had woken him up. He slept light, and he'd been thankful for it that night. He wished John had called, woke him, but it happened fast. Art thought about the alternate dimension where he had joined John and Will out there. Would they all still be alive? Or would Art have died with them?

He'd grabbed his rifle and flashlight and run out in his bare feet. They were cut to hell and back when he looked at them later, but he hadn't felt a thing at the time. There was still gunfire as he hurried out the door.

He didn't know what to expect. He remembered thinking "must be bears," because that's the only thing that made sense.

It hadn't been bears.

He saw Heather first, holding a pistol in one hand and a hunting knife in the other. She was covered in blood, so much blood. He had never seen so much blood. It was everywhere. She was surrounded by the bodies, seven dead wolves and two dead men, John and Will. Their throats were ripped out, any chance at saving them gone.

She didn't notice him. She was looking out into the darkness, somehow holding up the pistol and the knife in her shattered arms.

"Heather," he said. She didn't look at him. She peered out into the darkness.

"One more is out there," she said. "It's bigger." She pointed with her pistol. She was 12.

He turned with his flashlight, pointing. There was nothing. Then, a flash of *something*. It was big, much bigger than a wolf. He raised his rifle and fired, an educated guess. He raised his light again, searching, scanning. Nothing.

He waited a few more moments, and then tended to Heather.

The investigation didn't lead anywhere. The official decision was a rogue wolf pack, driven out of the wilderness by wildfires. It didn't make any sense. Wolves didn't act like that. They might get cattle, but gunfire should have driven them off. They would run.

They figured that Heather killed five of the wolves herself, trying to defend her father and brother, at first with a shotgun, and then the pistol and knife. She was "The Hunter" after that at school. She said she didn't remember any of that night now, whenever somebody asked. Art didn't think that was true, but he wouldn't want to talk about it either.

They had come back to the house to get her stuff. She had insisted, with her arms still wrapped in gauze and covered in stitches. She'd walked past where the attack had been, and walked through the house. She'd cried, and cried, but wouldn't leave. She picked out everything she wanted to take, said they could sell the rest.

They put the property in a trust until she was 18. Him and Emilia thought it was only right that she choose what to do with it as an adult. She turned 18 and promptly sold it.

He stood in the same spot as that night, looking out into the darkness. In the police report, they'd asked about the bigger one, the one she had been looking for when Arthur arrived on the scene. They'd asked her how big was it, and whatever size they suggested, she kept on saying bigger. They told her wolves don't get that big. She never backed down, and they stopped asking.

They'd asked Art the same thing. He had said he saw something, and fired at it, and then it was gone. They'd asked him the same questions, and he'd deflected. Said he thought he hit it, but any animal short of a grizzly would have been knocked flat by that rifle. They didn't find anything with his bullet in it.

He hadn't told them everything. He'd seen something, but it wasn't a wolf. It was big, shaped all wrong. It had only been a second, half a second. The light hit it, and he'd fired, and he'd heard the chunky sound of bullet hitting flesh. You hunt enough, you know the sound.

He didn't think about it at the time, but after, he'd realized he had saved both of their lives. The wound had scared the thing off, scared it enough for it to run. He didn't tell anyone that, not even Heather. She had endured enough trauma.

He went back to his truck and drove back into town. He still had time to get groceries before work.

17

Jefferson Hyde Bieter left the mine's offices proud of himself. He had put the fear of God into his son. This town would bend to his will, regardless if they liked it or not.

It was still early in the day, but JH was happy to see people still out and about, even as the fire encroached. That damnable fire. It was getting closer and closer every day. Why couldn't Coffey and his people do their goddamn jobs? He did his, and no one else in this fucking town could do theirs.

But then again, maybe it was for the best. Everything his family owned was insured, as were all the government buildings. There were a lot of old homes, and maybe the best thing that could happen was they got burned out, and he could get some new development in. Hell, with some of the forest gone, he could convince the county to give up some its land. And he'd get a pretty penny from all of it. A fresh start, and chance to build it up even bigger, make it something truly special. A legacy to be proud of.

Vision. That was what no one else had. That was what separated him from them, the wheat from the chaff. If some of the chaff got burned along the way, so be it. He wasn't responsible for everyone.

He looked out his window, at the bustling restaurants and shops. He'd built this out of nothing. Burns' Mine, hell, this whole fucking town, had been a hole in the ground where truckers stopped to fuel up and get their rocks off. Anyone respectable would drive right through. A dirty joke.

He'd built up Burns' Mine, taken on creditors, marketed not just his businesses, but the whole damn town. Those seedy motels now made beaucoup bucks, and he didn't see one red cent from them. They owed everything to him. He'd rebuilt it, cleaned it up; he'd brought people here and their precious, precious money. And what thanks did he get? He got Sheriff Bitch mucking things up. He got a faggot son who couldn't even do what he was told.

Barney Cochbrin had known the score. He'd received a cushy job, and he'd followed orders. Someone causing JH trouble? They suddenly had trouble with the law. Someone in town making accusations? What accusations? They didn't seem so substantial now. Barney had known where his bread was buttered. He's never bit the hand that fed him. JH could have pissed down his neck and told him it was rain. He just had to go and die of a heart attack on the shitter.

And they'd elected Hill to replace him. She was a folk hero, what was he gonna do? He couldn't run James yet— they didn't have anyone to replace him at the mine. Someone had to run that damn place. Her sob story had worked like a charm. She was an orphan, she had killed fucking wolves with her bare hands, she was from here. It was something she would always have over him.

Sure, he owned the mine, but owning the land and being raised here were different things. Truth be told, the mine was a last, desperate gamble with a portfolio that had wilted, and wilted, and wilted.

He wasn't from here. Didn't stop them from electing him mayor, though. But Hill wouldn't stop at sheriff. She had aspirations, ambition. She wanted more. He knew if she thought about it too long, his job was what she'd go after next. And she'd win it.

Can't have that. We cut her off at the knees. We oust her from the position, and then she'll move on. Go to the big city, where dykes like her could get along. She thought she was so secret about it, but his rabbits saw her. He hadn't used the information yet, but he would if he had to. She wasn't willing to get dirty, but he was.

It was for the good of the town. This was a simple mountain town, and there was no way he'd let a queer take it from him. It wasn't right. It was an abomination. Pastor Pearce had said so last Sunday. He'd do it, to keep this town clean.

He'd *have* to do it, because James couldn't take care of anything on his own. Just another burden laid on his shoulders. He'd have to steer his life in the right direction, whatever it took. He'd get that sow pregnant and he'd have a boy, and everything would be right with the world.

There was still police tape out in front of Sally's. He'd have to call Hill and tell her to take it down. The fires had caused enough trouble, and now they had to worry about stabbings too. What would he say? "An isolated incident of violence. The sheriff's office has it all in hand. Conquest is a peaceful town." Yeah, that'd work. Tourists didn't want to see the trouble anyway. They closed their eyes and went on vacation.

And the couple they'd found beyond the pass. He hoped it was just a wild animal. That was easy. "They took risks they shouldn't have, and angered the animal." Bear spray, make noise, etc. People never believed they'd be the victim. If it wasn't an animal—he didn't want to think about it. They couldn't have three attacks in one night. Not permissible.

He rolled into his office with purpose. His secretary Jane was wearing a skirt, and he took a long look at her legs as he entered his office. She tried to get his attention, but he needed to take his morning constitutional. It would have to wait.

There was a man in his office, sitting in one of the big leather chairs positioned in front of his desk. He stood as he heard JH enter. The man was taller than him, and built, his t-shirt tight on his muscles. His haircut made JH wince with jealousy. The motorcycle leathers he wore were stained with road dust.

"Sorry, Mr. Mayor, but your secretary told me you were free this morning. Told me I could wait in here for you," he said. He extended a hand for a handshake. "Jack Samson."

JH took his hand, but was already trying to cut him off at the pass. "I'm sorry, Mr. Samson, but you'll have to come back later. I have several meetings this morning—"

"Your secretary showed me your book," said Jack. "Told me you were free. I have some pretty serious business to talk about."

"I'm sorry, sir, but my secretary was wrong," he said.

"The town had quite a busy night last night, and I've got a lot of work to do."

The man frowned. "I talked to Sheriff Hill earlier, and she told me not to bother with you, said you weren't in charge anyway—"

"Wait just a minute," he said. *That bitch.* "Maybe I can help you—just give me a moment to get settled."

"Of course," said Jack, smiling now. JH sat behind his desk, putting the things he had been carrying in their proper place. Briefcase, newspaper, coffee. He was a little flustered, and he shuffled some papers around on his desk to give himself a moment to collect his thoughts.

"Alright, how can I help you, Mr—" said JH.

"Samson," he said. "Jack Samson. And you can help me by getting Sheriff Hill to release my friend from the county lockup."

"Your friend?" asked JH. "You mean the assailant from last night?"

"I don't agree with that term being used about him," said Jack. "But yes."

"He stabbed some boy over a dozen times," said JH. "Now, I appreciate he's your friend and all, but assailant is the correct term."

"I understand it doesn't look good at first glance, but can I tell you the way he explained it to me?" asked Jack. The man had a plaintive look in his eyes. "He's a good man, and this will ruin his life."

"Go for it," said JH.

"My buddy was defending himself," said Jack. "He felt his life was threatened, and he did what was necessary to defend himself."

"They have three witnesses," said JH. "If it was self defense, it'll work itself out in court."

Jack rolled his eyes. "One of them was the girl that caused the whole thing. She had been flirting with him all night, even though she was out with the Asian boy, and when my friend returned the attention, she got bitchy. Another was the bartender, who believed her over him. The last one was a female deputy, who was parked in a car down the street. And no offense to her or your sheriff, but I just can't trust a woman at policing. They're not reliable, you know?"

JH wavered at that. "I hear you," he said. "If it was up to me, she wouldn't be there. Young man, I do sympathize, I really do, but all of this will come out in the wash. If your buddy is innocent, our fine court system will work it out." JH thought about it for a moment, and relished in the idea of Hill's face being rubbed into dirt. It'd be hard to keep himself out of it, though. Trial probably wouldn't even be over before the election next year.

Jack sighed and grimaced, rubbing his eyes. He looked tormented.

"Mr. Mayor, can I level with you?" he asked.

"Sure, son," said JH.

"My buddy is a good man. We've ridden all over the country, and he's proven it time and again. We're not one percenters. We're not gangbangers. We're just men. He made a mistake, a long time ago, and now his ex-wife has sole custody of his son. He's almost through his probation, and another charge, even if he's innocent, will break it. He hasn't seen his son in years. She's even changed his name to hers. Imagine that. What kind of world do we live in? He breaks his probation—he'll never see his son again."

Jesus. JH looked at Jack, his eyes downcast. *This poor son of a bitch.* JH felt for him. He really did.

But he couldn't let him loose. It'd come out that he made the call, and if this guy even jaywalked later on down the road, JH's name would get dragged through the mud. And he didn't need any help with that. If Cochbrin had still been alive, maybe. But with Hill, no fucking way.

"Sorry, son," he said. "I wish I could help, but my hands are tied. I'll do my best to make sure your friend is taken care of."

JH saw a flash of anger, but only a flash. *That's right, boy. You keep that anger down.* Jack grimaced, and then turned it into a polite smile. This guy had some chops.

"Thank you for your time, Mr. Mayor," said Jack. "Have a nice day."

Jack stood, shook hands, and left empty handed.

18

That night was the worst in Kazuko's life.

Kazuko remembered the night Masaru died. It had been sudden. They were watching television, and he'd complained about some heartburn. She hadn't thought much of it. He would chew antacids like candy, in between puffs on his cigarettes.

She'd woken up next to his dead body the next morning. She had held him. Then she'd gotten up, and called the authorities. They were old, and they both had watched their friends die—to cancer, to heart disease, to old age, to entropy. They had lived long lives. They had raised a child. She was sad, but she was prepared.

She'd expected to outlive him. He had smoked three packs a day for 40 years. A part of her expected it, was ready for it.

When Alice came to her, and told her what had happened to Kyle, it was a shock. It was a set of expectations about her life, dying, all at once.

They got to the hospital, and the young woman translated for her with her phone. Kyle got out of surgery alive, but the next 24 hours would decide his life. She sat next to him, held his hand. She called his parents. They were on a cruise, and out of reach. They had joked before leaving that they would have a better vacation then Kazuko and Kyle. She supposed they were right. Kyle would live or die without them knowing. She left several long voicemails, if they somehow could get them.

Alice stayed with her. Kazuko respected her. She hadn't asked for any of this, but she stood by her side. Kazuko needed her. They could talk through the translator on her phone. Thank God for technology. It was magic.

"<Tell me what happened,>" said Kazuko.

"Are you sure?" Alice asked.

"<Please,>" said Kazuko. "<I need to know.>"

Alice told her everything. She started with when they'd met at the mine, and ended when she met back with her at the hotel.

"I'm sorry," she said. "This is my fault." Kazuko took her hands in hers at that. She shook her head, looking Alice in the eye.

"<Do not *ever* blame yourself for the actions of a man,>" she said. "<A man is responsible for his own violence. The only man who is at fault is the one they arrested.>"

They were quiet for a while. Alice turned on the television, but there were a bunch of war movies on for the holiday. She turned it off.

Kazuko beckoned for her, and after digging through her purse she pulled out a wallet. Alice was confused at first, and then realized she was showing her pictures. All of Kyle.

The first was a baby being held by his mother, the father over her shoulder. They smiled.

"<I was so happy when I heard the news. When Kyle's father Hiroshi left us, and came to America, I had never been so far from someone I loved,>" she said. "<But then Kyle was born. All that trouble his father had gone through seemed worth it, because it had created this beautiful boy.>"

"What did you think about your son marrying an American?" asked Alice.

"<I didn't care. I just wanted him to be happy,>" said Kazuko. "<Masaru, my husband, was upset. For a while. He held a grudge against Kyle's mother, Kate. But then she gave him a male grandson, and all was forgiven.>"

The next picture was in Japan, all of them together. Everyone was smiling, except for Masaru.

"<Masaru never smiled in pictures,>" she said. "<I teased him endlessly about it. I was so happy to see them all. All of us, together. I held him, little Kyle, and sang to him. He sang back! He couldn't speak, but he still sang. It was lovely. It was the only visit they made to Japan before Masaru died.>"

"Why did they never go back?" asked Alice.

"<Masaru and Kyle's father fought. Over everything. Over living in America. Over his career. Over Kyle. Over his wife. Neither would listen to me. They had come to show us this wonderful little boy, and still they fought. I do not blame Hiroshi for not visiting. He wanted to live his own life.>"

The next picture was just Kazuko and Kyle, Kyle held in her arms. She was singing to him, and he was looking back at her, wonder in his eyes.

"<Hiroshi was the best thing to happen to me. Having him, raising him to be a good man was the most impactful thing I could do. When I was young, a meaningful career outside of the home was impossible, but I was able to make Hiroshi a good man, independent, strong, smart, and kind. He in turn, with his wife, raised a thoughtful boy like Kyle, who is now a man.>"

"Would you have done anything differently?" asked Alice.

"<I don't really know,>" said Kazuko. "<But I don't regret my choices. I only regret other people's choices.>"

The next picture was Kyle in high school, an official prom photo. He was shorter than his date. They smiled, both gawky and awkward.

"<Masaru always saw Hiroshi, and then Kyle, as an extension of himself,>" said Kazuko. "<They shared his name so how could he not? I never knew how to talk to Masaru about it. About legacy. Maybe if I had they wouldn't have fought so much.>"

"Don't blame yourself for the actions of a man," she said. "Even your husband."

Kazuko smiled, her own words turned on her. Alice flipped through her phone, and showed her a picture they had taken the night before, Kyle and her. They looked happy.

"<He is a good man,>" said Kazuko. "<He will pull through. I know it.>" Kazuko believed what she said. Kyle was the end product of a lifetime of work. He was too important to die.

A nurse poked his head through the door. "I'm sorry to interrupt, but the sheriff is here to talk to you." Alice used her phone to translate, then followed Kazuko out the door into the central hall where Sheriff Hill stood.

Kazuko looked up at her. A foot's height separated the two of them. Hill extended her hand for a handshake, and Kazuko reached out and grabbed it. Alice explained the phone as translator.

"I'm sorry for all of this," said Hill. "And for the lack of a translator."

"<Do not be sorry,>" said Kazuko. "<Apologies will not heal Kyle. What will be done with the biker?>"

"He's in lockup. He'll see the judge on Tuesday, when he'll be formally charged and make an initial plea. Then they'll set a date for trial."

"<And that's it?"> she asked. "<That's all there is?>"

"I don't understand the question," said Heather. She looked at Alice, who only shrugged. The phone couldn't deliver the nuance a translator could. Kazuko felt herself getting frustrated. She wanted to slap this sheriff across the face, just for someone to *understand* her.

"<This biker, who tried to kill my grandson, who might very well prove successful,>" said Kazuko. "<He will see the judge on Tuesday, and then be formally charged, and then enter your court system.>"

"Yes," said Heather.

"<Does this kind of thing happen often here, Sheriff Hill?"> asked Kazuko.

"No," said Heather. "Most of the crime here is drunk driving. Very little violence."

"<Then how are you so damn calm?>" asked Kazuko. "<My grandson is in there fighting for his life and you're reading me the news!>"

"I'm sorry, ma'am," said Heather. "Sometimes I'm at a loss."

Kazuko looked at her, and saw another woman, her eyes shadowed, her shoulders tight.

"<I apologize, Sheriff,>" she said, collecting herself. "<I did not sleep much last night.>"

"Neither did I," said Heather. "It's been hard to come by."

Kazuko nodded. "<Thank you for your help.>"

She shook the sheriff's hand again, then rejoined Kyle in his room. Alice stayed out with the sheriff, talking with her a bit more. Kazuko felt powerless. She was angry at the biker, and she could do nothing about it. He could end up in prison, but would he ever understand what he had done? Would he ever truly comprehend the amount of pain inflicted?

She looked at Kyle. He needed to live. There was too much of her in him for him to die.

19

Heather tried not to vomit, but it didn't matter. The smell of death was still there, mixed with the smoke, and it was just too strong.

She'd wanted to see the scene herself.

They had waited to pick up the remains until she arrived. She'd brought Buzz with her. She wanted two sets of eyes on it.

It was an absolute bloodbath.

She threw up, and Buzz struggled himself, having to walk away from the scene. The hiker who had found the bodies found the dogs first, two hounds running up and down the trail, dragging their leashes behind them. He had taken a hold of them and then found what was left of the bodies.

Heather had seen countless dead animals, in between

her time on the ranch and hunting. She had field dressed deer. Only dead person was a poor homeless man frozen outside last winter. Grotesque, but sterile.

This was inhuman. The flesh was torn, ripped, but worst of all, mostly just gone. Bones were strewn everywhere, meat stripped from them. The ground was brick colored, the blood and gore soaked in.

"Your nose, sheriff," said Buzz. Heather reached up and realized she was bleeding again. She grabbed a handkerchief from her pocket and held it to her nose.

"Any thoughts, Buzz?" she asked him.

"It was probably bears, driven out by the fires," he said. "At least, I hope that's what it was."

"But so close to town?" she asked. On cue, a honking noise from a vehicle in town rang clear as day.

"Desperate animals will do desperate things," he said. "Like kill people."

"Wasn't a full moon last night, was there?" she asked.

"Nope," he said. "Waxing."

•

JH had called. Asked about the assault, the maulings. Told her about Jack coming to him and asking for self defense, for Runt to be released without a charge. It wasn't like JH. Was he trying to butter her up? She couldn't tell, and that just made Jack's behavior towards her even stranger. The bikers camped out at the Motel Marmot, their bikes all lined up out front. Darla had driven by and they were outside on lawn chairs, drinking. They smiled and waved as she passed. No crime in that.

Jack was playing games, trying to get Runt out before he was charged.

Heather checked for reports of maulings, starting out west, where the fire had started, coordinating with the time and date. Nothing. A few casualties from the fire itself and some sightings of animals running through populated areas, but no attacks, no maulings.

She stopped. Nothing. Just a random attack? She expanded her search outwards.

A hit! East. Two days prior. A lone hiker, found mauled. Severe attack. Flesh stripped. Finalized report as a rogue animal attack. 100 miles away.

She looked again, farther east. Another hit. Another two dead. Similar attack. On a trail, not too far from a town, near dark. 250 miles away. Finalized as an animal attack.

Another. 400 miles away. Two more. Animal attack.

Over the span of two weeks and 400 miles, seven people had been killed, all torn apart. All isolated hikers.

She opened up a map and charted the deaths. East to west, along Highway 2.

What had Jack said? "From Minnesota, west to the Pacific, and then back through the country." This pattern was a man's. Travel along the highway, pick off isolated people. But this violence wasn't a man's violence. It was an animal's.

She called the sheriffs responsible.

"The bodies were ripped apart, Sheriff Hill," said one. "Awful. Had to be a bear. Or a couple of bears."

"Most gruesome thing I've seen on the job, and I've been sheriff for 23 years," said another.

"There wasn't much body to look at," said the last. "The flesh, the organs—just gone."

She told all of them about the pattern.

"That is peculiar," said the first. "But no way a man did

that. Coincidence. All it can be."

"I mean, you're right," said the second. "Seems like man's work. But a man simply ain't capable of what I saw."

"Damn," said the third. "Call the FBI. I'm serious."

And tell them what? That she was starting to suspect a gang of bikers was massacring hikers as they rode across the country? The feds would laugh at her.

Her eyes watered. She rubbed them and poured herself another cup of coffee. She was running on zero sleep. There was a man in the hospital, another in lock up, two dead hikers, and bikers trying to play both her and the mayor. And the goddamn fires made everything even worse.

She closed her eyes and leaned back in her chair.

Her brother's shot hit the wolf, its jaws tight around her forearm. It yelped and crumpled. She pried its mouth off of her and it fell to the ground, limp. There were still more, and her flashlight circled.

"Over here, Heather!" yelled her father. "Give me a shot." She turned and shone the light in front of him. He tracked a circling wolf with the light and shot both barrels of his shotgun. The side of the wolf exploded and it fell over, dead. She heard a short, wet noise, and turned to see her brother on the ground, holding his throat.

It was torn open, a ragged hole from ear to ear. He tried to hold his throat closed, but it was no use. He was dying in front of her. He looked up at her, his eyes begging for help that she couldn't possibly give.

Her father reloaded his shotgun, unaware of his son's wound. He shot again, this time missing. He cursed, and glanced behind him, finally seeing his son dying. "No," is all he said before a shape darted from the darkness, and his throat opened. He fell, his shotgun tumbling from his hands.

Blood was still pouring from Heather's wounded arm. She didn't hurt right now. A wolf came in close and she threw up her other arm in defense. The wolf clamped down on her forearm, its teeth tearing holes in her flesh. It growled. She pulled the hunting knife from her dad's belt and plunged the blade deep into the throat of the wolf, cutting and digging with the razor-sharp knife. It gurgled, and then let go as it fell to the ground. Another approached, slower. She pulled the pistol from her now-dead brother's hand and fired a shot.

A knock on her door woke her up. This shit was getting old. Buzz poked his head in. "Fax came through. All the info on Runt, er, Mr. Iskilbitz," he said.

"Thanks, Buzz," she said. "Keep an eye on him."

"Yes, Sheriff," he said, handing her a sheaf of papers, still warm from the fax machine.

Everything the government had on Steven Iskilbitz. Born in 1931, outside of Kansas City. Arrested in 1961 for assault with a deadly weapon. Found guilty, sentenced to 8 years in prison. Suspected of several murders inside, but there was never any sizable amount of evidence. Pictures attached were him, if a little younger. Got out in 1969, and disappeared. Dropped off the radar completely. *He pops back up nearly fifty years later, looking maybe 10 years older?*

Another mystery. She looked at the picture of Runt, grimacing for his mugshot, in black and white.

What are you, Runt?

20

James stayed late at work, per usual. He started drinking after his father left, and he kept drinking all day.

By the time he left the office, it was dark. The normal late-summer sun was always blocked by the surrounding peaks, and the drifting black smoke choked out the rest of it.

He should go home. Talk to Susan. Apologize for his behavior, try and make it up to her. Take her out for a nice dinner. Try something.

He couldn't. He walked right past his Explorer and down the slight incline that led to the so-called "entertainment" district.

It was crowded—Fourth of July weekend, Saturday night. The sidewalks were packed. The smoke hung low, getting darker by the hour, but people walked through it, breathed it even as it stung their nostrils and burnt their lungs. He walked through the crowd, wearing his two-old day-clothes, taking a knock from his flask whenever it suited him. He didn't notice people eyeing him.

He did a few laps, and wandered into the Nine Ball, the oldest of two pool halls in Conquest, and by far the seediest. He'd taken Susan there on dates, but she had complained about it being scary, so they stopped going.

The Nine Ball was exactly how he remembered it. Wood-paneled walls, neon lights illuminating the darkness that surrounded the beacons of light that were ten pool tables. They served booze, and had a neglected dart board in the corner, but the pool tables were the main attraction. It was also an open secret that if you knew the right people, drugs could be purchased through a couple sets of doors.

It was one of the few places in town that still felt dangerous, a remnant of the town when it had been a truck stop. The rest of the town was manufactured: the Nine Ball was real. It was also air conditioned and emptier than the sidewalk, as most tourists who poked their head in decided against visiting.

James bought himself a drink, and scoped out the room. The bar had a smattering of people focused on their drinking, and the booths were half occupied. Two bikers played nearby, and James threw his quarter on the rail, reserving a spot for the next game. He watched them play as he drank.

Both of them were okay, the smaller of the two pulling out the game from the giant. James wasn't sure if he'd ever met a bigger man. Had to be 6'8", with broad shoulders and a bald head. There was a peculiar scar on the back of his head, a small knot of glaring scar tissue. The other looked strong, but no different from the average biker. He wore his sunglasses inside, a bandanna tied around his head.

The game ended, the smaller man winning. The bigger one only grunted, and then walked to the bar, raising his hand for a drink. He watched them play.

"You're next, friendo," said the winner. "Good luck."

James was half drunk, but he was very good at pool, and he played a little bit better drunk. He broke, and started on a roll. The biker got a few shots in, but James was just too good, clearing the table with ease.

"Some competition," said the biker. "Play again? Drinks on the line?"

"Sure," said James, enjoying the buzz. He reached out his hand. "James Bieter."

"Gunner," said the biker, taking it. He didn't remove his sunglasses.

They played again. Gunner shot better in the second game. James didn't think he was hustling, just trying harder. It didn't matter in the end, however, as James still won, a few balls ahead.

"Guess I owe you a drink," said Gunner. "Beer alright?"

"Suits me fine," said James. "Gunner your real name?"

"I treat it like it is," said Gunner. His lips barely moved when he talked. "I manned a helicopter gun in the war."

"You're a vet?" asked James. "No way you're buying me a drink." James paid for all three of them, throwing a twenty on the bar.

"I appreciate that," said Gunner. His big friend grunted as he got up and walked by them, heading toward a booth where several more bikers sat. "Excuse me. Gotta talk to the captain."

James watched as they walked toward the booth, where they bent over and spoke low with the three men who sat in it. He could barely make them out, but after a minute or two Gunner and his big friend sat down, and a new man got up, walking over to James.

He was taller than James, with piercing blue eyes. He wore a leather vest over a tight white shirt. The sleeves were taut on his arms, and he had a nice haircut. He was handsome, and James caught himself checking the guy out. His father's words echoed in his head. As he approached, James could smell him, leather and oil and earth. It set him at ease in a way he didn't expect.

"Saw you whoop my boy," said the man. He reached out a hand to James. "Name's Jack. Mind a game?"

James took his hand and shook. "James Bieter."

"That's what Gunner told me," said Jack. He smiled, and the pair started playing.

"You from around here, James?" asked Jack as he bent to take a shot.

"Yeah, I manage the historical village and mine tours," he said.

"Oh, wow," said Jack, an impressed look on his face. "Seems like a pretty big deal. This town certainly is packed. Business doing alright?" He missed.

"Better than ever," said James, bragging a little, his face warm. James lined up his shot and made it.

"Nice," said Jack. "You worried about those fires at all?"

"Yeah, but everything's insured," said James. "So we can rebuild if we have to."

"But what about having to evacuate?" asked Jack. "Word around town is that it could happen any minute."

"I know Joe Coffey, the chief fireman out there," said James. "They're keeping it at bay for now. Probably be wiser to evacuate ahead of time, but you only get so many summer weekends for the tourists." James took another shot, but miscalculated the angle, the ball rolling away.

"I'd be afraid of it moving in too quickly to evacuate," said Jack.

"I'm sure Joe will give us fair warning," said James. "Sheriff Hill is keeping her eye on it too."

James looked at him, smiling again. He had a nice smile. "She seems the capable type," said Jack. He took a shot, making his ball in the corner pocket.

"You've met her?" asked James.

"Oh, yes," said Jack. "Partly the reason we're in town. One of ours had a run-in with the law."

"The assault last night? You're friends with him?" asked James. He felt a little cold inside. The danger of the Nine Ball started to feel a little too real.

"Friends is a strong word," said Jack. "But we *are* brothers, so to speak, and you can't abandon your brothers, even when they do something colossally stupid."

"So you rode into a fire to help your brother?" asked James.

"When you phrase it like that, it makes us sound positively heroic," said Jack. "So yes." He winked at James, and James's heart fluttered. *Calm down, James, you're acting like a schoolgirl.*

"I chatted with your father for a bit as well," said Jack as he took aim at his next shot. He let go and the balls clacked, the cue hitting his next ball with deliberate strength. It went in.

James flushed. He hadn't thought about that when he'd given the men his name.

"Or at least I assume he's your father," said Jack. "Share the same name."

"Yeah, JH is my dad," said James. Everything fell out of him, all the ease and charm gone. Jack looked at him, studying him for a second.

"Well, pardon me for saying so," said Jack, "But your dad seems like a bastard." James smiled. Couldn't help himself. He caught himself, straightening his face.

"He," said James, picking his words with caution, "has a very specific way of doing things. His way."

"You're talking like he's listening to you right now," said Jack. "Does he have the town bugged?" He winked at James again.

"Maybe not bugged," said James. "But he has a habit of knowing everything that's going on, whether you tell him or not."

"That sounds awfully paranoid," said Jack. He missed his shot.

"You don't know him," said James. He took aim, but missed his shot as well. He was off his game.

"He's just a man," said Jack. "He can't know everything."

James didn't say anything to that. Jack walked around the table, and with precision laid himself down and snapped off a shot. His ball went in, but so did the eight ball.

"Your game, handsome," said Jack. "I do want a rematch, just give me a second with the fellas. I got to take care of some business, and I'll be back."

Handsome? James needed another drink. He ordered a whiskey on the rocks, and swallowed half of it right away.

Jack was still at the booth, talking to his three friends. It was dark, but James could see him talking to them, but couldn't hear any of it. They looked at him, nodding. The group left without a backward glance. Jack was the only one left.

"Sorry about that," said Jack. "All work and no play makes Jack a dull boy."

"You're in charge?" asked James.

"I guess you could say that," said Jack. "It's not very glamorous, though. That's the part people don't understand."

"Tell me about it," said James. "I bust my ass and I can't get a simple thank you."

"Heavy lies the crown," said Jack. He racked the pool balls in the triangle, then removed it with one swift motion. The balls stayed in place.

James broke, but he didn't make any. The alcohol was starting to get to him. Jack shot, taking solids.

"You like it here?" asked Jack.

James didn't know how to answer. At least not out loud.

"You're allowed to say no," said Jack.

"It's nice enough," said James, finally. "But sometimes I wish I could leave."

"Wife, kids, job," said Jack.

"No kids," said James. "But not for lack of trying," he added, under his breath, but Jack heard him.

"It's never too late to start fresh," said Jack. "All of us used to live in your world. It just didn't suit us. It tried to control us, tie us down, but we all realized, in our own way, that it was impossible. Men aren't supposed to live like this. Penned up, caged like an animal." Jack took another shot, making it.

"We are supposed to run free, be free. Not be held down by wives, or jobs, or fathers. Make our own way," said Jack. He took aim again, and made another shot. And another. And another.

"I used to be just like you," said Jack. "I had someone who told me how to act, how to think, how to feel. I lived that way for a long time, and it drove me crazy." He made another shot.

"It was a bunch of bullshit," said Jack. "I rejected it, and I've never felt better." He lined up his last shot, and made it. He'd run the table.

"Your game," said James. "That was incredible."

"I go on streaks," said Jack, smiling at him. "Let's sit."

They went back to Jack's booth, to the relative dimness away from the tables. James sat beside Jack, and it felt right. He could swear Jack pulled him in there.

They sat close. James could feel Jack's strength and warmth through his two-day-old shirt. Hell, Jack even *smelled* warm.

They talked for a while, and all of the past few days just fell out of James. The fires, the fights with both Susan and his father, everything. Jack just sat there and listened, as James leaned harder and harder into him. They drank some more. James could have talked to him for hours.

"Let's get out of here," said Jack.

"And go where?" asked James. Right now he'd follow this man to the ends of the earth.

"Good question," said Jack. "Follow me."

James followed him, out the back door of the pool hall, into the dark alley. Smoke hung in the air, humidity sucked up in the haze.

Jack grabbed him, pushed him up against the brick of the building, and kissed him. James returned it with enthusiasm. They kissed, and then they sat on Jack's motorcycle, James holding onto him, his arms squeezing Jack hard. They rode down the main drag, for everyone to see, and then parked in the front of the motel.

They got off the bike, James's head spinning. Jack opened the motel door and walked inside.

James followed him in.

21

"You just gonna let that bitch boss you around?" yelled Runt from his cell.

His voice slammed against Bill "Buzz" Sawyer like a wave crashing on the shore. He continued to read his book, and sip his coffee from time to time. Sheriff Hill had left for the day, leaving him alone in the station watching over their only tenant at the moment, Mr. Steven Iskilbitz. He would only answer to Runt, though. They had decided to keep him in the cell closest to the desk. Buzz was starting to regret that decision. He considered himself a patient man, but Runt was testing him.

"Why are you ignoring me?" asked Runt. "Ain't like you got nothing better to do."

"I'm ignoring you because you're a violent criminal," said

Buzz. "And if you don't like being bored, you're in for a rude awakening when you get to prison."

"I'm not going to prison," said Runt. "It was self defense."

"Yeah, sure," said Buzz.

"Why doesn't anyone believe me?" asked Runt. "It's a fucking disgrace I was even arrested in the first place."

"Uh huh," said Buzz.

"You the only one here?" asked Runt. "Having just three cops in a town seems dangerous."

Buzz didn't answer him, but for once Runt was right. It *was* dangerous. But no one expects to lose two fifths of their workforce within a week, although Buzz probably should have seen it coming.

He knew Tom Bennings. They'd worked together for years, since Buzz was hired by Sheriff Cochbrin. Tom loved Cochbrin, and loved the way he'd done things. He'd acted like they were still in the Wild West, and cracked jokes that Tom found hilarious. He'd laugh and laugh whenever Cochbrin told one, usually about women, sometimes about black people. They were funny the first time, but Cochbrin loved to repeat them, and Tom never got tired of them. Buzz had, after a while.

When Cochbrin died, and Hill replaced him, Buzz knew things would change. She was young and, to be honest, smarter than Cochbrin ever was. She was also a woman, which had rankled Tom. He hated taking orders from women. He'd had three wives, all divorced.

Buzz himself didn't care about any of that, as long as she respected him and he kept getting paychecks. But Tom couldn't help himself. Kept trying to do things the old way, which meant drinking on the job, and ignoring reports when it suited him, and repeating the same jokes that Cochbrin used to tell.

It wasn't going to work. Buzz tried to tell Heather that, but she tried to keep the same staff. She didn't want anyone to lose their job.

Tom blew up at her. Matter of time. Called her a bitch *and* a cunt, right to her face. Buzz probably would have beaten his ass if Tom said it to him, but Hill just fired him. Guess you had to have self-control if you were going to make it as a sheriff, with all the politics and such.

Tom had marched out. Worked a landscaping job with his cousin now.

Hank Griffin was the quiet type, but he'd quit after Tom got fired. Buzz figured it was because of Tom, but Darla had told him his wife had said she didn't want Hank working under a young woman like Hill. Felt the temptation was too dangerous. Buzz was fairly certain that Sheriff Hill packed a box lunch, but that was none of his business.

All that happened in under a week, and getting people to work in Conquest was hard, especially people from outside. Isolated, expensive, and boring. Suited him fine, but no young kid would want to work out here.

He didn't tell Runt any of that. Instead, he said, "Shut your mouth and let me read."

"Fucking shameful that you have a woman in charge here," said Runt. "I'll tell you, I've traveled all over the country, and I'm seeing it more and more. Women get elected, get put in charge. They ain't suited for it, biologically. And you know what happens? Men get blamed for everything. It's why I'm in here."

"You're in there because you're a piece of shit," said Buzz, head still in his book.

"Fuck you, pig," said Runt. "That girl in the bar, she was asking for it. And that boy shouldn't have hit me if he didn't want consequences."

"That girl you're talking about I've known since she was a baby," said Buzz. "And you're lucky Darla didn't shoot you on the spot for what you did that boy."

"Oh, because you've known her since she's a baby it changes everything," said Runt. He was on the bars now, head pushed right up as far as it could go. "Makes me fucking laugh. You hypocrite. Does everything change when it's a girl *you* know? Bet you're one of those motherfuckers who starts sentences with 'I have a daughter —' blaughty bla bla."

Buzz pursed his lips. He knew Runt was trying to get a rise out of him. Entertaining himself by making him angry. It was working. Buzz had once been ignorant, a stupid kid who didn't think about much outside of himself. Then he'd gotten married, had kids, a daughter who was close friends with Alice growing up.

As she got older, and he saw the dangers she faced every day, he learned. He realized how dangerous the world was for women. He was tasked with protecting her, by any means necessary, and he realized it was impossible. There were too many things out there trying to get her. Too many men. He taught her to protect herself, the only thing he could give her.

With that came shame. Shame of who he was, and further shame of *what* he was. He caught himself looking at women when he shouldn't. He caught himself questioning Hill and Darla's orders and suggestions. He became aware of every time he saw a female driver do something bad and thought it was because she was a woman, of his anger at it. He was a hypocrite, and there was no removing the hypocrisy. It was too late.

"They're here to serve men," said Runt. "God himself told us that, yet every day we get further from that truth."

Buzz dropped his book. Enough of this shit. He grabbed Runt by the collar, pushing him back from the bars and then yanking him forward, slamming his head into the cast iron. The metal rang with a dull thud as Runt's skull bounced off it. Buzz slammed him into it once, twice, three times, and then pushed him backwards.

"You shut your fucking mouth," said Buzz. Runt was on the ground, still smiling, blood running down his face, his forehead split open from the bars.

"Touched a sore spot, did I?" asked Runt. "Don't worry, I can't get to your precious little girl from here. Safe behind bars." The blood coated his face, but he did nothing to stem the flow. He laid down and blew a jet of air, the blood misting up from him. He laughed.

Buzz exhaled, trying to slow his breathing. He grabbed his book and retreated from Runt, into the main bullpen area.

As he walked away, he could hear Runt laughing.

22

Susan wouldn't go if James came home. She'd talk it out with him and try, try to find some kind of peace with him.

He didn't come home.

She looked through her wardrobe, digging deep into her closet. She tried on several dresses, but all of them fit a little too tight, each a little too unflattering. She had put on some weight over their marriage, like most people did, but she still felt guilty for not looking how she used to. Maybe it was the reason James never touched her anymore.

She found a red dress, never worn, bought for an event they'd never gone to. She did her makeup, wearing red lipstick to match, and curled her hair. She even wore matching underwear. She put on the dress, and she couldn't recognize the woman looking back at her in the mirror. It was an hour past when she would normally expect James home. No word. He had his chance.

She took an Uber to the Stone Buffalo, called that because the last restaurant there left a gigantic stone buffalo in the middle of the dining room, the statue weighing thousands of pounds. The new restaurateur had taken it as inspiration and named the restaurant after it.

She walked inside, the fresh air a welcome change from the thick smog that had settled into the town. The smoke was getting worse, and she couldn't help but look at the plumes of soot rising on the horizon from the burning forest. She put it out of her mind.

The place was busy, a subtle rumble of noise in the background as people's chatter filled the space. Her eyes went to the bar, looking for Andrew, looking for a beautiful man wearing leather. She couldn't see him, and her stomach fell when she realized it was all a sham, a ploy, and she had gotten all worked up and all dressed up for nothing.

Then one of the men at the bar turned his head, and it was him. He wore a sports coat, and raised his hand slightly to make sure she saw him. He smiled, soft and easy.

She walked over to him, sitting down next to him. He didn't try to hide his staring.

"You look good in red," he said. "It suits you."

"Thank you," she said, smiling. She felt awkward, on a date with a stranger. There was a ball of guilt still inside her gut, reminding her that she shouldn't be doing this. *Go home, Susan. Be a good wife. Good wives don't go on dates with handsome bikers.*

"They made me put on a coat before I could sit down," said Andrew. "I didn't know it was that kind of place."

"Conquest attracts a lot of rich tourists, so it has fancy restaurants," she said.

"I can see that," said Andrew, looking around. "Felt like the Blues Brothers in here when I came in."

"I've never seen it," said Susan.

"Everyone stopped and stared," said Andrew. "Much like I did when I first saw you."

Susan blushed. She hated that she did, hated not being able to control it. James never complimented her.

"That's terrible," she said. "Do you tell all the women that?"

"Only the ones I like," he said. "I'm glad you came."

"My husband didn't come home last night," she said, after a pause. "And I don't think he will tonight, either."

"I'm sorry," said Andrew, his voice unnaturally stilted.

"It's okay," she said. "I'm here, right?" The bartender dropped her off a glass of wine and she drank it down in one swallow.

"Where are you from, Andrew?" she asked. She squinted her eyes at him. "Or can you not tell me that either?"

"I usually tell people I'm from Atlanta, or Charlotte," he said. "But I'm really from a tiny-ass town in bumfuck Alabama," he said. "I didn't like it there, so I left."

"Just that easy, huh?" she asked. "You just left?"

"Well, I may have caused a little trouble," he said. "But it was because I didn't like it. And yeah, I just left."

"Do you have family anywhere?" she asked. "Anything anywhere?"

"My daddy left before I was born," he said. "And Momma died when I was 12. State watched me 'til I was 18. None of 'em loved me."

"That's sad," she said.

"You get over it," he said. "You have to, or you'll die." He swallowed the rest of his whiskey sour, and ordered another drink for each of them. They ordered their food.

"Why are you riding with a man that would stab people on the street?" she asked.

"You're asking me a bunch of hard questions, you know that?" he asked back.

"Handsome is only going to get you so far," she said.

"Genetics," he said. "The one thing my father gave me he couldn't take."

"You're not getting away from my question, however many folksy sayings you have," she said. "And honestly, as gorgeous as you are, I need a real answer."

"That's fair," he said just as their food arrived. "Can we eat first? That way if my answer isn't agreeable, it won't ruin the meal."

They ate, the array of food impressive and delicious. Meals here ran over a hundred dollars a person, not including alcohol, so she hoped it would be. Everything was amazing. They cleaned every plate. They talked, about everything and nothing. About Conquest, about the fires, about the food. They flirted. Susan could breathe.

"You want dessert?" he asked.

"I want your answer," she said. "If it's good, then we can get dessert."

He thought for a moment more. "The crew I run with is led by a guy named Jack. He wasn't the one who recruited me into the group, though. Guy who recruited me was named Shadow. Shadow saved my life."

"His name was Shadow?" asked Susan.

"I thought you wanted an answer?" asked Andrew.

"Sorry, sorry," said Susan.

"Anyways. He was kind of a hippie, long silver hair, spoke in deeper meanings, if you know what I mean. But he was smart, been around a long time. Worked out some stuff in his life. I've never belonged, anywhere I've gone. Anytime I've started to settle in someplace, something comes out of me and ruins it." He was struggling to describe it. "The bad in me. It was uncontrollable. It ruined my life for a long time." He stared at his hands.

"Shadow taught me how to control it, and he earned my loyalty because he did," said Andrew. "He had done the same for all the others, one at a time, and they reacted the same way."

"They gave him their loyalty, and joined the club?" she asked.

"Yes," he said. "And that man who stabbed that boy last night was one of them. But I was the young one of the group. Hence, Kid. Only been with them about a year. And recently, Jack took over control of the group. They had problems with Shadow, grudges, built up over the years. What was I to say to them? I was the new guy, so I let it happen."

"But —" said Susan.

"But—since Jack has taken control," he said. "The group has become something else. Something Shadow wouldn't recognize. And I don't owe any loyalty to any of those guys. I see my chance, I'm out of here. On my own again."

She looked at him for a long while, and he sipped on his whiskey sour. She flagged down a server.

"We'll have the blueberry tart," she said.

The tart was delicious. Once they were finished, they

started walking without direction. The smoke was heavy in the air, and as they wandered through Susan's familiar town, it grew into something different, unrecognizable. Landmarks became distant alien obelisks, known only when confronted face to face. They passed people, shapes in the smoke, strangers. The pair were all like them. Lost.

They ended up back at her house. She didn't know how. Susan Bieter bringing a strange man home. Scandal would erupt through the grapevine. She was pulling off his clothes before the door shut, kissing him hard.

The thought of her husband coming home did not cross her mind. James was gone, and so was Susan Bieter.

23

Heather needed a good night's sleep. A drink would also be welcome. So, she went to Sam's.

Sam was making dinner for them when she arrived. A glass of wine had already been poured. Some soft indie rock was playing on the small Bluetooth speaker in the corner.

"You know me well," said Heather, sitting down at the bar and looking into the kitchen.

"Have you slept at all today?" asked Sam, tending to the pan simmering on the stove.

"I took a nap at work," said Heather. "It wasn't very restful, though."

"You can sleep in tomorrow," she said.

"I can't afford to," said Heather. "Too much to do, not enough people."

Sam switched off the burner, moving the pan to a cool corner of the stove. She sidled over to Heather, sitting on her lap, straddling her.

"And there's nothing I can do to convince you otherwise?" she asked. She kissed Heather.

"Well, maybe," she said. "When you put it that way."

Sam kissed her again, and then moved back into the kitchen. "I just need to make the sauce, then dinner will be ready."

"You tease," said Heather.

"You say that like it's a bad thing," replied Sam, her back to Heather once again.

Heather drank her wine, the earthy red settling into her bones, warming her. They had only started dating a few months ago, but she felt a comfort around Sam that she had never experienced before. Sam understood her need to keep their relationship quiet, and understood her almost unrelenting workaholism, perhaps because Sam was so driven herself. Still, Sam would be leaving in two months, driving south for the winter, giving tours in Arizona and New Mexico.

She asked Heather to go with her. And part of Heather wanted to, even if leaving Arthur would kill him and leaving Conquest would feel like surrender.

"You're being quiet," said Sam.

"Just checking you out," said Heather. Sam shook her butt at her, eliciting a laugh from Heather.

"Dinner is ready," said Sam. She plated their food, and they started to eat.

"How was your day?" asked Heather.

"It was alright," she said. "Smoke hurt the ride some, but

everyone understood. We had to slow down because people were having trouble breathing. I'll have to cancel my bookings if it gets any worse. You hear anything from the front?"

"No updates since early today. It's bad, but they're fighting it. Joe's a good man, he'll do his best."

"What about that biker?" asked Sam. "What the hell was the story?"

"It's only gotten more and more confusing. The victim is still in critical condition. Seems like they were just fighting over a woman. Alice, don't know if you've met her. Works at the mine, gives tours. I was in Girl Scouts with her."

"But—"

"But today his biker buddies show up. Their leader talks to me and then goes and talks to JH, trying to play both ends against the middle. They're holed up in Motel Marmot, and been seen all over town. Big wolf patches they wear on their leather. They're up to something."

She didn't say a word about the hikers found up beyond the pass, or the various hikers who had died in the previous weeks. Or the fact that "Runt" was recorded as 86 years old. She didn't have all the pieces.

"Sounds like biker behavior to me," said Sam. "Bunch of macho grandstanding that eventually gets someone hurt or killed. Dick-measuring contests."

"It's not what we usually get here," said Heather. "Even the bikers who come through mostly just want to ride the mountain roads and get drunk."

"Men pretending to be outlaws," said Sam. "Gotta fulfill that mid-life crisis."

"That's not fair," she said. "Okay, maybe it's mostly fair, but still, they're harmless."

"My little country mouse, always seeing the best in people," said Sam.

"You say that like it's a bad thing," said Heather, sticking her tongue out at Sam.

They finished dinner.

"That was pretty dang good," said Heather. She was on her third glass of wine, and could feel her cheeks start to redden. She was beginning to grow numb, and it felt good after days of stress piling up on her. They laid on the couch, putting on a movie they'd seen a million times. They didn't get very far before they grew more focused on each other than on the movie.

They moved to the bedroom, Sam pulling Heather along. They touched each other, relishing the moment, taking it slow.

•

Heather was tired, drained, but couldn't fall asleep. Sam slept next to her. She envied Sam, who could close her eyes and fall asleep anywhere. Thoughts of the dead hikers, of her conversation with Kazuko, of JH, of Jack, kept popping up. She emptied her mind, trying to sleep, but the nightmares of circling wolves kept nipping at the edges. She started drifting off, on the precipice, when a clanking noise shook her awake.

Her eyes popped open, unsure if she had imagined the noise or not. It happened again, a noise of metal on metal. The trashcans? Was it raccoons? She sighed and got up, throwing her clothes back on, and slipping her under-arm holster on as well. Could never be too careful. She looked at Sam, still asleep. Would sleep through an earthquake.

She walked outside, using the small flashlight by the front

door to look around. The trashcans were undisturbed. There was nothing out there. The wind, playing tricks on her. She was about to go back inside when she heard a cough, farther out in the darkness, away from the small house. She pulled her gun, flashlight in one hand, pistol in the other.

The smoke was thicker, and the beam was hazy. She saw an ember redden out of the corner of her eye in the small copse of trees that bordered the property. She walked over to it, the light and gun leading the way.

A voice from the darkness called. "Please don't shoot me, Sheriff. I'm unarmed. Only want to talk."

Her light cut to the source of the sound, with her pistol following. It was one of Runt's friends, tall, a cigarette dangling from his mouth, his hands up in the air. His face was wrinkled, and he was skinny, like old men sometimes get.

"What the fuck are you doing here?" she asked, her gun still pointed at him.

"Jack don't know that I'm here," he said. "I couldn't just walk up to the Sheriff's Office, now could I?"

"So you track me out here?" she asked.

"You can put down the gun," he said. "I'm not gonna hurt you. If you're not quiet you're gonna wake up the whole neighborhood."

Heather lowered her pistol and holstered it. She dropped the flashlight so it wasn't directly in his face.

"You want to talk? Then talk," she said. "What's your name?"

"Abe," he said. "I ride with Jack. And Runt."

"And?" asked Heather.

"You need to let Runt go," he said. "Give him back to Jack. Put everything down as self-defense, then we'll disappear. You've got enough on your plate with this damn fire. You'll never see us again."

"Are you crazy?" asked Heather. "Do you think I haven't noticed the games you and your friends are playing? He's dangerous, and I'm definitely not releasing him on claims of self-defense."

"You don't have to believe it," said Abe. "Knowing Runt, he deserves to rot in prison. But Jack won't leave without him."

"You're not the Hell's Angels, you're not the Mongols," she said. "Maybe you like to play like you're outlaw bikers, but you're just a bunch of men in outlaw biker cosplay. What can Jack do that I should be so concerned with?"

Abe started. "He—we—he will do whatever he can—"

"Enough of this nonsense," she said. "I don't know how you tracked me here, but next time one of you shows up in the middle of the night I'm going to shoot first."

She turned, leaving Abe in the dark, his cigarette still dangling from his lip.

"I know what happened to those hikers," he said, Heather just on the edge of earshot. "The ones that got killed up beyond the pass."

Heather stopped, turned back on him.

His voice came from the darkness. "We killed 'em."

"Why shouldn't I arrest you right now?" she asked, marching back at him, hand on her holstered pistol.

"Because no one would believe you. Hell, you won't believe *me*. But you're clearly too smart for vague bullshit, so here I am. And if you want to arrest me, I won't resist. God knows I deserve worse than prison. But it won't make anything better. Honestly, it'd probably just make things worse."

"Why?" asked Heather. "Talk."

"You met Jack," said Abe. "By the way, any last name he gave you is bullshit. He's just Jack, always has been. Shadow gave him that name, and it's the only one he's ever had. This isn't about Runt, or even me, if you take me in. It's about Jack, and his principles. About what we are, and what we're supposed to be." His cigarette was mostly gone, and he popped another from a pack he had in his pocket, chaining it. He was falling apart. Heather could see it.

"Thought I was too smart for vague bullshit," she said.

"No, you're right, but I've been hiding all of this for sixty goddamn years. We don't even speak plainly around each other. Makes it hard just to switch it off."

"Start from the beginning," she said.

"It's a good place to start," he said. "I was born in 1899, in Missouri."

"Makes you almost a hundred and twenty years old," she said. "You look pretty good for 120."

"Thanks," he said. He puffed on his smoke. She couldn't even see the difference when he exhaled. "I was born in 1899, in Missouri. We were poor. My daddy beat me. Wasn't remarkable at the time. But one day he beat me, and something changed."

"What changed?"

"You believe in werewolves? Shapeshifters?" asked Abe.

"Is this a roundabout way of you telling me your whole gang is a group of werewolves?" asked Heather. "Because no, I don't. I don't believe in ghosts, or goblins, or UFOs, or vampires. There are enough monsters out there without me dreaming up new ones." Abe just looked at her, smoking his cigarette. His face didn't change. His wrinkled eyes just stared at her.

"I was thirteen. I had snuck some of my dad's booze, and he was pissed as a nest full of hornets. Wasn't me drinking that bothered him, but that I had taken some of his whiskey. 'This shit is expensive' were his exact words. I had to go pick the switch myself. I grabbed one, and he whipped me with it. More times than he had before. Think he was drunk. I don't really remember." He waved it off. "Don't matter. Something happened to me, something inside me, something that had been dormant, I guess. I don't really know. I changed shape. My bones, my muscles, my tendons imploded, exploded. I grew larger, stronger, faster. My clothes shredded around me. I can describe it, an odd hundred years later, but at that moment, I had no idea what was happening. I couldn't understand it, or control it. I became a beast, bigger than a bear, wolf-like, I guess, but monstrous. Nothing about it is pretty. My daddy didn't know what was happening. Probably thought it was the devil in me, or something. He tried to attack me. I don't know if it woulda mattered anyway, but he mighta lived if he had run."

"You killed him," said Heather.

Abe inhaled on his cigarette. "In an instant. He was dead before he knew it. It was instinct, and that's all I could run on then. I killed him, and I fed on him."

Heather couldn't help but grimace.

"It's a thing you should keep in mind," he said. "When we change, hunger overwhelms every other instinct we have. We burn through calories so fast, so damn fast. You don't care what you're doing, as long as there is something—anything to eat."

"My mother heard the chaos, and she ran in on it," he

said. "One small mercy is that I took off when I saw her. I ran, and I ran fast. I woke up in the forest, naked, just like in the movies. I snuck back into the house, stole some clothes, and left home for good. I didn't know what I was, but I did know I was a monster. And monsters don't live with people."

"I lived on the road. I couldn't control when I changed, or what I did when I changed. It's all a blur now. I'm sure I killed more people. But especially back then, it woulda looked like an animal did it, even if it didn't make any particular kind of sense. I went on that way for a while. Hell, decades. I tried to stay drunk. Seemed to keep the change at bay."

"I hated myself. I wanted to die," he said. "Then I met Shadow. Well, he found me. I don't know how. He kept his eyes open, and he found us. Reports of maulings, weird news, whatever. And Shadow changed my life."

"He was one of us," said Abe. "A shape shifter. But he could control it. He was older than me, maybe a hundred by the time I met him, hard to say. But he taught me how to control it, how to change only when I wanted to, or when I absolutely had to, how to rein it in, and even how to take control of myself when I was in the other form."

"Out of the goodness of his heart?" asked Heather.

"Actually, yeah," said Abe. "He knew there were others out there. He knew they were out of control, like he had been. And he wanted to support us, all of us, in getting that control back. There were rules, though, all of which were welcome when I first learned I would be able to control my life again. First rule was no killing people. Hard line. If you were defending yourself, and there was no other way, alright, but even then, no changing. Second rule was always to maintain control over yourself. You didn't give in to the other form, no matter how you felt. And the third rule was that you don't leave The Pack."

"The Pack?" asked Heather.

"Our name for ourselves," said Abe. "I would have signed my soul over to the devil to take back control. All Shadow asked was that I wouldn't be a monster anymore."

"You said before, 'was one of us,'" said Heather. "Shadow died? Or was he cured?"

"One and the same," said Abe. "Only cure is death. But yeah, Shadow's dead. He added to The Pack, one by one. Me, Runt, Gunner, Jack, Bark, Beast, and Kid, just last year. All of us in the same place, all of us desperate for control. Jack's the youngest of us. He was feral. Must have first changed when he was a kid. Parents abandoned him, but he survived. Shadow took him in, socialized him. He was more animal than man, but he learned fast. And we had all the time in the world." Something in Heather's mind turned, when Abe said that, but she was missing something.

"You don't age?" asked Heather

"Slow. Real slow," said Abe. "About one year for every five of yours. I imagine old age will eventually get us, but it would take a long, long time."

"What happened to Shadow?" asked Heather.

"We killed him," said Abe, after a long pause, another puff on his cigarette. "I'd like to say that Jack killed him, and technically that's true, but I might as well have done it my-self. I should have died with him." The cigarette shook in his fingers.

"Jack was tired of running, tired of keeping the thing inside of him on a leash. He was tired of feeling guilty for being born the way we are. And Shadow wasn't much on compromise."

"No women in The Pack?" she asked.

"Nope," said Abe. "Ain't no women shape changers. They don't get it, for whatever reason. Shadow always guessed it was genetics, dormant genes or something. 'Course, we ain't ever gone to the doctor. Government would chop us up into little pieces, just to see how we worked."

They stood in silence for a minute while Heather was working through all of it. It explained the hikers, it explained Runt's appearance despite his age. But still, werewolves?

"I know you don't believe any of this shit," said Abe. "I'd change right now, but it'd be dangerous. I haven't fed in a while." He believed what he said, that was clear. But he could also just be fucking crazy.

"I need to see it," she said. "Prove it."

Abe puffed on his cigarette, thinking.

"Alright," he said. "But if I don't start changing back real quick, run like hell."

Abe undressed. Heather glanced away. She pulled her pistol again, holding it at the ready.

"That won't do you no good," said Abe. "But if it makes you feel better, go on ahead. Watch."

Heather watched, her light showing Abe, naked now, skinny. And then he changed.

It was disgusting, ugly. Bones popped, muscles grew, burst, and then grew again. Skin stretched, exploded, hair spreading. He ballooned, an obscene, absurd growth. He rose taller, his bones stretching, thickening. She stepped back, almost tripping, catching herself.

And then he was done. A massive, ugly beast stood in

front of her, hoarse breathing and rotten breath. Grey skin, covered in coarse fur, stretched to the limit by dense, cartoon-like muscles.

"YOU, SEE," said Abe, and he changed back, just as fast. Heather turned away. She still heard it, his body changing, organs, bones, all sliding back into place.

It was true, everything he said. It was real.

"Christ," said Abe, fully human again. He was breathing hard. He put his clothes back on.

"How does it feel?" asked Heather.

"It's burning alive," said Abe. "The whole time."

She let him collect himself and finish dressing.

"You've been riding around the country for 60 or 70 years and no one's ever caught on?" asked Heather.

"We don't go to cities , and we mostly stay out of towns. There's a lot of road in the US, and mostly people ignore us," said Abe. "Part of what Jack wanted to do different than Shadow was to dip our toes into civilization."

"Turned out great," said Heather.

"Jack is pissed at Runt," said Abe. "Might even kill the guy himself once he gets him out, but he can't let him stay locked up. Makes Jack look bad to the rest of us, and he might reveal us, knowing how weak Runt is. Neither is allowable. That's why I came here, why I'm talking to you."

Heather stared at him.

"Just let Runt go," said Abe. "There will be bloodshed if you don't. Jack has only talked so far. As Runt gets further and further outside his grasp, he'll do worse to get him back."

"There's a boy in the hospital," said Heather. "And sure as shit Runt is guilty."

"Justice ain't always the right choice," said Abe. "Throwing good money after bad."

Heather studied Abe. She knew he meant what he said. She could let Runt go. Make things easy. She thought of the grandmother. Thought of those hikers. Thought of Joan Seymour, and when she'd decided to run for sheriff. And Art's question.

She had been drinking coffee with Art on a Saturday morning.

"Is this worth fighting for?" he asked. "Because if you're serious, that's what this is gonna be. A fight."

"Of course," she said. "Joan deserved better, and I—"

"I'm not talking about Joan," said Art. "You're right about her. But I mean this town. Conquest. Is this a hill you're willing to die on?"

Joan Seymour was a friend of Heather's, a local. She waited tables. She dated a lot. One night, she went home with a wealthy tourist. She accused him of rape the next morning.

Cochbrin and JH couldn't sweep it under the rug. Joan refused to quiet down, refused to drop the charges.

It never went to trial. The little evidence the cops had disappeared overnight. Joan couldn't find work anymore, and she left town. Most people shrugged. Heather couldn't stomach it.

"It's worth what we've put into it," said Heather. "And I'll make it better."

Art stared at her then, a long look.

"But would you die for it?"

"No one's gonna die, Dad," she said.

"You're trying to change things, Heather," he said. "And change is life and death to some people."

But would you die for it?

Abe was staring, waiting for an answer.

"No," said Heather. "I can't."

Abe returned her look for a second, and then looked down, finishing his cigarette. He dropped it and stomped out the ember underneath his boots.

"I tried," said Abe. "I can only do so much before he notices. He's smart. I'm not even supposed to be here. I'm supposed to be finding Kid, but he's disappeared. I'll do my best to stop Jack if it gets serious."

"It already is serious!" she said.

"No," he said. "Not yet." Abe walked away. Heather reached for her pistol, thought about stopping him, arresting him, doing *something*. But she didn't, and Abe walked away through the darkness and the smoke.

She went back inside and took a long drink of water in the kitchen. Sam was still asleep, like a log. She laid back down next to her, and Sam shifted slightly.

Heather's heart rate was elevated, and she wasn't sure if she'd be able to calm herself down enough to sleep, exhausted as she was. Shapeshifters, wildfires, murder.

She did sleep, drifting away. She slept hard and deep, her body weary.

When she woke up, the town was on fire.

24

Joe Coffey and his men fought the wildfire with everything they had, but the fire burned on regardless.

They'd worked sixteen-hour shifts for weeks now, and it was starting to wear on them all. Even Joe, known for a ridiculous level of endurance, was finally starting to tire. They had fallen back ten miles in just the last day, and he was starting to lose any hope of saving Conquest.

They were in hell. The sun hung low, and the smoke whipped by them, ash falling from the sky. Joe didn't know what the apocalypse would look like, but he couldn't imagine it being much worse than this. Gray, black, orange saturated his vision. The few green trees felt wrong, a freakish break from this new paradigm of color sent down by God himself. The trees demanded to be burnt, by existing, not being eaten up by the beetles, by remaining alive in this hellscape.

The wind was pushing too hard, their breaks not wide enough. There were only so many of them, trying to fight too much. Joe thought they had pulled back far enough, but he was wrong. And it was costing them. The fire pushed and pushed, and they desperately tried to clear the area. If it jumped them again, he'd call JH and force the evacuation through, consequences be damned.

He took a short break, trying to absorb as much water as he could into his body. Five minutes every hour, he told all his men. Stop, drink as much water as your body can hold, and get back to work. No help to anyone if you collapse from dehydration or heat stroke.

Wilburn took his break as well, guzzling cup after cup of water. It spilled down his shirt and under his gear.

"Got a hole in your lip, Wilburn?" asked Joe.

"I still think I can drink faster than I can," he said, making a bizarre kind of sense to Joe. "Are we actually going to stop this fire, Chief?"

"We're damned sure going to try," he said. "Ask God for His goddamned wind to stop for just a fucking second, and we might have a chance." Wilburn was the unofficial Chaplain of the group. He conducted the group prayers every time they went out. Joe counted a couple atheists in his twenty-man crew, but they didn't mind the ceremony. Firefighters would take all the help they could get.

"I've been asking, Chief," said Wilburn, gasping after another massive swallow of water. "But he hasn't answered yet."

"He might listen if you weren't such a goddamn dirty

sinner," said Joe, smiling. Wilburn was also dating three different girls at the moment. Being a young, handsome firefighter had its advantages.

"It ain't a sin if they know it's not serious," he said.

"You think they'd agree with that if I asked 'em?" asked Joe. Debating modern relationships in hell, with men thirty years his junior.

"I am very clear about the nature of our relationships," he said. "My only commitment is to my Lord and Savior, Jesus Christ."

"Well I hope he's fucking listening," said Joe, gulping down a final cup of water. He slipped his gloves on, getting ready to get back to work, but froze when something changed. It sounded different, felt different. Joe slipped a glove back off, stuffing two dirty fingers into his mouth. He held them up for a moment, and then smiled. The wind had stopped.

"Thank the fucking Lord!" he yelled at Wilburn, and then called to all the crew within earshot. "Now's our chance! Double time, boys! Let's lick this thing!"

Word passed down the line through the crew, and they put their nose to the grindstone, forcing weary muscles to push through the aches and pains of hours hacking through vegetation and dirt, trying to fight nature itself. They were spread thin, but this proved that God was on their side.

The boys worked hard, the dead wind a sign. They put their heads down and hacked at the underbrush, adding accelerant where it needed it, and setting the boundaries of the control.

They all wore their gear, heavy jackets and pants, gloves, and even helmets, with oxygen tanks. Joe was strict about that shit. It was hot as fuck with all that gear on, but if he caught any of his men trying to cool off, or get by without it, they'd be getting their pay docked. Not wearing your gear was dangerous, and could kill you in a second.

It was heavy, it was hot, it was uncomfortable, but it saved their lives every day. It also made hearing difficult, even without fires roaring nearby, and chainsaws revving, and trucks idling.

Joe didn't sit back at the cooler, or at the truck. He put his head down and worked with his men. He worked with Tommy Doheny nearby, but the rest of the crew were spread over a mile. They each had a radio, but his crew was quiet. Well trained, and disciplined for the roughnecks they were.

"You hear that?" asked Tommy.

Joe stood up, listening. "Hear what?" he asked.

There was a whistle, coming from the west. Then it ended, cut off.

"Whistle," said Joe. He grabbed his radio.

"Johnson, come in," he said. No response.

"Johnson, answer," he said. Still nothing.

He called out again. "Anyone," he said. "Come in." Silence greeted him. He looked at Tommy. They stared out to the west, where the rest of the squad were, and they couldn't see a thing. Visibility was next to nothing, but Joe had seen Miller at the edge of his vision not five minutes ago.

The control burned around them. "Let's go find them."

Joe and Tommy hustled toward the rest of the crew. It wasn't radio malfunction. Someone blew their alarm whistle.

His eyes scanned the horizon, looking for any movement in between the pine trees that towered above them.

The trees were tighter here, clustered together. The men had sawed them down so the fire couldn't spread through the tree tops.

"Chief," said Tommy.

"What?" asked Joe.

"Chief," he said again, grabbing Joe's shoulder.

"What, Tommy? Jesus Christ," said Joe, looking back, and finally noticing that Tommy was pointing. Not toward movement, but up, in the boughs of the nearby trees.

His first thought was of Christmas. His family, every year, would set aside a Sunday, and they'd put up their tree and decorate it. The wife and the kids handled most of it. He'd go out and buy the tree every year on the way home from work. Always a live tree. No plastic trees for Joe Coffey.

They'd decorate it with the lights, and the ornaments. His wife loved the decorations, and he'd haul bin after bin of bulbs and Santas and all kinds of crap out of storage every year for his wife and the two girls to decorate. He'd lay on the couch and watch football. After they were done, they would call him in for the "inspection." He'd poke and prod at the tree, and decide if it was worthy. It was always declared worthy, if only after Joe had teased his wife and daughters a bit. But the tree wasn't ready then, not yet. There was one more step to finish.

The tinsel. It was his duty. He would wrap the tinsel around the tree, from the base all the way to the star that graced the top. The whole ritual was the same thing his father had done when he was a kid, and Joe could still feel him as he wrapped the gaudy silver strings around the tree. He looked forward to it every year.

The pines that surrounded them were much too big to be

Christmas trees, but they resembled them nonetheless. You could even compare the sparks of the fire floating among the needles to resemble crude lights. It was the tinsel, though, that made him think of Christmas. Tommy was pointing up, among the boughs, at the long ropes of intestines that were strung between the trees, hung over branches, dangling, blood dripping from them to the forest floor, sizzling as it hit the embers. Long lines of them. 30 feet of small intestine in the human body, an old biology class ringing in Joe's mind.

"Oh dear God," he said. He looked back down, and he saw shapes moving through the smoke. They were big.

"Chief," said Tommy. "Orders?"

Joe didn't have a master thesis that explained why he became a firefighter. If pressed, he would say that they help people in a very simple way, and that he got a lot of pleasure out of performing a civic duty. Most people would thank him when they learned he was a firefighter, and tell him that he was brave.

He'd thank them in return, because he was goddamn polite, but he didn't think he was brave. He knew the dangers of what he was facing, but fundamentally, a fire was a big thing, especially forest fires. They took teams of men to beat back, to defend against, to ultimately extinguish. And mostly, he didn't stand up to the fires, like a medieval knight fighting a dragon. Mostly, he looked into the heart of this thing, saw its size, and ran.

"Run, Tommy," said Joe, his voice just above a whisper. "I have a shotgun in my truck."

They ran.

Joe tossed aside his small oxygen tanks and mask, risking

breathing in some smoke to shed the extra weight. Tommy followed his lead, and they sprinted through the forest, the control blazing around them. They stomped through the embers. Joe's truck was a few hundred yards away, not that far, but they were exhausted when they started this morning, and then they'd worked all day. Joe didn't look behind him, but he could hear the shapes, loud footfalls smashing through burning underbrush.

He could see his truck, parked along the trail leading into the woods. He had a shotgun tucked into the narrow cranny behind the seats. He didn't know what was chasing him, but two barrels of buckshot would kill *anything*.

He heard Tommy scream and then gurgle. Joe shouldn't have looked behind him, but he couldn't stop himself. A grotesque, misshapen beast had gutted Tommy, now dragging him on the ground. Tommy's eyes were open, and for a brief moment Joe thought he was somehow still alive. God had some small amount of mercy, because no, he was dead. The two other shapes were still after him.

Joe looked ahead, running still, but like Lot's wife, the looking had cost him. A sharp jolt of pain cut through his leg and he fell. The wind was driven out from him. It grabbed his ankle and pulled, and he screamed. It began dragging him. His shovel was still in his hand. He reached and swung it at the beast. The blade of the shovel embedded itself in the arm of the creature, but it didn't let go. It growled in pain, then pulled out the shovel and threw it aside like a toddler playing on the beach. It squeezed Joe's ankle, and he could hear his bones snap. If he escaped, he would never walk without a limp.

It dragged him back toward the line his men had formed.

He did his best to twist his face away from the forest floor, but he was still covered in burns and cuts by the time the beast let him go. The two other shapes hunched over bodies. He could see one of the bodies. It was Wilburn. The one crouched over him was gigantic, at least ten feet tall, distended body and muscle dwarfing the small human. Its maw was buried in his torso, pulling up every so often to choke down bloody chunks of flesh.

One picked him up, flipping him over and pushing him up against a tree. Joe closed his eyes, waiting for the end to come. Instead, the creature wrapped its mutated hand around his face, and an elongated claw opened his eye. It made him watch. It wanted him to know that he had lost.

He didn't look at Wilburn's poor, desecrated body. He looked at the creature holding him. He looked past its mutated, enormous frame, past its bizarre musculature, right into its eyes. The eyes narrowed as it realized it was being studied, and it stared back into Joe's. Its eyes were dead.

It forced Joe to watch his crew being eaten. None of them had to endure being eaten alive. Joe did, the shapes digging into his abdomen. He screamed until he had no breath.

The three creatures fed until their bellies swelled. There were twenty bodies strewn over 500 yards. The fires built and raged around them. The creatures took the cans of fuel the firefighters had used and spread the liquid over the bodies and the trees.

When the wildfire caught up to the firemen's control, it subsumed it, feeding on the fuel, eating what was left of the firemen's bodies.

The wind picked up.

July 3rd

25

The Battack house was the oldest original house still standing in Conquest. It had been built after the discovery of the mine, and Ambrose Battack lived there until he died. His son and widow had remained there until after the mine dried up. When the last of the Battacks died, the house became state property. During the truck stop days it was a roadside attraction, unnoticed by everyone but the most eagled-eyed visitor.

With the rebirth of the town, it was one of the many features the town offered tourists, a peek back in time at the life and home of a silver miner. It was built on land now protected by the state, technically outside the city limits, with all profit going to the state park system, and not the county or town coffers, and definitely not the pockets of the Bieters. For that reason, it was never featured prominently on advertisements for the town, usually only as a bullet point far down in the brochure.

The town's volunteer fire department stopped the erstwhile blaze, but not before the Battack house burned down.

The town was chaos. Visibility was gone, smoke thick. Tourists abandoned the town in droves, and all the guides and tour buses were either leaving or had already left. Heather passed the Battack house on the way in. It was a burnt wreck.

She called Darla.

"What the hell is happening, Darla?" she asked. "Why did we not get a warning from Joe?"

"Joe and his men are missing," said Darla. "Presumed dead. The fire moved faster last night, and they must have gotten caught up in it. By the time someone realized what was going on, houses were on fire."

Goddamnit. She had talked to Joe yesterday. More dead.

"Do we have it contained?" she asked.

"It was errant embers carried in the wind," said Darla. "But we don't have long before the wildfire gets here. Hours, county said."

"When do reinforcements arrive?"

"Um—they said they couldn't send anyone else," said Darla. "Said they had to give higher priority to larger communities being threatened."

"Fuck!" said Heather.

"They suggested evacuation," said Darla.

"Well, no shit," said Heather. She swore she could hear Darla's wince over the phone. "Prepare for evacuation. Cruise down every street, and announce at full volume that evacuation is highly recommended. Announce a full time-table for the fire's arrival, and say there's no help coming. Tell them they have to get out now."

"But what about the mayor?" she asked. "Doesn't he have to approve any evacuation?"

"By the time you're announcing it, he will have," she said.

The parking lot at the mayor's office was empty, but JH's SUV was parked out front. He was behind his desk, on the phone, his face two shades redder than normal.

"Well hello Ms. Hill," he said. "Normally I would prefer a knock on the door before you come into my office, but I suppose with the current state of affairs I can forgive it. I've been on hold for twenty minutes with the county trying to get in touch with someone, anyone."

"Don't bother," she said. "They're not sending anyone else. We're on our own."

"What?" asked JH, slamming the phone down. "That's unacceptable. I will—"

"There are larger towns being threatened by the fires," she said. "They get prioritized."

"Prioritized?" asked JH. "How much goddamn money do we bring to the county? Hell, to this state?"

"They suggested immediate evacuation. I agree," said Heather.

"Oh, you agree. Surprising," said JH. "We can't evacuate the town. It's a holiday weekend—"

"We have *hours* before the fire gets here," said Heather. "The town could be half gone by midnight. This is our last chance."

"Just two days ago, Joe Coffey said we had a week," said JH.

"Joe Coffey is dead, JH!" she said, raising her voice. She advanced on his desk, leaning over it, and him. "His body is out there burning in that fire somewhere. He died trying to save our lives and this town."

"Dead?" asked JH. "No, that's impossible. There must be some miscommunication."

"I've already ordered my deputies to start the evacuation," she said, staring at him. "We have to get everyone out while we still have time."

"You have no such authority," he said, standing up. He looked up at her, his eyes narrowing. "You have no right." Heather felt the anger rise in her gut. She should stay calm, but she just couldn't take it anymore.

"*Someone* had to show some leadership," she said, looking him dead in the eyes.

His eyes widened, his eyebrows digging down into his face. He poked his finger into her chest, tapping hard. "Now listen here you bitc—"

Heather grabbed his finger with her left hand, rotating it and bending it up. With her right hand she jabbed twice, hitting JH hard, her knuckles pounding the soft tissue in his face. His nose was bleeding, and within an hour he'd have a black eye. It would have been enough force to knock him down, but she held him up with his finger. He was staggered, and the look of fear on his face was gone, replaced by pain and confusion. This was a bad decision, but it felt good.

"One. Don't touch me. Ever," she said. "Two. Sheriff. I'm the duly-elected sheriff, and you will address me as such. Three. We are evacuating this town. You can either agree with me and save face, or I can embarrass you in front of the town by doing it anyway." She let go of his finger, and he fell back into his chair. He squinted his eyes at her again, quiet. He was angry, but he couldn't muster any real outrage.

"Declare the evacuation," he said, his voice low, barely audible.

"Glad we could come to an agreement, Mr. Mayor," she said with a forced smile.

"You will pay for that," he said, his teeth gritted. He grabbed a tissue and wiped the blood away from his nose.

Heather walked out, without a glance back.

Arthur was drinking coffee and reading the paper when she walked into his house.

"Hey, sweetheart," he said.

She hugged him, holding him tight. He hugged her back, not expecting it.

"Everything okay?" he asked.

"No, Dad, no, everything is not okay," she said. "Look outside, for God's sake. We're evacuating. The fire is coming, and fast. Joe Coffey is MIA."

"I know," said Arthur. "But I'm not leaving. Not without you."

"What?" she asked. "Grab what you can, throw it in the truck, and get out of here. The roads are already backing up."

Heather looked at him. His hands were in his lap, and his age finally hit her, his eyes downcast. He looked up at her, not with obstinance and anger, but with open, honest eyes. She smiled. She couldn't help it.

"I will not lose you," he said. "Sorry if I'm making your life hard."

"You won't lose me," she said. "I don't intend to burn down with this town. You want to help? Go track down

Darla and help her spread the word about the evacuation. Help the older couples who need it."

"I can do that," he said.

"But," she said, taking his hand and squeezing, "You *will* get out of this town. I'll be right behind you, but I have to be the last one out. I've got to escort our prisoner. I can't leave it to anyone else. Can you handle that?"

"Yes, Sheriff," he said, saluting.

"We're not the army," she said. "We don't salute."

"I'm just teasing," he said. "I'll get to work."

"Shouldn't be too hard to find Darla. Her PA should be audible as soon as you step outside. I'll call her and let her know you're helping. But pack your stuff before you go help. Once we're gone, we're gone."

Arthur stood up and hugged her again, engulfing her in his frame. "Be careful. Love you."

"Love you too," she said, and she was gone again, out the door and leaving him to his work.

She called Buzz, who was still at the lock up.

"Any changes with our tenant?" asked Heather.

"No," said Buzz. "He finally got tired of talking."

"Do not let any of his crew near him," she said. "If they try and force the matter, you have authorization to use lethal force if necessary."

"Understood," said Buzz. "Is this because of the Yamamoto boy?"

"What do you mean?" asked Heather.

"Oh, I thought they told you," he said. "He died early this morning."

26

Kazuko watched as they loaded Kyle's body into the bag, and then onto a gurney, and then onto a van. He was further and further obscured.

Still, she stayed with him as long as she could. She was there, awake, when his heart had stopped. Nurses had run in and tried to resuscitate, but it didn't matter. He had absorbed too much punishment, too much pain. He couldn't overcome it. His wounds did not care that Kazuko had invested so much in him. They bled all the same.

She didn't need to know English to know the words the doctors told her afterward. We did all we could. I'm sorry for your loss. How can we help?

The tiny hospital was mired in chaos, even without Kyle's death. They were evacuating, Alice explained to her through her phone. The flames had moved in, and the town would be on fire in hours. Everyone was getting out. The doctors took Kyle's body, taking it out of the town, away from the fire.

Why did it matter where his body was? He was gone. He would never have children, or grandchildren of his own. He would never make his own life.

Alice stayed with her the whole time. Kazuko wished she could show her appreciation, but she had nothing but grief and sorrow, and it was hers alone to bear.

"We have to leave, Kazuko," she said. "We need to pack our things and get out of town. It's dangerous to stay here much longer. You probably don't want to do anything right now, but we *have* to move."

"<I only have a few things at the motel,>" said Kazuko. It was clothes, and her bathroom stuff. A suitcase full of clothes. There were Kyle's things as well. She should not leave them to burn. It was all that was left of him.

"I should pack up my apartment," Alice said. "I don't have a lot, but I should get what I can, then check in with my parents. How about we go to the hotel, grab your things, and then go to my place, real quick. Then we can head out of town. We can make sure everything goes smoothly with Kyle's body in Wattle Hills."

They sat in the hospital's lobby, people rushing back and forth while pushing out wheelchairs and stretchers with the few occupants of the hospital. They went into waiting ambulances and sped away. Orderlies loaded the most expensive mobile equipment into vans. Everything was moving around them.

"<You do not have to help me anymore,>" said Kazuko.

"<You have done so much for me. You must worry about yourself and your family.>" Kazuko would not dump her care on another young woman.

"Who is there to help you if I leave?" she asked. Alice looked at Kazuko.

"<No one,>" said Kazuko.

"Then I will help you until there is someone else," she said.

"<You've already done so much,>" said Kazuko. "<And this is more still.>"

"It's the decent thing to do," she said. "Now let's go."

They drove through town in Alice's hatchback, and Kazuko stared at the hordes of people fleeing. The smoke was everywhere, on everything. It poured out of the ground, and clung to the people as they tried to leave. Traffic was slow, but it was moving. For all the people there, it was no worse than a big stadium clearing out. Given enough time, they'd be gone.

They passed a police cruiser announcing the evacuation through its PA as it idled its way through the small neighborhoods surrounding the central tourist hub.

The biker was still here. The sorrow in Kazuko turned to a sudden rage. He was sitting in a cell, waiting to be moved, taken away. He had stolen from Kyle, from Kyle's parents, and from *her*. Did any of that matter to him? Had it even crossed his mind?

They arrived at the motel and gathered Kazuko's things. She packed Kyle's few belongings as well, refusing to leave them behind.

They left the motel. It was deserted, the tourists fleeing ahead of the evacuation orders. The small, local roads were mostly empty as they cruised to Alice's apartment.

It was small, but well decorated, and Kazuko sat and drank water as Alice worked. She packed bags, throwing clothes and keepsakes into a big suitcase and multiple backpacks.

Kazuko had Kyle's things—his wallet, his keys, his phone. Kazuko could only look at the lock screen. He had changed it the other day, a selfie of them together on a mountain trail overlooking the town. They both smiled.

Her hands cradled the items as totems, as memories. She dropped them in her purse.

She had miscarried, before Hiroshi. It was early in their marriage, with Masaru under pressure at work, back before she realized that it would not change, no matter how many promotions he got. They had celebrated the pregnancy, and Masaru had a hop to his step, less tension in his shoulders as soon as he heard. He would have a child, a boy if he was lucky.

Then one night Kazuko woke up, her legs wet. Masaru turned on the light for them, only to see the sheets coated in blood. She screamed. She thought she was dying. Masaru rushed her to the hospital. She had thought that maybe they could save the baby. She was seven months pregnant. It was not unheard of. She decided, in the car ride, as the towel beneath her sopped up blood, that she would tell them to prioritize the baby's life over her own.

They did not give her the choice. The baby was already gone, dead inside of her, but the doctors did everything to save Kazuko. It worked, but she was in the hospital for a week, recovering. She went home heartbroken.

Masaru had his work to throw himself into. She had

nothing.

She almost killed herself. Not because of the loss of her child, but because of Masaru. She was lethargic, lost for weeks, months after the miscarriage. Masaru appeared to become his old self. Addicted to work, stoic. She asked him, finally, how? His answer was short.

"The child was a girl," he said after a moment of thought, his face like stone. "We will have another. It will be a boy." That was all he said, then resumed eating, assuming his answer was sufficient.

It chilled her inside, and her heart sank.

Divorce wasn't an option. The shame it would bring her and her family was unfathomable. Suicide was the only way. She planned to hang herself after Masaru left for work the next day.

But he didn't go to work. It was winter, and there was a rare day of heavy snow in the city. He was trapped inside, and her plan was impossible. And then he apologized.

"I have thought over my words from last night, Kazuko," he said. "And I spoke poorly. What I said is what I try to tell myself to make myself feel better. That we will have another child. I want a boy—you know that. But the pain in my heart is still there from the loss of Kumiko. And it will not heal."

"Kumiko?" asked Kazuko.

"It is what I thought of naming her," he said. "After your mother. It is what I call her when I dream of her birth, in a better life."

Kazuko burst into tears, embracing him. They cried together. The snow had saved them. Led to Hiroshi, and to Kyle. And to losing him.

Taken from them by some stranger, with no clue or thought to what he had done. Kyle did not have a name, a family. He was only an affront, to be ticked off a list of grievances because the stranger had nothing else except his anger. It was all he had accrued in his life, and in a second he had stolen the life's work of two generations.

He needed to know what he had done. Someone needed to tell him the true impact of his actions. Not just someone, though. Her. He would hear her rage, know that it existed. Hear her sorrow.

She looked up again, to Alice. She was rummaging through her belongings, looking for something. Alice would be better off without her, better off without having to care for an elderly woman. She got up, carrying her cane and purse, and left, the door quiet behind her.

She would find the man who killed Kyle, and make him understand his violence.

27

James woke up, naked and alone. The hotel room was empty, except for him and his now three-day-old suit. Jesus. What had he done?

His head was pounding, a flood of memories from the night before washing over him. Pool, Jack, kissing in an alley, the motorcycle, the hotel room. Jack was gone, no trace of him in the room. James could still smell him, the overpowering scent. It was still in his nostrils. He smelled something else. He got up, naked, then looked out the front window of the room. Smoke.

The main drag was directly in front of the hotel, and beyond that was the forest that separated Conquest from the highway. The smoke was thick now, and the line of motorcycles in front of the motel was now gone, only a solitary bike remaining. Not Jack's, though.

He found his phone, still in his pants pocket, low on battery. No signal. The fires must have taken out the towers.

He threw on his clothes, chewing on some aspirin. The pain coalesced behind his right eye, and he tried to push it away. His crumpled suit smelled of whiskey and smoke and of Jack.

What had he been thinking? He needed to go home. What day was it? Sunday? That couldn't be right. Sunday meant church, and there were no church bells this morning.

He needed to go home.

He walked away from the motel, taking in shallow breaths, the smoke burning the back of his already scorched throat. He could still taste Jack. He walked back toward his house. He needed to talk to Susan, he needed to tell her. Tell her everything, about the Lion's Den, about the extortionist, about Jack. It wasn't fair to her anymore.

Whenever he left the Lion's Den, early in the morning, before the sun was up, shame would return. That was the greatest thing about the Den—whenever he was there, the shame was gone, forgotten, cast aside. All of them faced it. With their families, their jobs, their friends. It was the only place they had the luxury of amnesia.

It always came back when he left. He would turn up the radio and drink some coffee, but it boiled up in his guts, the shame, the fear, the pain. He would drive through the early morning, back to his normal life, back to the constant performance of what a man was *supposed* to be, his guts roiling. Inevitably, he would pull over, throw up, the tension and the nerves too much.

He would get back in his truck, drive through the sunrise, and become *normal* James again, the aberrant sinner left behind in the Lion's Den.

He walked back to his house through the smoke. The aspirin was dulling his headache. Had anyone seen him embrace Jack in the alley? How many had seen him ride behind him to his motel? How many saw him go inside, and did any watch him now, watching him walk up the street?

He arrived at his house, Susan's car in the driveway. She was probably sick with worry, knowing her. His fault. He was responsible for that pain, but he wouldn't be anymore. He would lay it square with her, and they would come to an agreement. Somehow.

The anxiety in his stomach was rising, but he pushed it down, taking deep breaths as he walked up the stairs, onto the porch. He unlocked the door, and into his house. It was dark, the lights off. It looked the same as he had left it, two days before.

Maybe she was still asleep. He walked upstairs, down the hall, the bedroom door shut. He opened it.

Empty, bed made.

"Susan?" he asked, his voice loud in the quiet house. No answer. He repeated it louder, loud enough for anyone inside to hear. Nothing.

Where could she be? A neighbor's? With his dad?

The anxiety in him fell away, the confrontation delayed and replaced by confusion. He looked outside, and the lights were out in all of his neighbors' homes, their cars gone.

A sheriff's car drove by.

"ATTENTION: A FULL EVACUATION OF CON-QUEST HAS BEEN DECLARED BY SHERIFF HILL AND MAYOR BIETER. PACK UP NECESSITIES AND LEAVE

AS SOON AS POSSIBLE IN AN ORDERLY FASHION. DRIVE CAREFULLY OUT OF TOWN AND HEAD EAST ON HIGHWAY 2. MAKE ARRANGEMENTS WITH FAMILY AS NECESSARY. THE WILDFIRES ARE APPROACHING RAPIDLY. WE CANNOT FORCE YOU TO LEAVE, BUT ALL AUTHORITIES WILL BE EVACUATING WITHIN TWO HOURS, AND WE EXPECT CONQUEST TO BE CUT OFF SHORTLY THEREAFTER. GET OUT WHILE YOU STILL CAN."

Christ. Christ. Panic hit him all at once. Susan was gone, and the town was going to fucking burn down. *Breathe, breathe. Pack up what you can, load it in into Susan's car.*

There was a knock at his door, and he jumped. He went back downstairs and answered it. It was Arthur Stone.

"James," he said. "I'm helping with the evacuation, and noticed your lights on. Everything alright? Need any help?"

"No, Art," he said. "I've got a terrible hangover, through. Slept through all the bad news. I'm packing now."

Arthur looked at him with a sad, half-manufactured smile, one he was used to from his employees. "Cell service is down, but if you need something, we'll be circling for a bit longer. You can flag us down and we'll help if we can." He turned to go back to his idling truck.

"Actually, Art," he said. "I—I don't know where Susan is. I woke up, and she was gone. Has anyone seen her?"

"She's gone?" asked Art. "No, I don't think so. We'll keep an eye out for her. Maybe she's helping at a friend's house. I'll keep an eye out." James could see the other questions Art had, questions about why his wife would leave without saying a word, but thankfully the older man didn't ask any of them. He just nodded a goodbye and retreated to his truck.

James took the time to shower, washing away the smells from the last few days. He was short on time, but he needed to be clean. He crunched a few more aspirin while the hot water pelted him. Clean clothes after three days made him feel human again. Jack's smell still lingered.

He emptied dresser drawers into suitcases, grabbing Susan's jewelry box, and the contents of his safe. He grabbed his pistol as well, tucking it into the back of his pants.

There was another knock at his door, and he went back downstairs, expecting to see Arthur again.

He opened the door to find his father. He had a black eye.

"What happened?" asked James.

"I fell," he said, pushing past James and into the house.

"And hit your eye?" asked James.

"Yes, damn it," he said. "Where's Susan?"

"I don't know," said James. "She left."

"What the hell do you mean she left?" he asked.

"She's not here. I woke up, she was gone," said James.

"Jesus Christ," he said. "Can't even handle your wife. But maybe, for once, we can work this in our favor."

"What?" asked James. "We need to pack up and get the hell out of here. Susan is probably already out, waiting for us."

"We have a golden opportunity here," said JH. "A perfect chance for some free press. The first thing that'll happen once the town is rebuilt is the election. And I had a stroke of genius, the perfect slogan for your campaign. The Last Man Out. We make sure you're the last man out of town. Hell, rescuing Susan is perfect. Those stupid fuckers will eat it up with a spoon." His eyes were wide, staring off into the distance.

"Would you stop thinking about the goddamn election for once?" asked James. He looked at his father. His eyes, one normal, and one half closed, darted quickly, scatter shot.

"I'm thinking about our future, boy," said JH. "Someone has to goddamn do it. And you're gonna leave your wife in the town while it burns? Hill is out there right now, working, and you're in here packing bags. That bitch is showing more balls than you. We're gonna get another four years of *her* at this rate. I will not allow it."

JH was looking at him now, his eyes burning a hole in James. The anxiety was overwhelming him. He just wanted to leave. He thought back to the night before, the freedom, the energy he'd felt next to Jack. Anything had been possible then. Now he was back here, his father pushing him, again. He was powerless. He was going to go insane. He needed a way out.

JH snapped his fingers in front of his face. "Wake up," he said. "You're gonna go out there and volunteer to help Hill, and look for Susan like a good boy. You'll find her, and then you make sure you are the last one out of town. Technicality or not, I don't care, just make sure it happens."

"Okay," James said, and JH broke his glare, but looked back when James started talking again. "But I want you with me. Father and son, last ones out. Mayor and future sheriff. That should make for even better headlines, right? No way Hill can match that." James eyed his father. If he wanted James to stay, then JH would stay with him.

JH looked uncertain, thinking. Then he nodded. "You're finally showing something. We'll whip her ass with that.

Finish packing, and then throw it in the Navigator. I'll talk to Hill."

JH slapped him on the back and headed back outside. James hated it, but it felt good, his father's approval.

He finished packing and climbed into the vehicle with JH. A walkie talkie buzzed in the middle console.

He needed a way out. The pistol was still tucked into his pants.

28

The town of Conquest was emptying as the smoke got thicker and thicker. Heather's handkerchief was spotted red, her nose dripping blood.

Arthur and Darla still drove the circuit around the town, and both the elder and junior Bieter men had joined them. She didn't know why they did, but she wasn't going to turn down help. The volunteer firemen directed traffic at the highway. She had called the highway patrol and the police out east to let them know about the influx of people.

Her conversation with Abe was fresh on her mind, and she waited on Jack to do something, anything. But he didn't. She saw The Pack on the road, leaving town. Jack gave her a friendly wave as they drove by, a smile on his face. Abe was among them, though he didn't even glance in her direction.

Her people would be on their guard with Runt, but what else could they do?

She couldn't worry about it. She needed to get the town to safety.

A couple residents refused to leave, but there was nothing she could do about it except try and convince them otherwise. Her father had worked on a couple, and they'd changed their minds, packing up what they could. Otherwise, Conquest was becoming a ghost town. The fires were close now, and they made her nervous. Still, they tracked ahead of schedule.

Sam was already packed when Heather stopped by her apartment.

"Why are you still here?" asked Heather, hugging her and then kissing her.

"I was waiting on you," she said. "I've already booked a hotel in Missoula. Figured we could split it."

"I can't go yet," Heather said. "Hell, I don't know what tomorrow looks like. The rest of the county is in just as much hell. You should get out of here while you have the chance."

"You're right, I should," said Sam, and kissed Heather again, this time with tender force, holding it, savoring it. Heather closed her eyes and returned the kiss.

Heather broke the kiss, looking at Sam. Without the town, there was nothing holding them together. Sam would leave, could leave, with ease, without a second thought. This wasn't home to her. It was just another job. How long would Sam stay in the area, before she moved on to something richer? Heather suspected it wouldn't be long. And it would always be that way, as long as Heather was in Conquest. There were always greener pastures. Maybe the fires were trying to tell her something.

She wanted to ask Sam what this meant for them. If Sam would stick around for her, if she could commit to Heather long enough for Heather to figure all of this out. But she didn't have time. Instead, she kissed Sam again, hard, and tried to commit the moment to memory, just in case it was one of their last.

"You should go," she said. "I'll call you when I can."

"I love you," said Sam.

"I love you too," said Heather, then Sam was out the door, and in her Jeep, and on the road.

Still parked in Sam's driveway, Heather checked in with Darla on the radio.

"How's it looking, Darla?" asked Heather.

"Still a couple of old timers who won't go," she said. "If we leave 'em, they'll die."

"Have JH talk to them," she said. "Tell him to use whatever lie will work. Any word on Susan Bieter?" JH had said they were trying to find James's wife, who'd disappeared that morning.

"Still nothing," she said. "Mrs. Dannen—you know, the retired lady who plays organ for the Baptist Church—heard she was out with one of those bikers last night."

"Oh, Jesus," she said.

"Also, Alice Ames flagged me down, told me the old Japanese lady, grandmother of the dead boy, walked out into the smoke. She's been looking for her, but I told her that once we came back to get Runt out, we were out for good. She told me she understood."

Heather squeezed the bridge of her nose, and blood began trickling from her left nostril. She held her handkerchief up to it.

"Do what you can," she said. "One more sweep, and then gather at the station. We'll be taking Runt out, and getting out of here."

"Roger," said Darla.

A flash of movement blew through her peripheral vision. She looked over, but there was nothing except the overwhelming smoke. Ash was raining down now. She got out of her car and moved through the haze, covering her mouth with her blood-stained handkerchief. She waited, holding her breath, listening. There was a noise out there. The layers of smoke obscured and deflected sound. She could hear engines, whispers, and rasps floating through the air.

The fire was close, and she couldn't chase phantoms. She got back in her car.

Heather drove around town again, doing a complete sweep. She passed JH, who was standing on an old couple's porch, convincing them to leave their old house. They looked sad, but he was working on them. James was next to him, his face a mask of sorrow. He looked at her as she passed, their eyes meeting.

They were cordial to each other, despite the rumors she'd heard about him coming from his employees. He wasn't a small man, taller than his father, but he looked defeated, crumpled, a sad shell. He was running for sheriff against her, but how much of that was JH doing the pushing, she didn't know. James broke eye contact, looking back down on the ground, waiting for the old couple to finally crack and get out of town. They all cracked if they talked to JH long enough.

Darla was still circling, and announcing, but the town

was empty except for them and smoke. The ash was piling in the gutters. She passed Art's house, and he was outside, in the lawn, just looking at it. She pulled over and walked up to him.

"It's time to go," she said.

"Just getting one last second with her," he said. "But I'm ready as I'll ever be."

"You head out," she said. "We have to escort our guest. We're going to set up shop at Stone Mill. I'll call you when we're settled."

He hugged her. "I'm proud of you. I love you."

"I love you too," she said. "Be careful."

Arthur got into his truck and drove off. Heather steered to the office. Darla was already there, waiting for her. James and JH waited by their SUV.

"They insisted on following," she said. "Still no sign of Susan or Mrs. Yamamoto."

"Let's get Runt," she said. "He's the number one priority."

Buzz was in the lockup, waiting for them. Runt laid still in his cell, face-up on his cot.

"Is it time for a field trip?" he asked as Heather and Darla walked in. Heather grabbed two shotguns from the cabinet and loaded them with shells, throwing extra ammo in her pockets.

"Shut your mouth," said Heather. She looked at Darla and Buzz. "Buzz, you walk with him. Darla will stay in front, and I'll be in the back with the riot gun. You know the drill."

"Are we expecting trouble?" asked Buzz.

"I don't know," said Heather. "But I want to be ready if it finds us."

"Oh, it's already here," said Runt, smiling again, staring

at the ceiling. "You can feel it. Feels good."

She grabbed her pistol from the holster, pointing it at him through the bars. "Get down on your knees, hands on your head. I won't ask twice." Runt looked at her, cock eyed, and then got up, easing his way off the cot and moving to the floor, doing as she asked. "Buzz, handcuff him. I'll cover you."

"All of this for little ole me," said Runt. Buzz unlocked the cell door, his handcuffs out. He grabbed one hand, locking the handcuffs in place around Runt's wrist, and then moving the other and doing the same. Runt didn't resist. Buzz pulled him to his feet.

"Don't know why y'all are so jumpy," he said. "Law and order all the way, that's me." He stuck his tongue out at Heather as he passed her.

They walked through the station. Heather locked it as they left, for what it was worth. Buzz marched Runt in front of them, one hand on Runt's wrists and the other on the butt of his pistol. Darla led, with Heather behind her, her shotgun held in front of her.

The car was close. They get into the car, they head out of town, and this part of the nightmare was over.

A voice from the smoke. "Not so fast, Sheriff," it said. A figure emerged, ash falling around them. Jack.

"Hold," said Heather. They all stopped, and Heather got closer, her shotgun pointed at Runt's head.

"Leave while you can," said Heather. "The town is going to burn."

"Oh, I know," said Jack. "But I can't let you leave with him."

"He's a murderer," said Heather. "And he'll face justice

for it."

"Let's just go, Sheriff," said Buzz. "He's unarmed. He can't stop us."

Heather was waiting for the other shoe to drop. Jack wouldn't have come out here all alone. She heard noises in the smoke. The same particular blend of noises from earlier.

"This is your last chance, Sheriff," he said. "Let him go, and everyone can walk away."

But would you die for it?

"That ain't happening," she said.

"So be it," he said, raising a single finger in the air, then gesturing forward. Out from the smoke came shapes. Four of them. They surrounded Jack. They were huge, each of them ranging from eight feet tall to ten, but their true height was impossible to gauge, as they hunched, arms hanging low enough to touch the ground as they moved.

Heather had watched Abe change, had seen the abomination he transformed into. She knew what they could be. She still wasn't prepared for them.

These creatures were misshapen, bones and muscles bulging, asymmetrical, arms and legs, torso and head, bent, twitching. Jagged claws and fangs too big for mouths. Grotesque exaggeration—the word *shape* was the best way to describe them, because they defied classification.

"What. The. Fuck." said Darla. Buzz said nothing. James and JH froze, adjacent.

"Now," said Jack. "We feed."

29

Alice wandered through the smoke, looking for Kazuko. The town of Conquest was now a shadow of itself, but she couldn't leave without her.

She had turned around, and Kazuko was gone. She looked out into the smoke, listening, but there was nothing. Why had Kazuko wandered away?

She wasn't senile. Kazuko was sharper than most people, period. She wasn't the type to stray. Alice needed to find her.

She finished packing and threw her things in her car. She'd find Kazuko, and they'd get out of here.

The smoke had transformed the streets, the town, into something new. She had grown used to them, over the years. The town was invisible as she walked to work and back every day.

Alice had been a teenager when the town changed, when it grew, exploded. Her dad would drive through Conquest when she was small, and he wouldn't let her leave the car while he stopped at the mechanic, or at the small convenience store when they needed milk in a pinch. It was full of strangers, of transients, of truckers. A little girl should not be left alone.

By the time she was a teenager the town was unrecognizable. The Revitalization Project was all everyone within 50 miles talked about, about the town that had been a joke now being a success. Tourists flocked there in droves, and Alice and her friends would walk the streets of Conquest on the weekends, going to the movies or hanging out. It was safe now. It grew as she did. It still grew, new buildings replacing old. The last gasp of businesses from the old days was dying out, being replaced by chain restaurants or tourist shops, offering rooms along with jobs.

Still, the old Conquest was here under the surface. In the houses of the old timers, who had lived there for forty or fifty years, and saw the value of their property skyrocket. In places like Sally's. In the old gas stations, that never moved and refused to sell.

Most of them wouldn't come back.

She'd still have a job at the mine, once they rebuilt, but what to do in the meantime? She could finally take her parent's offer and go to school, if one would have her.

Darla and Art passed her multiple times, and she told Darla about Kazuko missing. Darla told her that she wasn't responsible for the old lady, and that losing someone just made some people break. The town would be cut off soon. She should get out while she can and get in touch with her parents, who had left early that morning.

She knew she wasn't obligated to help Kazuko. There was a version of her that left Kazuko after Kyle died, taking the out that Kazuko had offered. That Alice would have followed her parents out, and never talked to Kazuko again.

But that was a version of herself she couldn't stomach. Her parents had always told her that she was too kind, too nice, too soft. She loved her parents, but she couldn't understand it. Too kind? She didn't tell them she was staying longer to help Kazuko. They would have told Alice to abandon her.

Where would she have gone? Kyle's body was already out of the city. They had left the motel room empty. She couldn't speak or read English. There was nothing else here for her.

No.

There was still one thing here. The biker. Runt. The man who had killed her grandchild. But what could she do?

She could wait for him outside of the police station, and stab him while he was defenseless, in handcuffs.

Alice hurried toward the Sheriff's Office, where Runt was being held. Would she be hidden? The park was next to it, and the rest was surrounded by businesses. A boutique hotel stood across the street to the north. The smoke made the search impossible. Kazuko could be five feet in front of her, and Alice would never see her.

Alice walked the circuit around the office, looking for anything. She saw Darla and Art pass her by, now with JH and James behind them in the mayor's big SUV.

She walked through the park, which had the clearest sight lines to the office. "Kazuko," she said, finally. "If you can hear me, please answer. We need to leave."

She heard a noise then, a metallic tapping noise coming from her north, the center of the park. The carousel. It dominated the middle of the park, but she had never ridden it. It had been installed ages after her carousel riding years were over.

Kazuko was sitting in one of the bench seats, where parents could ride with smaller kids or infants. She was tapping the metal railing, sending the noise through the park.

"Kazuko," she said. She sat next to the older woman. "Why did you leave me?" She still had her phone, and thankfully the translation app was locally stored.

The phone spoke to her. "<I need to do something. You would not have allowed me, so I didn't say anything. Please just go, Alice. Do not be burdened by me.>"

"We have to go," she said. "The town will be cut off, and we'll be stuck here, waiting for a fire. Vengeance isn't worth your life."

"<It is not vengeance. I just want him to understand his actions," said Kazuko. "He needs to understand the torment he has caused.>"

"And how would you talk to him?" asked Alice. "He doesn't understand Japanese. He's not going to wait for an app to translate for him."

"<It is not for him. It is for me,>" she said. "<Leave if you must, but I will say my piece.>"

Alice looked at her, and then back at the station. She had picked a good vantage point, able to see all the comings and goings at the station, even through the smoke. The ash was piling up on the floor of the carousel, on all the carved animals.

Alice didn't know what to do. Kazuko was calm, placid.

But she worried that Darla was right. That losing Kyle had broken her.

"<I will leave with the police force,>" Kazuko said, finally. "<I will say my piece, and then we will follow them out of town.>"

Darla and the Bieters rolled in, parking in front of the Sheriff's Office. Sheriff Hill followed.

"<They are moving him,>" said Kazuko. "<It is time.>"

"Wait!" Alice said, holding her and pointing at a figure in the smoke. It was one of the other bikers. How were they still in town? Kazuko struggled for a moment, but then saw the figure, and held still.

They watched as Runt and the police came out of the office. They watched as Jack made a final offer. They watched as the shapes emerged from the distant smoke.

"Monsters," she said. The translation app was still running.

"<No,>" said Kazuko. Alice looked at her. Her face was still calm, near expressionless. "<This makes sense. About why these men took my Kyle.>"

"What?" asked Alice, dumbstruck. Kazuko met her eyes, the figures of the carousel around them, while the shapes in the smoke closed in on the station.

"<These are not monsters. They are demons. And we must send them back to Hell.>"

30

It was early, the sun still down. Susan woke up in her and her husband's bed with another man. She had made a terrible mistake.

She looked over at Andrew, who was still asleep. She was naked, and shame washed over her. She needed to get dressed, needed to cover up. She dressed, throwing on clothes as fast as she could, before he woke up, before he saw her again. She had betrayed James. No matter what happened between them, she had committed the unthinkable.

Dressed, she could think again. She needed to get Andrew out of the house. He was still. Slept like the dead.

She touched his shoulder. "Andrew." No response.

"Andrew," she said, and shook him harder. His eyes fluttered.

"You need to leave," she said.

He looked at her in confusion. "What?"

"You need to get out of my house. My husband could be home any second. I made a mistake last night," she said.

He furrowed his brow. "Where do you think your husband was last night?"

"What?"

"How many nights has he been gone for?" he asked, sitting up in bed.

"Two," she said, walking away from him.

"Where did he sleep?"

"I don't know," she said.

"Wherever he slept," said Andrew. "It wasn't alone."

"You don't know that," she said. Andrew stood up, out of bed. He was still naked, and the memories of the night before flooded her thoughts. He walked up behind her, burying his face in her neck. His touch was devastating, and her cheeks flushed with shame again. She thought of all the business trips that James took. Of the way all the girls at the salon got quiet whenever she mentioned his name. It didn't matter. You took a vow.

She turned around, and pushed him away with a gentle touch.

"I thought we had something," he said, an honest look on his face. "There's something between us."

"This was a mistake," she said. "I'm married. You should get dressed then leave. I need to find my husband."

"Are you sure?" he asked.

"Yes," she said, not looking him in the eye. "Please go."

"Alright," he said, sighing. He got dressed, picking up his clothes that had been strewn across the floor from the night before.

She wouldn't look at him. She had lost her mind. The whole town would be talking about it before long. What would she tell James? How would she be able to face him?

"I have a feeling that this town is going to get a lot more dangerous, real soon. Be careful out there."

She didn't say anything. *Please, just go.* She closed her eyes, waiting for him to say something else. She finally opened them, turning around, and he was gone. She heard the front door open and close.

She straightened the bedroom, then changed the sheets. She removed any trace of Andrew from the house. From her life. From her mind.

It was 6 AM. The oppressive smoke hid any sign of sunrise. She could hear sirens in the air. Something was wrong. She needed to find James. They needed to talk, to rebuild. They could still salvage this. She was sure of it.

Regardless of where he'd slept, James would go to the office first thing. He always did. She would go there, and wait for him. She'd meet him head on. They would figure this out.

She grabbed her purse and left. She would walk to the office. It was a short walk, and she could use the time to clear her head. She headed uphill to the offices of the mine. She could feel the smoke in the air, like walking in molasses. Ash was falling from the sky, and pieces landed on her face. She wiped them away, the ash leaving streaks of gray.

She *would* fix her marriage. Her mother always said that marriage was about perseverance. About being dutiful to your husband. About accepting what they gave you, and giving back all you could. She wiped away ash from her mouth, and then she was a child again, with her mother.

Her mother wiped away blood from her mouth. She was holding a hand towel from the kitchen to it, looking down on little Susan.

"Are you alright, Mommy?" she asked.

"I'll be fine," her mother said. "Are you ready for school?"

"Yes," she said. "You're bleeding."

"I said something bad to your father," her mother said. "I shouldn't have done that. I'll be fine. You better go and catch the bus before it's too late."

Susan was older now. Her mother's eye was black and blue. They were at a Fourth of July BBQ, and she was playing in the sprinklers with the other kids, running back and forth, jumping through the cold, cold water. Her mother was wearing sunglasses. The other adults had noticed anyway. She told them she'd fallen. They didn't ask any more questions.

It was winter. She was hiding under the bed. There was screaming coming from her parents' bedroom. Her mother would scream, her father would yell, and there would be a loud thud, followed by more screaming. It went on for a long time. Her mother went to the hospital that night. They talked to the pastor after that.

Two years later. She overheard them talking. They thought she was asleep.

"Lyle told me you were out with that boy from work," her father said.

"We were talking business," said her mother.

"Business my ass," he said. "Put out your hands."

"Please, Stan, please," she said. "It wasn't anything."

"Put out your hands," he said. "What is adultery?"

"It's a sin," she said, and a thin whipping noise filled the room. Her mother cried.

"You want to wake your daughter?" he asked. Susan had covered her ears, but she could still hear it. Her mother missed a week of work. Her hands were black.

Susan wiped the ash away from her mouth. She was almost to the office. James's truck was parked there. Maybe he was already there. They could work it out.

She took her spare key for the office and opened it. It was dark inside. She turned on the lights. She had worked there in the early days of her marriage. When JH had become mayor, James had convinced her to stay home. Told her a woman's place was in the home. She liked working, but she'd ended up agreeing to it. He made enough money for them both.

There was no one here. She went into James's office and sat down in front of his desk. He would come in, and she would confront him about both of their behavior. They would go home, and they would make up. Their marriage would survive. Their family would still have a chance. She waited.

No one showed up. It was 7 AM, and no one was there. Something was wrong.

Susan got up and went around to James's side of the desk. His computer was on. Maybe there was something, anything there that would tell her where he was.

She rifled through the desk, but only found old folders filled with receipts, expense reports, and forgotten paperwork. Buried in the back was a manila envelope, with James's name on it. It was crumpled. It had been shoved back there. She pulled it out.

She ripped it open, dumping the contents out on his desk.

It was a thumb drive, and a note, folded up. She plugged the thumb drive into James's computer. It auto-opened.

The folder was full of pictures. Full of pictures of James. Full of pictures of James with other men. Touching. Kissing. Sex. She stared at them, tabbing through them for a long time.

She looked at her husband in the pictures. He was unrecognizable. He was passionate. Lost in emotion. He looked free.

She pushed away from the desk, her hands shaking, her eyes tearing up. She took a deep breath. Closed her eyes, concentrating on her breathing. She read the note, then dropped it back onto the desk. She ripped out the thumb drive, dumping both it and the note into her purse. She held it tight, her knuckles turning white.

Her heart hurt. She couldn't catch her breath. Her marriage was a lie, a facade, a cover. He had used her to appear normal. He had trapped her. There was no fixing their marriage. Their marriage barely existed. Years of her life, gone.

Her mother's voice in her head. "Marriage is what you make of it."

No. No, she refused.

She got up from James's desk, turning off the lights as she left. She locked the door behind her. She wandered into the smoke and ash.

As she vanished into the haze, Kid followed her at a distance.

31

Heather held Runt at gunpoint. The Pack surrounded them.

Heather moved up to Runt, grabbing a hold of the handcuffs. She placed the barrel of the shotgun to his temple. Everyone else was still frozen. The beasts circled them. They needed to get back in the station.

"I'm betting you can't change faster than a shotgun shell," she said to Runt. "Back off, or your friend loses his head."

Jack raised a hand again. The beasts paused. "Oh, come on Sheriff, if you kill him, there's nothing stopping us from slaughtering you in the street."

Heather's mind raced. They had two shotguns and a pistol against these bastards. She started pulling Runt back. "Darla, Buzz, aim at Jack. If any of these *things* get any closer, kill him." They did as ordered, and Jack put his hands up.

He began to retreat into the haze and out of sight.

"Stay where you are," she said to him. He ignored her and kept backing up into the smoke. James and JH finally moved as well, getting behind the three with guns.

Jack kept talking, but Heather wasn't listening at this point. Her eyes were glued to the four beasts that surrounded them. He was trying to distract her, distract them, keep them outside. But he was also fading back into the smoke. He'd be out of line of sight in a few seconds. And then his men attack.

"Focus fire," she said to Darla and Buzz. "They're not invincible. One at a time."

Jack was gone, back into the smoke. His voice came from the smoke. "Kill 'em all."

The beasts moved, spread out, and Heather dragged Runt backwards faster, his heels dragging on the cement. The barrel of her shotgun was still pressed to his skull. They were close to the office. The Pack was trying to cut them off. *If we fire, they'll pounce.*

They weren't going to make it. The beasts had out-positioned them. Maybe if she dumped Runt they'd have enough time to run. But it'd be their death sentence. She didn't think Jack had any intention of leaving them alive.

There was a sound in the distance, getting louder. An engine?

The beasts heard it as well, and they turned to look as it came into view. A truck drove full speed through the park, clipping through shrubs and taking out decorative fences. It wasn't slowing down, the smoke rushing past it.

It hopped the curb surrounding the sheriff's office parking lot and plowed into the largest of the creatures at nearly

60 MPH. The sound was horrendous, metal crunching and bones snapping. Now was the time. She clubbed Runt in the back of the neck, and passed his unconscious body to Buzz, the strongest of them.

"Drag him inside. Darla, cover me."

Darla fired her shotgun at the next beast, and it snarled in pain. The Pack didn't know what to do. Heather fired her own shotgun at the one closest to her, and ran over to the truck. Art was inside. He fought against the airbag, pinned against his seat. She racked another shell, fired again in the general direction of the creatures, and then pulled her knife out of her belt and stabbed the airbag, forcing the air to rush out of it.

She racked another shell, but the creatures were gone, even the one Art had crushed with his ruined truck. Black blood was mixing with the spilled oil from the crushed engine. They had fled, retreated. It didn't matter, though. She and her crew were sitting ducks out here. They needed to get inside.

"Inside, Dad," she said, covering him with the shotgun as he shook off the impact of the crash.

"What the hell is going on?" he asked, all of them piling back into the station.

"Good question," said JH.

"Barricade the doors," she said. "Buzz, put Runt back in lock up. He'll wake up eventually."

They pushed desks and filing cabinets in front of the doors, the only way in or out of the small building.

"What the fuck was that?" asked JH. "What were those things?"

"Werewolves," said Heather.

"They didn't look like any fucking wolves to me," said JH, gasping for breath, his face red. James had taken a chair and was sitting in the corner, his head down, face in his hands.

"Shapeshifters, then," said Heather.

"No," said JH. "That is bullshit. Must be something else. Trained gorillas, or bears."

"I've been to the zoo down in Boise," said Darla. "Those were not goddamned *gorillas.*"

"Those things aren't possible," said JH.

"Then explain to me what those monsters were," said Darla. "And if you say the word gorilla again, so help me—"

"I don't have to take this from no deputy," said JH.

"It doesn't matter what they are, other than wanting to kill us, which is fairly clear at this point," said Heather, trying to stop an argument. Buzz came back into the room.

"Runt's locked up again, Sheriff," he said. "Still unconscious."

"Why don't we just give him up again?" asked JH. "It's all he wanted. Guess that explains why Jack was trying to sweet talk me."

"Because he's the only leverage we have. Why do you think they want him back in the first place? It's because he's one of *them,* and they don't want their secret getting out," said Heather, trying to stay calm. "You saw those things. We all did. If they want a clean break, we all have to die."

"Jesus," said JH, sitting down. "Why here? Why my town?"

"Buzz, Darla, don't feed Runt anything," said Heather. "Not until he is literally dying. They need calories to change."

JH looked up at her with that. "Oh, that is some horseshit. You're just making this up now."

Heather grabbed her map from her office and slammed it on the table. "Seven dead hikers over the span of ten days, including two, here, on Friday night. Remains torn apart. No animal sightings at all." She pointed out each and every one, marked on the map.

"Are you saying those things killed and ate all those people?" asked Darla.

"Yes," said Heather. "And a crew of twenty firefighters went missing yesterday, just outside of town. Not one, or two, or five, but twenty, including Joe Coffey. The fire didn't kill them. I don't believe it for a second."

James sat up in his chair, looking like he was trying not to vomit.

JH looked at her still, but his doubt was wavering. "What do we do?"

"We find a way out," said Heather. "There's only so many of them."

"Only so many?" asked Buzz. "One of them is enough to kill all of us. Hell, Art ran that big fucker over with his truck, and it walked away."

Arthur was in the bathroom, washing his face and cleaning out a cut. He walked back into the main office area. "It seemed like a good idea at the time."

"It's the only reason we're still alive. But they're hurt, healing, trying to regroup. If we can organize quickly, we can ride out of town before they know it," said Heather.

"That'll be a problem," said Arthur.

"Why?" asked Darla.

"I tried to get out on the road, but it was blocked. Smoke got thicker and thicker, and then I ran into a literal firestorm. The trees on both sides of the road were on fire, and some fell and blocked the road. Can't go that way, not unless we had a tractor or something that could haul the timber. And definitely not with those things on our tail," he said.

Heather looked at her map of the town. They were surrounded by mountains, by burning forest, by those *things*.

They.

Were.

Trapped.

32

The shotgun blast had ripped through his abdomen, but Abe's body was healing the damage. The buckshot was being pushed out of him, the shot plinking on the floor. He howled in pain, but it was nothing compared to what Bark was going through.

Bark was big, and even bigger when he transformed. Nearly ten feet tall, and weighing a metric ton, he had done severe damage to the truck when it hit him, but he had paid the price. His hips and pelvis were shattered, ribs and shoulders dislocated. Abe had grabbed him and run when the gunfire started. Bark's body was healing itself, and he howled loud enough to wake the dead. The pain must have been astronomical. Bones realigned as muscles knitted themselves back together.

They had set up shop in the mayor's office. Jack was sitting behind his desk, feet propped up on it. Abe, having healed, transformed back into his human form. Beast and Gunner were still out roaming, keeping an eye on the police station. Kid was MIA.

Abe dressed, his body sore. He was hungry, weak. He hadn't fed enough to change. He didn't eat any of the hikers outside of town. He needed to make Jack see reason. Maybe he could convert him back. Once upon a time, Jack was Shadow's most loyal man.

Bark healed. He stood tall again, his chest heaving with exertion. A massive howl erupted from him as he beat his chest. He looked at Jack. "HUNGRY," came out of him, his chest and throat rumbling. Bark couldn't talk in human form, but he could manage a few words after he'd changed.

"Go down to the grocery store," said Jack. "Eat your fill of the meat, and then relieve either Beast or Gunner, whoever wants to eat more. I want at least two of you on the streets at all time. And find Kid, goddamnit. We need him. If you come across anyone else on the streets, feel free to take them out."

Bark howled again and padded out, loping like an orangutan out of the office and into the street.

"That was a hell of a thing," said Jack.

"It was," said Abe.

"You don't look so good, 'ole boy," said Jack. "You feelin' alright?"

It was 1966. Abe looked up. He couldn't make out the face, the sun beaming bright behind the figure, silhouetted. He was numb, two gallons of wine circulating through his body. *Leave me alone.*

"You feelin' alright?" asked Shadow.

Abe didn't answer him. Looked back down, stared straight ahead. The man would wander away, given enough time. Maybe kick him a few times first. He could take the punishment.

"You don't look alright," said Shadow. "You look like shit, to be honest."

"Go away," said Abe, mumbling the words through slurred lips.

"No can do, partner," said Shadow, kneeling down in front of him. Abe studied him. The man was older than him, long silver hair hanging down in front of his face.

"Man oh man, I can smell the burden on you, but you've done a good job covering it with wine," said Shadow.

"Burden?" asked Abe.

"I carry it too," said Shadow. "But we can carry it together, if you want."

"Don't know what you mean," said Abe, the words stumbling out of his mouth.

"Yes you do," said Shadow. "That girl last night. Do you remember?"

That cut through the red fog of the wine. He had changed last night. It had been too long. He had run out of booze. A girl, on the outskirts of town. Ripped her throat out, and then fed.

Abe stared up and squinted at him. "You police?"

"No, brother," he extended a hand down to Abe. "But I can give you back control."

Abe looked at the hand, deciding whether to take it or not. He finally did. Can't believe it led him here, to this, with Jack.

"Feeling my age," said Abe. "You think this is a good idea?"

"What do you mean?" asked Jack, his feet still propped up. He was cleaning his fingernails with a boot knife.

"All of this," said Abe. "Orchestrating this chaos to get Runt back."

"We can't let them keep him," said Jack. "He knows too much."

"He's a fucking idiot," said Abe. "And he don't have any proof of anything. If he ever changes, they'll put him down, and then they *still* won't have any evidence."

"That's a possibility," said Jack. "We could leave, leave our brother, and we might get off scot-free. Or, the feds will dig around, find him, use him for science experiments, and then come for us. I don't know about you, but I don't want to get dissected."

"We're already down two men," he said. "We should cut our losses and get out."

Jack tucked his knife back into its sheath, reflecting for a second, and then looking across the office at Abe.

"We're not *down* anybody," said Jack. "We'll find Kid, get Runt out, and we'll be right back where we were. This heap of trash will burn to the ground, and we'll be gone. Good as new. We can drive south. Get away from the goddamn smoke for a while."

"Can you not see where this is headed?" asked Abe. "How much damage has been done since we killed Shadow? Someone will notice. We can't keep up this pace."

"No one has noticed. The only reason we're in this situation is Runt's stupid ass," said Jack. "And once he's back, he will straighten up and fly right, or we'll kill him too."

"Dozens of deaths won't go unnoticed, Jack," said Abe. "That's what Shadow understood. He understood that any other life besides the one we were living would get us hunted, killed. You don't want to be dissected? That's where we're heading."

"I will *not* go back to that," said Jack, staring at Abe. "That was a prison. It was contrary to our nature."

"We're killing innocent people," said Abe, finally. "Starting with Shadow. It ain't right."

Jack spit to the side. "Shadow? Innocent? Did he ever tell you what he did before he found you?" asked Jack. Abe's face must have told him the answer. "Oh, he didn't. Believe me, he was no innocent. All that happened was that he got scared."

Abe had nothing to say. He always considered Shadow close, the closest person he had. Shadow never told him about his past, at least nothing explicit. Jack continued.

"And those people?" said Jack. "They are food, nothing more. I feel the same as I did when we slaughtered cattle in a field. They're calories, Abe." He was close to Abe now.

We're gonna die here," said Abe. Jack closed the distance between them. He studied him. Abe eyed him.

"You talked to her," said Jack. "I can smell her on you."

"What are you talking about?" asked Abe.

"The sheriff," he said. "I know her scent. What did you tell her?"

"I didn't tell her anything. I was just trying to put pressure on her. To get her to release Runt. So we could go. So it wouldn't come to this." Jack's eyes stayed locked on him.

"I guess it didn't work," said Jack, breaking eye contact.

"I guess not," said Abe. "I thought it was worth a shot."

"You couldn't find Kid, either," said Jack. "Not having a good couple days, huh, Abe?"

"There was no sign of him anywhere—" said Abe. Jack interrupted him.

"And now you want us to flee, like a bunch of cowards," said Jack.

"I—"

"This town is ours, Abe. Might makes right. We are better than them. That is what Shadow never understood."

"I get it," said Abe, defeated. He would never get through to Jack. He was a fool for even thinking it.

"Good," said Jack, quickly pulling out his knife and thrusting it into Abe's neck. Abe struggled, gurgling, starting to change. "I don't think so," said Jack, twisting the knife and ripping it through the rest of Abe's throat. The blade caught on his spine, and Jack used both arms to lever the knife between the bones, twisting again and decapitating him, the spine snapping. Blood was everywhere, pouring out of Abe's body, pooling on the floor. His head lay on the ground next to him.

"Shame," said Jack, to no one. He undressed, taking off his vest, then shirt. Then his boots, followed by socks, belt, and pants. Underwear last. He put them on the desk, keeping them from getting bloody.

He transformed, and fed on Abe.

33

James was trapped. He needed to get out.

The sheriff's office was a mess. A pile of desks, filing cabinets, and bookshelves covered the only doors into the building. Sheriff Hill, the deputies, Art, and his father all stared at a map of the town, laid out on a table in the center of the space.

"The fire is coming in from the west."

"No way we'd make it."

"We could cut through the pass."

"They'll be waiting for us."

"They're waiting for us either way."

James heard a banging noise, coming from lockup. He followed his ears, and found Runt, awake and banging on the bars of his cell.

"Who are you?" asked Runt. "You're not a cop."

"No, I'm not," said James, looking Runt over.

"I can smell Jack on you," said Runt, with a short smile. "Bet none of them out there know that." *Even after the shower?*

"We talked last night," said James. "Before all of this spun out of control."

"You did more than talk," said Runt, his tongue sticking out the corner of his mouth.

James didn't answer, but his cheeks flushed with shame.

"Don't you worry, boy," said Runt. "Your secret is safe with me. I've been to prison, done things I'm not proud of. You have anything to eat?"

"Sorry, I didn't think to grab something from the store when I was running for my life," said James.

"No need to be a smartass," said Runt. "I'm fucking starving."

"You need the food to change," said James.

"I need the food to live, goddamnit," said Runt. "I'm not magic, for fuck's sake."

"I think you'll live, for now," said James.

"I can't wait to get the fuck out of here," said Runt. "Never would have come into this town if I'd have known what was waiting for me."

"You're not going anywhere," said James.

"Funny you saying that," said Runt. "How long have you lived here?"

"My whole life," said James. He could sense what Runt was drawing him into, but he couldn't stop.

"Your whole life," said Runt. "Spent in this godforsaken little town. This little tourist shithole."

"I won't be lectured by some biker," said James, getting up to leave.

"Some biker," said Runt. "Fuck you, pal. I'm just trying to give you some truth. Maybe you can't see it, but this kind of life is a trap. A trap to make you feel safe and secure, but the whole time it's just digging into you, pulling out every bit of happiness you got."

James stopped. He wanted to yell at Runt, but he knew it wouldn't get him anywhere.

"The only difference between us is that I had the guts to do something about it, while you've let your life waste away."

James left Runt in his cell, Runt cackling as James walked into the other part of the building. Everyone was still clustered around the map. His father was arguing with Hill.

"Are you saying all we got are pistols and shotguns?" he asked. He had isolated Hill, ignoring the deputies and Art. "Why don't we have any assault rifles? Or submachine guns?"

"Because we didn't need them! We're not fighting wars out there. We're calming down drunk tourists," she said.

"Absolutely ridiculous," he said.

James walked up to them, their argument unimportant. "I'm going out there."

"What?" asked Sheriff Hill. "That's suicide."

"No you are not," said his father.

"Susan is still in town, somewhere," said James. They hadn't seen a whisper of her out there. God knows where she went. "I'm going to find her, and I'll bring her back here."

Hill was silent.

"You'll be killed before you walk ten feet," said JH. "Susan is dead, James. There are fucking monsters roaming the streets, and we haven't heard from her in hours. People don't just walk off. She's in the belly of one of those things—"

James slapped him, hard, one time. The sound echoed through the room. "You shut your fucking mouth." He walked past his father. "Sheriff, I'm going out there. I'm not asking for approval. I'm aware of the risks. Would you help move the furniture?"

If James would have looked at his father, he would have seen an expression of utter shock. JH was trying to speak, but the words wouldn't come. He was left to sputter.

Hill looked at James. "There's a heavy access door on the roof. You can get out that way. There'll be a small jump, but nothing you can't handle. I'm going to lock it behind you, and I'll only let you in if it's safe. Understood?"

"Yeah, understood," said James. He refused to look at his father. His palm still hurt from the slap, but his chest was bursting from the rush. He struggled to keep his breathing measured.

"Do you want a pistol?" asked Heather.

"I have one," he said. "I hope you'll forgive the open carry."

"I think we can excuse it for now," she said.

JH had finally found his voice. "You son of a bitch, you come back here."

James left, following Hill into the small room with roof access. He didn't look back as the door shut and JH didn't follow them.

The heavy door swung open on the room, and the smoke was thick, unctuous, choking. With the vantage point, James couldn't see farther than fifty feet.

"Good luck," said Hill. "Two sets of three knocks, and I'll

let you back in."

"Thanks, Sheriff," he said, and walked over to the edge of the roof, looking around for a second before jumping down.

The town was a labyrinth now, covered in smoke. Everything that had been so familiar was unrecognizable. He heard nothing but his own footsteps. He knew the fire was approaching, but he didn't see it. He covered his face with a bandanna and walked.

He didn't know where Susan was. A part of him loved her, but he wasn't her savior. Not anymore. He wasn't looking for her.

He was looking for Jack.

The town would burn soon. The glow of the fires was visible through the smoke. Ash landed in his hair as he walked down the middle of the street. He didn't know where Jack was holed up, but he wasn't going to waste time on any of that. He wanted out, and he was going to find the only man who could help him.

He pursed his lips, a loud wolf whistle erupting from him that rang through the air, bouncing around off the ash and smoke hanging in the air. He whistled again, and again.

A few more whistles, and a few more minutes, and he heard the padding of feet coming towards him from the north. Runt had smelled Jack on him. One of these things should be able to do the same. They were afraid of Jack.

He put his hands up high in the air, waiting for the creature to approach him. Maybe it'd pounce on him and rip his guts out before he could say a word. A different way out than he wanted, but a way out nonetheless.

But it didn't. It stopped, puzzled by his behavior. It reached out a massive clawed hand and wrapped it around

James's throat.

"I want to talk to Jack. I want to make a deal," said James. The creature tightened his hand for a second, but then loosened it.

It barked a word, "FOLLOW."

It turned, leading James through the smoke. Another creature approached, ready to attack, but the first waved it off. Its bent face studied James for a moment, and then the creature loped away into the smoke. The creature stopped and pointed. They were at his father's office. How appropriate.

James walked in, following the familiar path to his father's office. It stunk of blood and death, and James immediately saw the scattered remains of a corpse as he entered. There was meat and gore everywhere, and he struggled not to vomit. He swallowed back the bile in this throat and pulled the bandana tighter around his mouth. Jack was sitting in his father's chair.

"Wow," said Jack. "Wasn't expecting you to walk through the door. Sorry I left without saying goodbye. We were in a bit of a rush." James was doing his best to ignore the mutilated remains left in the corner.

"I would normally get that cleaned up, but I don't think we'll be here long," he said. "You're lucky you ran into Gunner and not Beast."

"They all look the same," said James, finally, through his bandana. "You used me."

"I don't think that's fair," said Jack. Jack leaned back in JH's chair. "I think we both had a good enough time."

"You used the information I gave you," said James. "You killed Joe Coffey and the other firefighters."

"I wouldn't feel too bad," said Jack. "If you hadn't told me, I would have gotten it somewhere else."

James pulled the gun from his waistband, aiming it at Jack. "You used me."

"Whoa whoa whoa," said Jack. "Don't be stupid, James. That isn't going to solve anything." Jack got up from the chair and walked up to James, at ease, relaxed. "Did you really come here to threaten me with a pistol?"

James wavered, and pulled the gun down, letting it hang at his side. He couldn't think, Jack on his mind again. The man was intoxicating.

"I came to find a way out," said James. "A way out of Conquest. A way out of this life."

"Well, I can do that for you. I control this town and I can get you out of here," he said. "But—I can't do it for free. I need something."

"You need Runt," said James, not able to meet Jack's eyes.

"You get me Runt, and I can get you out," said Jack. "Easy as pie."

"No," said James, after a beat.

"No?" asked Jack. He was closer now, his hand caressing James's cheek.

"I don't want to just get out of the town," said James. "I want to be like you. I want your power. I want your freedom." Jack stared into his eyes, his fingers tracing James's jawline.

He spoke with a confident smile. "I can do that for you."

He kissed James, soft and tender on the lips. James didn't resist, the gun still hanging at his side.

"Now go get me Runt."

34

Susan had fulfilled her dream on her wedding day. It was beautiful.

They were married in the First Baptist Church, with Pastor Pearce residing over the ceremony. She had picked out everything. Purple and white were their colors, and it was absolutely perfect. The flowers made the church smell like spring. Their families were there. Everyone was so happy.

It was all she ever wanted. Since she was a little girl, her wedding was all she'd dreamed about. Walking down the aisle in a perfect white dress, everyone's attention on her. Her mother told her it would be the most important and best day of her life. She would tie her fate to her husband, who had decided that he wanted to spend his life with her. What a blessing. And James let her design everything, decide everything about that day. His father was paying for it, not him, and he was happy to let her spend JH's money.

She now stood in front of the Baptist church, the thick smoke wafting by, and she couldn't coalesce those memories with her reality. The big wooden double doors stood in front of her. She breathed in, and her body was wracked with coughs. The smoke was becoming too much to bear. She pushed the doors open, and she met no resistance. The church was lit, smelling of disinfectant and of the chlorined pool of water that sat behind the pulpit. The baptismal was a relic of the pre-Revitalization days, and had never gotten updated with recirculating water. God smelled like chemicals.

She had been baptized as a little girl in that pool. Sundays were the only day where the entire family would come into town—when any people living out in the country would come into town, those days. The Church was the largest Non-Mormon church in the county. The Mormons were not strong in Conquest. Old Charles Burns was a holy roller himself, and had kept them from setting foot in the town before it went to the pits. Baptists were tradition.

She had smiled, beamed at the altar. James was handsome, charming in his nervousness. She saw the dark edge to it now. His father in the front row, his default smile there, always there. Had he known? Did James tell anyone, ever?

She wanted to feel sorry for him. She wanted to feel pity. But anger was all she could muster.

They didn't have sex on their wedding night. They had remained pure before their wedding. Not that she wasn't willing, but James had always reminded her of their Christian responsibilities, and she agreed. She didn't think much of it that night. They were so tired. They had been on their feet all day.

It continued. They tried. They wanted a baby. It didn't happen, and as they failed, James's lack of enthusiasm only got worse and worse. Easy to see now. He didn't want her, only pushed through by some combination of pressure and shame, pressed hard into him often enough that the lie became the truth.

She sat in the pew. The church was empty.

She had played in the pews while her mother and father attended a counseling session with Pastor Pearce. She had flipped through the hymns, through the Bibles, ran up and down the stairs surrounding the pulpit. She had watched the stained glass as the sunlight poured through them. Her parents were in there for a long time. Her mother's eyes were red from tears. They went back to the pastor for more visits, but she was left with her grandparents after the first time.

She flipped through the hymnals. So familiar. Pages worn, reliable. She looked to see a shotgun in her face. She yelped. It was Pastor Pearce, a sawed-off pump in his hands.

"Oh, Jesus, Susan," he said, lowering the gun. "I thought you were one of those things."

"Why are you still here?" she asked, knowing he could ask the same of her. He was talking crazy. What things?

"I couldn't leave the church," he said, his gaze suddenly down, ashamed. "And it's a good thing I didn't. I need to defend it against whatever the devil is wandering our streets. Why are you here? Where's James?"

"I don't know," she said. "He hasn't been home since Friday night. I went out to look for him —"

"Oh," said Pearce. He put his hand on her shoulder.

"James is like his father. Driven to succeed, but with the drive comes a cost. Before she passed, James's mother would come to me for guidance about what to do with JH."

"What did you tell her?" asked Susan, the hymnal still in her hands. She thumbed the cover, the raised lettering.

"I told her to have faith," said Pearce. "That God tests us all. That He wouldn't have guided you to marriage unless it was part of His plan."

Her mother's voice rang through her head again, "Marriage is sacred. Your father is only serving God's will." She squeezed the hymnal, feeling the fake leather bend in her hands.

"Bullshit," she said, beneath her breath.

"What?" asked Pearce, the shotgun still in two hands, pointed down.

Susan looked up at him. "Bullshit," she said again, this time louder, venom in her voice.

"I—I—" he said, stammering. He took a step backwards, the force of her words pushing him.

She stood up now. "This is God's plan?" she said, raising her arms, gesturing to everything around her. "My husband abandoning me in a wildfire is God's plan?"

"God moves in mysterious ways," said Pearce. "We can't see everything like He does."

"Does God see my sorrow?" she asked, stepping toward the pastor. "Does he see the torture my mother was put through? The broken bones, the bruises, the mental torment? Did God see those things?"

"I know it's difficult sometimes," he said, but she stopped him.

"I don't know if God saw them, but you did, Pastor," she

said, taking another step towards him. "You saw them all. You saw the black eyes, the arguments, and you told the women to abide, to have faith, to practice patience."

"I did only what the Word told me to," he said, the shotgun moving up.

"Are you going to shoot me, Pastor?" she asked. He realized what he was doing, and lowered the gun again. His eyes wavered.

"I've only done what I thought was right," he said. "The world is hard. I was only trying to protect them."

"Bullshit," she said. "You protected men." She pointed out, toward the door. A colossal noise came from behind as she pointed.

"Behind me, Susan," he said. "God will save us."

She didn't move. "What are you talking about?"

"Please, please just get behind me," he said, his hand on her shoulder. She resisted until there was a louder noise, something heavy being moved. She stepped behind him, eyes still on the door.

"What is it?" she asked.

"It's one of them," he said, his voice low. "They heard us."

"One of who?" she asked. "What the hell is going on?"

The doors burst open, and Susan saw what he was talking about first hand. It was huge, ghastly. It stood on two legs, but was hunched over, like a great ape. Its skin was mottled, grey and white, covered in coarse fur. Its proportions didn't make sense. The muscles of its chest and arms were distended, grotesque, enormous. The hands and mouth were big as well, with fangs and claws that grew past utility into absurdity. Its shape defied reality, defied how animals existed.

The creature's dark, beady eyes narrowed at the pastor,

at her. It howled, a terrible noise that echoed inside the old church. Pearce pointed the gun at it, and it stared at him, its off-kilter head tilted, studying him.

"Stay back!" he shouted. "Whatever you are."

The beast grunted at that, then started shambling towards them. Its steps were small and tentative, but still toward them. Its legs were uneven, the muscles lumpy and odd.

"Not one step closer," said Pearce, holding the gun ready. Susan was climbing up the stairs of the vestibule, backing up, away from the thing. The thing's mouth opened, widening. It took a second for Susan to realize it was smiling.

"Shoot it," she said, to Pearce. "Shoot the damn thing!"

It leapt, a burst of movement and agility Susan wouldn't have expected, pouncing on Pearce, the shotgun clattering away from him. He put up his arms to defend himself, but it did nothing. The creature buried its two spade-like hands into the guts of Pearce and started digging, flesh and entrails flying out of him. He screamed once, but then was gone.

Susan looked on in horror. The creature was tearing through what was left of Pearce in glee, a dark chattering noise ringing from the creature. It was laughing.

The blood was everywhere, and the scent was mixing with the chemical smell that already filled the church and the smoke that wafted in through the open doors. It was too much, and Susan threw up.

The sound was enough to grab the beast's attention. It looked up, seeming to remember she was there, and its mouth smiled again—not curving upwards, but opening wider. It pulled itself out of Pearce's corpse and advanced on her, the slow crawl it had done before, one she now recognized as the predator about to pounce.

The shotgun on the floor, ten feet away from her. It was her only chance. The creature saw her eyes, its unnatural eyes looking at the gun. She scrambled for it, but the creature was faster, and closer. Its clawed hand wrapped around the short metal barrel of the gun and threw the gun away, hitting the ground somewhere in the rows of pews.

She was close to it now, and she could smell the blood on it, Pearce's blood soaking into its straw-like hair. It faked a lunge, and she fell backwards. It chattered again. It was playing with her. She scooted backwards as fast as she could, but it maintained its position on her. It was too big, too quick. She tried to move farther back, but hit the wall. There was nowhere else to go.

It heaved forward, slower now, looming over her. She could feel its hot breath, rot and copper covering her. She turned her head and closed her eyes, waiting for the end.

"Beast," said a familiar voice, from the entrance of the church. "Leave her."

The creature turned from her toward the voice. It was Andrew. The creature roared at him, but moved a step from her. Andrew had followed her, to protect her. He would be killed.

And then he changed. His muscles exploded out, swelling, growing. Even thirty feet away, she could hear bones snap and pop as they grew and re-socketed themselves. His face mutated, a half-formed snout with heavy fangs, his flesh unmelding. It happened fast, ten seconds of torment, and Andrew was gone. He was one of them. He roared, and Beast joined him. They charged at each other, and they met in the middle of the church, a tremendous thud filling the space.

She scrambled across the room, past the corpse of Pastor Pearce, and grabbed the shotgun. She heard the noise of them fighting as she cowered between two pews.

She had wandered away from her home, and into Hell.

35

James didn't smell the smoke on the way back to the sheriff's station, even as it thickened around him. Jack's scent was the only thing on his mind.

The fire had hit the edge of town. He could see it burning from the roof of the station as he climbed up, his gun still tucked in his waistband.

He rapped on the door three times, and then three times more. After a few seconds, a bolt retracted inside the door and the door opened, Darla's head visible through the crack.

"Alone?" she asked.

"Yes," he said. "For good and for bad."

"Fair enough," she said, and opened it for him, letting him inside. She locked it again after he came in. He could feel the tension back inside the station. The sheriff was pacing, clearly anxious. In contrast, Jack had been so calm, so sure.

"No success?" she asked him.

"I couldn't find her," he said, his head down. "It's toxic out there. The edge of the town is on fire. I couldn't find anything."

"You tried," said Sheriff Hill. "She may turn up yet." He knew she didn't believe it. He didn't either. Susan was gone. It was for the best. Less holding him back.

JH was stewing in the corner. He was outnumbered and outmaneuvered in this group, and all the political clout in the world wouldn't help him. Even Buzz wouldn't help him. Served him right. Art was playing cards with Darla in the corner by lantern light. The station had an emergency generator, but Hill didn't want to use it unless absolutely necessary.

James looked at his father, but he wouldn't even glance back. Too much disobedience. *Fuck him. Let him burn in this damnable town.* James would be out, free, finally. His father couldn't reach him when he was with Jack, riding out of here.

James left the main office area, into the holding cells. He walked past Buzz, who was nose deep in a book. Buzz looked up and nodded at him as he passed, and then returned to the paperback. Runt was sitting on his bunk, his dark eyes staring ahead, into the void. If Runt smelled Jack on him, he didn't let on.

The break area was tiny, just enough to hold a fridge, microwave, a small table, and some chairs. The counter area held a tiny sink. A few dirty mugs sat inside of it, collecting water. He opened the drawers, one by one. Leftover packets of salt and pepper. Soy sauce, chopsticks, napkins. A few ragged dish towels, folded. He worried for a second, but then found what he had been looking for. There was one in every break room.

A kitchen knife, four inches long. Tossed in with spare silverware. It was dull, but it would do. He pocketed it, then rolled up his sleeves.

He walked back out of the break room. Buzz was still lost in his book. Runt stared at him now, through the bars in his cell. He smiled at him. He zipped his lips, and mimed throwing away the key.

Buzz was one of the old guard, one of the good old boys that Cochbrin had hired, a man who maintained the status quo. Everyone knew that Buzz fed JH information whenever he was pressed, but no one had ever done anything about it.

Buzz and his wife had been over to eat a couple times, along with James's father and some of the other men who ran the town in the early days of the Revitalization Project. He had learned a little about Buzz. He had two kids and a wife, who sold quilts on the internet. Buzz liked to read trashy thrillers.

James walked past Buzz again, and Buzz didn't move this time, still engrossed in his reading. He pulled the knife from his pocket, and in one smooth motion moved behind Buzz, grabbed his thinning hair, pulled his head back, and slid the knife deep into his throat. He pulled it hard across, the dull blade ripping more than cutting the flesh. A look of shock was on Buzz's face, and he struggled, blood pouring out of his neck. He reached up, trying to protect what was left of him, but it was too late.

James dug in with the blade, cutting deeper and deeper. Needed to cut through the vocal cords or he'd make too much noise. Buzz could only gurgle and grunt as the blood pumped out of him. James held onto him until he stopped moving. Runt, true to his word, didn't say anything, just watched, his eyes gleaming.

James arm was covered in blood, elbow deep. He moved fast now, jogging into the kitchen, soaping up quickly and washing the blood away, watching it flow down the drain. The knife was next, bits of Buzz's flesh still stuck to it. All down the drain. He returned the knife to the same drawer he'd gotten it from, and toweled off. He rolled up and buttoned his sleeves again. He jogged back into the cells. No one had intruded. Good.

He grabbed the keys from Buzz's belt, avoiding the blood, and unlocked Runt's cell door.

"Give me five minutes," he said. "Two exits, either a stairwell to the roof, or the front door, lightly barricaded."

"No worries, boss man," he said. "I'm gonna need some time with our friend over here." Runt started changing, his body stretching, bones snapping, muscles growing taut, and then exploding out. James didn't want to look, but he needed to know what the change was like. It would be him, soon enough.

Within ten seconds, Runt had turned into an asymmetrical monster, muscle, hair, fangs, and claws. He was ugly as sin. Runt ignored James, and began feeding on Buzz's corpse, lapping at the blood and swallowing whole huge chunks of flesh. The room smelled of blood and gore.

James left, walking back into the short hallway that connected the two areas of the building. He ducked into the stairwell that reached the roof, unlocked the deadbolt, and walked back outside. He couldn't lock the door behind him, but it didn't matter. He wouldn't be coming back.

•

Arthur shuffled the cards again, his hands doing the motions over and over without thinking. Cut, firm, float, bridge, firm. Over and over.

Darla had left five minutes ago, retreating from his winning streak. She had gone off to replace Buzz on watch, give him a break.

They were all on guard. Heather was pacing still, leaning over the map of the town from time to time. Being inside was killing her, he knew. Doing nothing was killing her. He left her alone. Trying to distract her would only make it worse. He shuffled.

JH was pissed because he wasn't getting his way. He wanted to run. It was suicide. Arthur ignored him. He shuffled. What was taking Darla so long? Buzz should be out here by now.

The sprinkler system suddenly turned on, water pouring down on the three of them from the pipes along the ceiling.

"What the hell?" asked Heather, and then the door from the holding cells opened, an object flying through the air, tumbling across the floor, and landing at Heather's feet. It was Darla's head.

"Fuck," she said, running towards her shotgun, which was sitting on her desk. Arthur looked over at the door, only to be hit in the chest with a sack of dry concrete. He tumbled backwards from his chair, falling to the floor with a thud. He pushed the sack off of him, and realized it was actually Darla's torso, the limbs torn off. He scrambled to his feet and then was hit again, this time with a desk flung at him from the barricade at the front door. Runt was out, and he had transformed. The side of the desk grazed Arthur's head, and he fell to the floor, woozy.

Heather was in her office, shotgun in hand. She aimed at Runt and fired, but missed as a chair hit her in the arm. She cocked and fired again, this time hitting him in the flank, black blood seeping out from his mottled skin. Runt screamed in agony. He grabbed another desk in two hands, and then charged Heather with it, using it as a shield. She fired into the desk, once, twice, three times, the desk falling apart in Runt's clawed hands.

He dropped the remains of the desk, getting ready to attack Heather. She pumped the shotgun, but was out of shells. Heather drew her pistol and backed up into her office again, firing shots into Runt. They didn't slow him down.

Arthur's shotgun blast did, and he yowled again as the shot ripped into his side. Arthur got to his feet, loading the riot gun. Runt hesitated, and Heather shot several more rounds with her pistol, hitting him in the head and eyes. His right eye exploded as a round passed through it, and Runt screamed in pain. He lashed out with a claw and caught Heather, knocking her off her feet. Art let off a series of shotgun blasts, racking shell after shell. Runt ran, half blind, smashing through the remaining furniture that had blocked the front door.

Arthur followed up to the door, popping off shots into the smoke as Runt ran.

Arthur went back in and checked on Heather. Her eyebrow was busted and she clutched her side.

"I think that bastard broke some ribs," said Heather. Arthur helped her up. She leaned in the doorway, surveying the damage.

JH still sat in the corner, speechless. He was looking at Darla's head. It sat in the middle of the floor. She stared up at the ceiling with dead eyes.

"Fuck."

36

Kazuko stood in the middle of the street, waiting. She carried nothing but her cane. She would say her piece.

Runt crashed through the front entrance of the Sheriff's Office, with Arthur shooting after him. The gunshots, both inside and outside the station, could be heard through the town. The blasts echoed through, and bounced off the smoke, but Kazuko knew where he was. So she waited for him, in his path.

After the standoff outside of the station, the beasts had retreated, moving slowly through the smoke. Kazuko moved as fast as she could, but Alice still slowed down to not leave her behind. They ducked into an alleyway, hiding behind a dumpster.

"We need to stay out of sight," she said. "Find a good

place to hole up." Alice looked at Kazuko, and realized that she couldn't understand her. She reached for her phone, but Kazuko grabbed her wrist, stopping her.

"No run," she said, in broken English. "Fight." She mimed a rifle. "Where?"

Alice sighed, and shook her head. "We can't win against those things, even with weapons. We have to run, have to hide. Or we will die." The duo were outnumbered. The monsters were bigger, faster, and tougher than hell.

Kazuko shook her head She put her hand on her own heart. "*I* stay." She put her hand on Alice's heart. "You go. Live."

Alice paused, looking out into the street. The smoke drifting in was darker, thicker. The fire was approaching town, if not in it already. The only way out of this alive was to make their way to the pass. Kazuko was still staring at her, her eyes earnest. She believed what she said. She also thought the town was beset by demons.

Was she wrong?

Whatever the beasts were, being armed was better than not. Her and Kazuko would be running anyway. And she couldn't leave Kazuko to fend for herself. Deluded or not.

Alice squeezed Kazuko's hand. "Follow me."

Wilson's Guns and Hobby was a new store, built in the wake of the Revitalization Project, but Tom Wilson had lived in the city limits of Conquest his whole life. He had owned a pawn shop in the space this store now stood. He was friends with Mayor JH Bieter, and took the town's money to remodel the space, and change the scope of the store.

Tom Wilson had left town, and his store was dark, empty, deserted. Both the front and back doors were locked. They could have broken the front glass, but that would have made noise. Alice knew the secret of a lot of these old buildings, in that they had basements, and basement windows that were rarely locked.

The store's basement window thankfully wasn't locked, and she snuck inside, opening the door for Kazuko. The store wasn't large, but it was dense, packed floor to ceiling with guns, knives, and bows.

Alice looked at the guns on the wall, an array of rifles and shotguns. She knew what she wanted. Her last boyfriend had taken her in there, enamored. The item had that effect on everyone. Tom Wilson used it to get tourists to come in, to buy overpriced camo jackets and thermoses.

There was a glass case, separate unto itself. Inside rested an elephant gun, a massive rifle that fired gigantic shells used to hunt big game and stop charging animals in their tracks. If anything could kill these things, this could. If it didn't break her shoulder every time she fired it.

Alice didn't own guns, but her father had taught her to shoot. If you grew up in this county, you learned.

The case was locked. She grabbed a display dagger and smashed the glass with the handle then pulled the massive rifle out of the case and shouldered it. It must have weighed over twenty-five pounds. Alice walked behind the counter and found the shells, massive metal bullets that looked like they belonged in a tank. Alice grabbed an ammo pouch and loaded the rifle with the heavy metal.

Kazuko walked over to her, then ran her hand over the massive gun. She nodded with approval. "Demon killer," she said. Kazuko had grabbed a knife and sheathed it on her belt.

And now Kazuko stood in the middle of the street. She would say her piece.

Runt burst out of the sheriff's office, half blind, running from shotgun fire. The smoke was thick, noxious. She saw him first, and yelled, her voice echoing down the deserted street.

"<Demon! You will hear me.>"

Runt looked to the source of the voice, of the language he didn't understand. Kazuko stood in the street, five feet tall, leaning on her cane. He didn't break his sprint, charging straight toward her.

He healed as he ran, his eye reforming inside his skull, the shotgun pellets and bullets pushed out of him and landing in the ash. At a full sprint, his speed was incredible. He loped, the brutal strength overcoming the awkward gait. He'd be on her in seconds.

Kazuko watched him and waited. She stood, the unbreakable stone. She would say her piece. She would make him understand.

Runt was mere seconds from her, his mouth open, still covered in blood. He would feed on her.

Alice stood on the roof of the nearby cafe. On a normal July 4th weekend, the rooftop would be packed with people eating, drinking, celebrating. It was empty now, the chairs stacked on the tables.

She pulled the rifle snug to her shoulder, aimed down the sights, and pulled the trigger.

The sound was deafening, like artillery fire, a localized cosmic explosion only six inches from Alice's ears. The gun jerked back into her shoulder, but she held it tight, just like her father had taught her.

Alice didn't worry about hitting Runt in any particular place. She aimed for center mass, and let the gun do all the work. The shell ended up hitting Runt in the upper left portion of his torso. Runt didn't know what hit him. He only felt the impact, heard the explosion, and then his arm and shoulder, were missing. The bullet ripped through his flesh, hitting bone and pulling it out of him. He fell, his body sliding to Kazuko's feet. She remained.

Alice didn't hear Runt's scream, her ears still ringing from the shot. Black blood was pouring out of his shoulder, cascading down his haunches. Runt's body was trying to heal itself, to knit itself back together, but it struggled. Alice could see the morass of cells inside his distended abdomen working, regenerating. She broke the barrel, popping out the shell, and slid in another.

Alice gave him credit for his resiliency as he rose to his feet, struggling with the pain and trauma. He grunted, squelching noises emerging from inside his chest. He looked at Alice just as she aimed and pulled the trigger again.

The second shot was less momentous, but just as damaging. It hit his right hip, the shell obliterating the bone and exploding out the back of him. He fell again, a catastrophic yowl tearing out of Runt's throat. She broke the gun again, inserting a new shell. Runt struggled, the damage too much, his body in shock.

Alice ran downstairs, joining Kazuko. She remained.

Alice pulled the rifle to her now-bruised shoulder and aimed it at him. He wouldn't survive another shot from the cannon.

Kazuko walked up close to him. She could smell his blood intermingling with the smoke in the air. Runt was struggling to breathe, but his eyes were still clear, and they focused on Kazuko. She stood over him. Even rendered harmless, his size was still remarkable.

She opened her hand, and revealed a photo, holding it out for Runt to see. It was the prom photo of Kyle. Her fingers gripped the picture tight, the photo a weapon.

"<You have stolen two generations from me,>" she said. "<You have taken thousands of hours of love and care thoughtlessly. You have erased the future of a family. You deserve worse than this, than a death in the street, with some momentary, fleeting pain. The trauma you have left on the world will not heal.>"

She paused, but Runt didn't react.

"<I cannot deliver what you deserve,>" she said, finally. "<But you will receive it, in Hell.>" Kazuko threw the picture at Runt, and then pulled the knife from its sheath and plunged it into Runt's eye, deep into his skull. Runt stopped moving, his resilience at an end.

Kazuko stood over his body, looking down at it. Tears rolled down her cheeks. She made no effort to wipe them, only looked as the creature turned back into the recognizable form of the man that killed her son.

"Let's go," said Alice. Her ears still rang, and she could barely hear herself speak as she looked at the dead body of Runt, just the biker, again.

Kazuko nodded. She had said her piece.

Alice began to walk, but then heard a short cry, and a grunt. She turned around to see another creature, twice as large as Runt had been. Despite its size, it had snuck up on them. Kazuko was dangling in the air, trying to scream, but unable. The great monster had plunged its arm straight through the elderly woman. She looked into Alice's eyes, trying to say so much, and died.

He threw her to the side and roared, a horrifying sound that Alice could barely hear. She didn't hesitate, pulling the rifle to her shoulder and firing again. The sound, like a mortar, rang again, and a gigantic hole opened up in the side of him. He did not fall, however, but the roar turned into a bellow of pain, and he ran, leaving Alice alone in the street with blood, ash, and two corpses.

37

The two creatures tore at each other, ragged claws ripping chunks of flesh and splashing black blood across the church. Susan gripped the shotgun tightly in her hands. She didn't know what to do.

Andrew had changed. He was larger than the other one, and was dragging it around, smashing it into the walls as the smaller struggled in his grasp.

The creature that used to be Andrew looked at her and shouted, "RUN," his voice three octaves lower than normal, but it was all she needed to hear. She picked herself up from the floor between two pews and ran for the heavy wooden double doors.

The first creature saw her and broke free from Andrew's grasp, sprinting at her, panting as it crossed the rooms in several large strides. She turned to fire, but Andrew grabbed it from behind, and they engaged in a frantic, desperate struggle. The first creature raked its claws across Andrew's eyes, and he shouted in pain. It scrambled back to its feet. It looked at Susan again, a wide smile on its face, even as it bled from a half-dozen wounds on its body. It shook its head as it covered the door. There was no way she could get past it.

She backed up away from it, behind Andrew, who was on his feet again. He bore no resemblance to the man she knew. His shape echoed the one who had killed the pastor, but it was different in a thousand small ways. He was ugly, none of his handsome features transferring over to this new form.

Andrew had been honest, yesterday in the park. He *wasn't* like most men.

Andrew looked at the other creature. His eyes were open again, blood caked on his face. "BEAST. LEAVE," said Andrew. The other creature—Beast?—didn't move, just stared, chattering again, his mouth wide.

"TRAITOR," Beast finally said, and then ran at Andrew in a burst of speed and agility much like when it had attacked the pastor. Andrew was prepared for it, however, grabbing Beast's right wrist as it tried to gouge him. He couldn't grab the other in time, as Beast's left hand dug into Andrew's torso. Andrew grunted in pain, and then seized the left wrist as well, pulling Beast's claws out of his body. Beast snapped at him, Andrew ducking away in time to avoid Beast's fangs.

Beast pulled his hands away, and swam past Andrew like a defensive lineman, trying to get to her. Susan dove under a swinging claw as Andrew lost hold of him. He wanted her, and Andrew was doing his best to protect her. Andrew grabbed the legs of Beast, dragging him back, Beast flailing, his claws outstretched, swiping at Susan, who was just out of reach.

Beast struggled, spittle flying out of his mismatched jaws. He wanted her, wanted her blood, wanted to feed on her. He kicked hard, catching Andrew in the throat. No matter their power, they still needed to breathe. Andrew let go.

Beast smiled at Susan as Andrew gasped for air. The hard, wooden floor was taking a toll on her, the repeated impacts with it leaving bruises. He charged at her, free of Andrew's grasp, and she turned the shotgun toward him and fired. The blast echoed, the gun nearly flying out of Susan's hands. The blast hit Beast in the chest and he yelled in pain, but he was still up, bleeding from the chest. He nattered, a low burst of noise.

Susan dove again, her knees smashing against the wooden floor as Andrew brought a pew down on Beast, the bench breaking in half over Beast's head and back. He grunted and fell. Andrew swung again and again, destroying the bench over Beast. He was breathing hard, panting, but Beast was on the ground, struggling to move. The laughter began again. Susan looked at Beast, on the ground. The nattering laughter rose from him, even as his body was broken.

Beast moved with another burst of quickness to his feet and his hand around her neck, lifting her up and off the ground, then pinning her against the wall. She struggled to breathe.

Andrew moved to help her, but Beast raised a finger toward him, looking away from her, waggling it. Andrew dropped the bit of bench he still held onto. Susan looked at him, urging him toward something. His face was mutated, distorted, but she saw the humanity in his eyes. He would not trade victory for her life.

Alright. Susan held the shotgun, feeling the weight in her hands. She pumped it once, racking a shell. Beast either didn't notice or didn't care. She had shot him in the chest, and it had done nothing. *Soft tissue it is, then.*

She extended the shotgun and pulled the trigger, blowing off Beast's balls. She dropped from his grasp immediately as he screamed in pain, cradling what was left of his genitals. She pulled herself off the floor and racked another shell. Andrew smiled at her, the same way Beast had. It was unnerving. She walked over to the writhing body of Beast. She put the barrel of the shotgun in his extended, bat-like ear, and pulled the trigger. The blast ripped through the church, and half of Beast's head disappeared in a cloud of black ichor.

"What the fuck is happening?" she asked.

An enormous howl entered the church from outside. Close. The church was filling with smoke. Beast's body was now human again, his head half gone. Andrew looked outside, listening.

"GUNNER," he said, a deep rumble. "HIDE. DO, NOT, COME, OUT."

"I can help," said Susan.

"NO, YOU, CAN'T," he said. "HE IS, NOT, BEAST. HE HAS, CONTROL." Susan couldn't see much emotion in his face, but she could hear the fear in his voice. She hid, sinking down underneath the risers where the small choir would sing, in front of the baptismal.

Gunner walked into the church, his monstrous form

crouching to fit through the doors. The creature's eyes looked over the dead bodies of Pastor Pearce and Beast, then glanced back to Andrew. Gunner was big, bigger than either Andrew or Beast. His arms hung low, his knuckles grazing the ground as he crouched. The muscles in his chest flexed, looking like they would burst through his skin. His legs were askew, one larger than the other. His ears and nose were small—curled even. The change made him look like an inbred dog, eyes unable to open fully, mouth that couldn't shut. His breaths were loud harsh wheezes.

Andrew bled from a dozen wounds as he squared up to Gunner. The fight with Beast had taken its toll.

Neither spoke, staring at each other. Then, Andrew charged, taking two massive gallops before leaping into the air. Gunner moved with astounding quickness, grabbing a hold of him in the air and smashing him into the rows of pews, breaking several of them as the weight of Andrew fell. Gunner was on top of him in an instant, and Andrew tried to fight him off. The collisions were thunderous, hundreds of pounds of animal smashing into each other. Susan hid.

Gunner wasn't laughing like Beast, or playing games. He was trying to rip out Andrew's throat. Andrew sliced at Gunner's eyes and Gunner released his grip, Andrew scuttling away while he could.

Susan hid, staying quiet, watching these two monsters slice each other to the bone. She wanted to turn her head, close her eyes, the two demons filling the church with sounds of death. But she watched. She watched them destroy each other.

Andrew charged again. He didn't leave his feet this time, his claws and teeth leading the way. Gunner grabbed Andrew's jaws, keeping Andrew from biting out his throat, but Andrew's claws were free, and he began digging into Gunner's torso, ripping open his stomach.

Gunner pushed the jaws open, and Andrew screamed in pain, but continued to dig, cutting through muscle and cartilage, until intestines began spilling out of Gunner's stomach. Gunner grunted in pain, but did not stop stretching apart Andrew's mouth, even as Gunner's belly was ripped open, blood pooling around them on the floor.

Andrew dug, ripping through organs, the viscous flesh piling on the floor, catastrophic damage to Gunner. Gunner's massive arms and chest strained, Andrew's jaws opening wider and wider, obscene, like a snake. Susan watched. One would soon break, their absurd biology pushed past any conceivable limit.

Andrew's jaw cracked, and then shattered, an awful burst of noise. Susan winced, tearing up. His arms stopped clawing, stopped digging, hanging limp as Gunner pulled harder, ripping off the top of Andrew's skull with a deep snarl. He let Andrew fall to the floor, his intestines still caught up in Andrew's claws. Gunner's chest heaved, his breath coming in short, ragged chunks. Susan held her breath, repressing tears.

He looked down on himself, and began piling his guts back inside him, holding them in with one massive paw before he began shoving meat from the three corpses into his maw, swallowing hungrily.

Susan gripped the shotgun tight in her hands. Andrew was dead, slaughtered. Gunner's back was to her. This was her chance.

She crawled out from her hiding space, holding the shotgun in front of her like a ward. Gunner continued to eat, holding his guts inside of him.

"Back off, fucker," she said.

Gunner turned and growled, and saw the shotgun. He bared his teeth, brown, covered in blood. The wound in his stomach was healing. Still, it was grievous. He didn't move, challenging her. Fuck it.

She pulled the trigger, the spray of shot hitting him in the stomach and the hand that was guarding it.

"Get out," she said. "Feed somewhere else."

He snarled again, but his eyes stayed on her shotgun. She pumped it again, but felt the difference. There were no more shells. Hopefully he didn't know it.

She raised the gun again, walking closer to him. His lidded eyes narrowed as he snarled again, but ran, a hand snaking around the ankle of Pastor Pearce as he went, dragging the body behind him. He was gone.

The church was a charnel house. Andrew had returned to his human form, but the once beautiful body was mutilated, unrecognizable.

She walked to the door, then looked outside. The town was burning. Soon, the church would be gone too.

38

The town was burning as James returned to Jack. He heard the gunshots that followed his escape from the station, but it was behind him. The town was behind him.

He held his shirt over his mouth as he walked back, the smoke growing thicker and thicker. The late afternoon sun, always dim in Conquest, was all but gone, erased by the smoke filling the sky. Ash piled in the gutters.

Buzz's death rattle echoed between his ears. James's hand was still warm from his blood. He felt the jerk of Buzz's head as he pulled the knife across his throat. Guilt, shame, death.

No.

Buzz was complicit in this. They all were. They ran the system that had kept James here, kept him in prison. Now he was out. He had found a way out.

Jack. Jack would get him out of here. He'd have agency, have *power*. He needed to get back to him. Town Hall was still standing, still unblemished, the three-story white building standing out in the smoke.

Jack was in his father's office, staring out a window.

"James," he said without looking back. "You came back."

"Of course," said James. "Of course I did."

"I wasn't sure you would," said Jack. "I didn't know if you could do what was necessary." He looked back, over his shoulder. "Did you do what I asked?"

"Yes," said James. "Runt is free. He's behind me somewhere, probably wreaking havoc."

"Good," he said. "Now we're at full strength again. How many are left alive in the sheriff's station?"

"There were four when I left," said James, guilt and shame in his gut rising. He pushed it down. "But Runt might have changed that."

"Was the sheriff one of them?" he asked. "And your father?"

"Both were still alive when I left," said James. All these questions. He wanted his end of the bargain. He wanted their power.

"I've done what you asked me," he said, heading off any more questions. "I want what I'm due."

James turned around and walked toward Jack, and his smell was strong again in James's nose. The memory of Buzz's blood splashing on the floor evaporated inside it.

"That is fair," said Jack. "You've done exactly what was asked of you."

The doors in the outer hall opened, and footsteps echoed through the space. "Boss," said a voice, quiet.

Jack's face changed, grew a look of concern, an expression James didn't recognize.

Gunner stumbled up behind James, in human form. He was naked, and he looked weak, even gaunt. As he moved into the room, he fell onto the floor. He was gasping for air.

"What happened?" asked James, walking up to him.

"Beast, Kid, and Runt," said Gunner. "All dead." James stomach fell. He'd freed that monster, and for what? For Runt to get killed in the street. He could feel the weight on his shoulders, once nearly gone, returning. Gunner climbed to his feet.

"What?" asked Jack. "All three?"

"Killed Kid myself. Turned traitor, trying to rescue a woman from town. He killed Beast. Found Runt's body on the street. Looks like he was shot with a cannon."

Jack didn't say anything, just turned away and walked over to the heavy desk, which he flipped over without effort.

"Where's Bark?" he asked.

"Didn't see him," he said. "Came here to tell you about Beast and Kid and found Runt's corpse on the way. Kid and the woman almost got me. Had to run without finishing her."

"You, me, Bark," said Jack. "We were seven. Now we're three."

"We can be four," said James, walking toward Jack. "Turn me. And then we can leave. Wash our hands of this town."

Gunner looked at James confused, but James didn't notice.

"We're not leaving," said Jack.

"What?" asked James. "Why not? It's burning down around us. We need to get out."

"We are not leaving until we get some justice. Once this town is burnt to the ground, and we're sure everyone is dead, we will leave."

"I don't—" said James.

"It's the principle, James," said Jack. "We will not run with our tails tucked between our legs. We aren't cowards."

James was going to explode. He wanted out. He'd *earned* it. He paid for it in blood. *Fine. If this is what it takes, then I'll do it. Anything.*

"Okay," said James, finally. "Let's do it."

Gunner spoke up, having held his tongue long enough. "What the fuck is he talking about, boss?"

"We struck a deal. He gets Runt out of jail, we let him into The Pack," said Jack. "Make him one of us. Don't work like that, though. You're born with the change or you're not." He took a deep breath. "It's very unfortunate that Runt is dead. We could really use him right now. Unfortunate that James went to all that trouble for nothing." He reached into James's waistband and grabbed his pistol, holding it to James's head.

No no no no no, no. James's heart sank, his hands shaking. He'd done everything he was told.

"I'm sorry for the subterfuge," said Jack, "But I really needed Runt out of jail."

"We—" said James. "We had something."

"No," said Jack, staring at him dead in the eyes, pistol outstretched. "We had sex."

Tears welled up in James's eyes, and he could barely contain them. He blinked hard, trying to keep them back.

"I killed for you!" said James. "I cut a man's throat. Buzz Sawyer. He had a family."

"He was just a man," said Jack. "Like you. Not much to

you humans. I'll tell you something, maybe you'll feel less guilty."

"Fuck you," said James.

"I'll ask a question first. Do you know what pheromones are?"

James just stared at him, tears now rolling down his face.

"I think you know what they are," said Jack. "You're smart. Now, men have pheromones, just like animals. Usually don't mean much. But for us, they're much stronger. They make people highly suggestible."

Jack's smell. Followed him everywhere. "You fucking drugged me," said James.

"Oh, I wouldn't say that," said Jack. "I just gave you the warm and fuzzies. A little extra oil for the engine."

James wiped away his tears. Composed himself. He looked into Jack's eyes, and there was nothing there. No anger, no sadness, no love. Cold, dead eyes. He'd forfeited everything for this.

"You're a monster," said James. There was no way out.

"I have mercy in me, James. You did what you were told, and don't think I don't appreciate the time we spent together."

"Can I leave?" asked James, hope entering his heart.

"No," said Jack, then shot him between the eyes. James's body crumpled to the ground.

Gunner watched. Jack looked at James's body for a second. "Feed on him. I need you at one hundred percent. We find Bark, and we hunt. No one leaves town."

39

The church was burning when Susan left. The fires moved through town, hopping from building to building. She left the bodies inside, taking the remaining shotgun shells.

Susan walked down the ash-filled streets of Conquest, burning down around her. Her house was gone by now.

She could see the blood of Gunner, a trail of gory ash following behind him. She saw figures in the smoke around her. Were they real? She held the shotgun ready, but none of them came toward her. A silhouette of James flashed in the distance, but just as soon as it appeared, it was gone.

There were creatures out here, and she heard them all around her. Or were they fires, the soft gasps, the muffled footfalls, teeth ripping through flesh, all vague messages from the fire, all illusion. Her sweater was over her mouth, keeping the ash out, if not the smoke.

Susan passed her parents' house, smoke rising from the eaves. She stopped and stared.

Her father needed a wheelchair now. Diabetes took his foot first, and then his leg up to the knee. His force of will, his determination, his anger, his abuse, none of it could overcome the amputation. His power, his yelling, all of it was a paper tiger now. Her mother took care of him because no one else would. She did it for Susan. She kept that burden for herself.

He had cried when he'd woken up from surgery. It was the first time she'd seen him cry. He didn't cry after the second. He had already had lost what was there. He refused to use a prosthetic. Susan loved her father, despite everything, but she was glad the day they took his foot.

His venom was there, Susan knew. The rage was there, but he was no threat. He never learned how to take care of himself, and now he was helpless. Her mother now exercised control. Susan had walked into their house, then, after the surgery, and it was different. The air felt lighter. The monster was contained.

He would live the rest of his life underneath the care of her mother. Susan took solace that he finally understood what it was to be powerless.

They were long out of town, all the keepsakes and fine china in their special van that could carry a wheelchair. This wasn't their house anyway. Not really. The real one had been sold years ago, and was already gone. They wouldn't come back here. They'd take the insurance money and sell the property.

She and James would have money coming to them as

well, for both the house and the mine properties. All of it in James's—and by extension, her name. What were *they* anymore, her and James?

She needed to get out first.

A shout came through the smoke. At her. "Don't move any closer." A female voice. Susan stopped.

"It's Susan Bieter," she said through the smoke, calling out to the figure

"Susan," she said, a moment of recognition. "What are you doing here?"

Susan walked closer, the figure becoming clear. Alice Ames stood in the street, holding a massive rifle. It was tight to her shoulder, Alice ready to aim and fire if a threat presented itself. She stood over a body, ash gathered around it, encased in it. An elderly Asian woman was dead, killed by a creature, judging by the hole punched through her chest.

"Alice?" asked Susan. Alice lowered her weapon, letting it rest on the pavement. Her eyes were red, though from the smoke or crying, Susan couldn't tell. They had once worked together at the mine, enough to know each other.

"I couldn't leave her," said Alice, without explanation. "She came so far. This isn't where she belongs." Susan saw the man's body then, a few feet away.

"Who?" asked Susan, gesturing toward the woman's corpse.

"Kazuko," said Alice. "She deserves better. She lost everything. Conquest took it all from her. I won't leave her behind."

"Those things are still around," said Susan.

"Yes," she said. "This can hurt them. They know it." She raised the gun, a massive hunting rifle. Susan looked into

Alice's red, ash-encrusted eyes. They moved, jumping from place to place. She was in shock.

"Was he one of them? One of those creatures?" asked Susan, pointing at the other body.

"Yes," said Alice. "We killed him. Justice. But Kazuko paid for it. I chased off another. They are afraid."

Susan felt calm now. Alice needed an anchor, or she wouldn't make it. Susan would be that for her.

"We have to get out of here," said Susan. "We have to get out of Conquest, Alice. It's burning down, and those things are roaming around. There's nothing here for us."

"I won't leave Kazuko," she said. "Someone has to take care of her. There is no one else." Alice was crying now, again. The barrel of her gun dragged along the ground as she spoke, a soft scraping noise rising as it carved a path in the ash.

"She's dead, Alice," said Susan. "We need to go."

"I'm not leaving this town without her," she said, every word punching through the smoke. Alice had grabbed the rifle again with two hands, now assuming a defensive posture. Susan couldn't force her. The body of Kazuko was still lying on the pavement.

"You've done all you can do," said Susan. "If we carry her with us, we will die."

"I tried to p-p-protect her," said Alice, stammering.

"What would she have wanted you to do?" asked Susan.

Alice was quiet for a moment, both hands still on the massive rifle. "She told me to go. To live."

"Then let's do that. We'll come back and get her. I promise," said Susan, looking into Alice's eyes

It calmed her. "Okay," Alice said, her eyes fixed on Susan.

"Let's go," said Susan. "Keep an eye out with that gun. Keep those creatures at bay."

"Demons," said Alice. "Kazuko had told me they were demons. I didn't believe her. I'm not sure anymore."

"Demons can't die," said Susan. "They're only men. When they die, they're just men."

Alice nodded, understanding Susan's logic. "Where are we going? The pass? It's the only way out."

"Those things will know that. We'll be sitting ducks out there. It's over a mile long and we can't outrun them," said Susan.

"Then where?"

"Into the mountain," said Susan. "Into the mine."

40

Heather couldn't identify Buzz's body. Runt had destroyed it, ripped it apart. The room was covered in gore and blood, and smelled like a slaughterhouse.

Heather entered the room with her gun drawn, but there was no one there besides what was left of Buzz. The paperback book he had been reading was on the floor, soaked through with blood, among the bones and viscera. She looked for signs of James, but there was nothing. He was gone.

She came back to the central area. They were soaking wet, water pooled on the laminate floor. Art had manhandled the remaining furniture in front of the entrance, but Runt's escape showed how flimsy their barricade had been. They weren't safe here.

"Any sign of James?" asked JH.

"Nothing," said Heather. "No sign of him. Not his clothes. Nothing."

"He has to be somewhere!" said JH, getting up from his seat in the corner. "People just don't up and vanish!"

"You can go in there and check yourself," she said. "But you won't find him. He's gone."

"That thing must have taken him somehow," JH said. "Why would James just leave? He just got back!"

Art was loading their remaining shotguns and pistols in the corner, stuffing ammo into packs. "Your boy betrayed us," he said.

"That's impossible," said JH.

"He went in there," said Art, putting down the shotgun, looking at JH, and pointing at the lockup. "And ten minutes later Buzz and Darla are dead, Runt is free, and he's missing. Add that up and tell me what makes sense."

"Why would he betray us?" asked JH. "It's insane. In-sane!"

"Maybe he wanted you dead," said Heather. "And he saw his chance." She was pulling out the spare body armor the station had stashed away. It was old, but it would have to do. She winced as she strapped it around her torso. Her broken ribs screamed with every breath. Stars filled her vision as she tightened the armor around her. She bit her lip and her vision cleared. There was a single flashbang in the supply, old arms left over from Cochbrin. She clipped it to her belt.

JH started to speak, but then stopped. He shook his head, murmuring to himself. He finally broke out of whatever thought cycle his mind had diverted to.

"And what are you two doing?" he asked.

"We're getting ready to leave," she said.

"You're going out there? With those things?" he asked. "We're safe here. They have their friend back."

"We're leaving, Mayor," said Heather. "We're taking shotguns and body armor, and we're heading for the pass. We are sitting ducks in here, so we're going to get the hell out of Conquest. You're welcome to stay, but you'll be alone."

"Now I don't—" said JH.

"Don't want to be eaten by those big monsters," said Heather. "I know. So you're coming with us." She threw him a protective vest, and then a helmet. "Put them on. Can you handle a shotgun?"

"Yes," he said, strapping the vest around him.

"Good," she said. "Because we'll need all three of us armed to stand a chance at putting even one of them down."

They left by the roof. The fires were close now. The visitor center was burning, the grass smoldering in the park. The totem pole had fallen, burnt away.

"We run for the pass," she said. "Call out if you see any of them. Focus fire if we do."

"See any of them?" asked JH. "I can't see a damned thing."

The smoke was oppressive now, pressing in on them. They climbed down onto the street. The ash had piled up like snowfall, and they left a trail in it with every footstep.

Heather led the way, with JH in between, and Art taking the rear guard. All of them were wheezing after a block. Heather stopped at a corner, huddled next to a building.

"You're bleeding," said Art.

Heather reached to her nose, blood dripping like a broken faucet. She wiped it away with a sleeve, but she knew it wouldn't stop. It burned, every breath cascading pain through her sinuses and into her chest.

They continued through the town, the fire chasing them. The town sloped up as they ran. The smoke thinned as they moved through town. The streets were quiet, no sign of Jack or his brothers.

They cut across the street, but then JH stumbled and fell. He picked himself up before realizing he had stumbled over a corpse.

"Jesus," he said. It was Kazuko. Heather and Art gathered around the body.

"She didn't make it out," said Heather. She had been killed by one of the creatures. Another casualty.

"She didn't die alone," said Art, kicking ash off the dismembered body of Runt.

"Well, we know they can die," she said. She spit on his corpse. They had allies out here, somewhere. She passed her sleeve over her nose again, wiping away some more blood. Her sleeve was crusty, layers of blood drying.

"We need to keep moving," she said. "Only a mile or so and we'll be at the trailhead."

The trailhead was the beginning of a system of paths that snaked through and around the town of Conquest. It went for miles, connecting to other trails, valleys, lakes, and peaks all around the area. It had always been a beautiful way to see the town. It burned.

Heather turned and looked into the town. Half of it was gone, the fire eating the oldest buildings at the edge of the city limits, and the newer development as it burned through. The sheriff's station was now surrounded by it. They still saw no sign of The Pack. With Runt gone, did they flee?

They pushed up the gentle incline, JH straining with every step, his face beet red. Heather realized she was crying, the smoke forcing tears from her eyes. It was too much. It was going to kill them.

"I can't, I can't," said JH, repeating himself, his breath coming in fits and starts.

"You will," said Heather. "We can't carry you."

They pushed on, a high, wheezing whistle coming from JH as they got closer and closer to the trailhead. The pass would lead them out of town to an adjoining road. They could make it.

The smoke grew thinner and thinner, and Heather could feel a hint of fresh air in each breath, pushed down from the mountains. They were almost out. She could see the pass, the small park information display. The Pack must have fled. Heather would have seen them by now.

"Are we there?" asked JH. He was doubled over, trying not to vomit.

"Stand up to breathe," said Art. "You won't get any air doubled over."

"Almost out of town," said Heather, and then her eyes caught something. A flash of movement in her periphery, in the smoke.

"Contact," she said, her voice cutting through the soot.

"What?" asked JH, still trying to catch his breath. Art backed off and readied his shotgun.

"They're here," she said. "Get ready."

There was nothing, and then they were there, shapes emerging from the gray. There were three of them. Big, distended, exaggerated muscles and bones, teeth and claws, gray fur and leathery skin. She had seen them, seen them up close, but it wasn't something you could get used to. They were massive, directly in their path to the trail. They were close, and then began to spread out.

"They're trying to flank us," said Heather. "We have to fall back."

"Fall back where?" asked JH.

"We can't go back," said Art. "The fire will kill us."

"Then through the village," said Heather. "Cut through it to the mine, then out to the pass. We can lose them inside."

The historical village was nearby. They could make it if they ran. It was close quarters, and unfamiliar to the creatures.

"Run," said Heather.

The creatures exchanged a glance, and followed.

41

Arthur entered the historical village for the last time on July 3rd. Fire was dancing on the rooftops of the nearby neighborhoods. The historical village would burn soon.

The village was all new construction, despite its appearances. Built to resemble the mining town of early Conquest, the facades of the buildings were all mid-19th century frontier construction. Some, like his smith and the stables, kept the appearance inside as well. Most of the other buildings, the shops and restaurants, all segued into modern niceties when you entered. It had the appearance of antiquity, of authenticity.

The village was four square blocks, walled off except for the entrance to the street, with adjoining parking lot. You could walk directly into the mine from the village, and that's where they headed. The sun was setting, the mountains and smoke blocking out what little light remained. Their flashlights, taped to the barrels of their shotguns, bobbed as they ran through the smoke and ash.

It was a half mile to the entrance of the mine, where the size of the creatures would be a hindrance. They just needed to get there. The creatures were fast, and would be on their tails quick enough, but they could do it.

"I can't go any farther," said JH, his breath now coming in ragged whoops. "I'm gonna pass out."

They moved down the central thoroughfare of the village, and the mine wasn't much farther. The creatures stalked them. If they stopped, they'd die.

"We can't stop," said Heather. Arthur looked at her, and saw the pain, saw how she was guarding her torso as they ran. She was hiding it better than JH, but she was struggling too. They both needed time.

"Please don't leave me," said JH, coughed out between choking breaths. "I don't want to be eaten by those things. I can't die like this. I'm the mayor, goddamnit."

JH looked like death. Heather's face was smeared with blood and ash. Conquest could burn, but Arthur wasn't going to let Heather burn along with it. He wouldn't lose her too.

"Take him," said Arthur. "Hide. I'll get their attention, and you run for it. I'll keep them busy, and then catch up later."

"No," she said. "We stick together."

"Sweetheart," he said. "I know it ain't the best plan, but it's all we got. Take JH and get out of here while you've got a chance."

"You versus those things?" she said. "That's not a fair fight."

"I know," said Arthur. "They don't stand a chance."

"You're not funny," said Heather.

"I'll be right behind you," he said. "I know this place like the back of my hand. I'll lead them on a wild goose chase, and then I'll catch up to you."

"I—" she said.

"No arguments. Not this time," he said. "Go."

They looked each other in the eyes, and something she saw kept her silent. She held his gaze, and then left.

Heather grabbed JH's arm and ducked down one of the small alleys that weaved between the buildings. Arthur watched her go, tears welling in his eyes. He wiped them away.

Arthur walked to the middle of the street. He saw two of them. The big one, the one he had hit with his truck, and one other. Those injuries had healed, but it was still wounded, a massive entry wound on its flank that was slowly closing. They were at the far end of the street. Arthur waited until he was sure they saw him, and then he ran. He knew where to go.

His job in the Burns' Mine Historical Village felt like manna from heaven. Arthur had worked metal his whole life, but previously had worked for himself, making and selling pieces independently, doing freelance fabrication. The job at the village was safe though, and it came just as they adopted Heather. It allowed them to buy a house in town, to make sure he had a steady paycheck and insurance for all of them. Money poured into Conquest, and some of it went to him.

Sure, he only got to work with silver, but he made some spectacular pieces, sold in the village, and he got a cut. No accounting, no taxes. Just him and the metal. He got to talk to the tourists as well. He used to think that he wanted isolation when he worked, but he learned to like the company.

It was hard after Emilia died. The work carried him through. No matter how many waves of grief swept through him, his hammer, the oven, the metal were always there.

He looked back behind him, and the big one gave chase. The other hung back, waiting, looking. He couldn't worry about it now. Too late. He'd have to trust that Heather and JH could find their way out. Fire burned behind them.

Arthur had a minute, maybe two, to prepare. He ran into his shop and turned on the furnace, as hot it would go. He opened up the locker in the corner. Safety gear, to protect against the heat. He only wore gloves and the helmet on most days, even though regulations said otherwise. He put on everything today. It was going to get very hot. He pulled the silver sword down off the wall. It would have to serve as a weapon today.

When the huge creature smashed through the entrance a minute later, the room was on fire. A second later, a bucket of molten silver hit it in the face, and it screamed in pain. Arthur didn't give it time to recover as it thrashed in the hole it had made in the wall. Arthur was armed with his heaviest hammer, and he smashed the creature in the knee. It shouted in pain again, the loud scream filling the room.

Arthur brought the hammer down on its knee again, the second blow enough to shatter the bone, making it explode out of the skin. The creature fell, one leg crippled. It swiped out with one huge claw and knocked Arthur backwards, still blind. The molten silver, the melted sword, burnt its eyes and face, its quick healing only doing so much. It swiped again, but missed, and Arthur brought the hammer down with all his might on the back of the creature's neck.

It howled and swung again, claws raking through the heat protection but not through the protective vest underneath. It was vulnerable, and Arthur swung the hammer fast and hard. He hit the beast straight in the temple, and it finally seemed to have an effect, the blow getting through the thick skull.

It staggered, and its injured leg gave out as it tried to right himself. The beast thrashed on the ground, blind and stunned, and Arthur swung the hammer like he was chopping wood, first breaking its flailing arm, and then bringing the tapered point of the hammer down on its temple, over and over again. Its skull cracked on the third hit, and shattered on the fourth. It stopped flailing on the sixth. Blood flowed over the cooling silver, molded to its inhuman face.

Arthur gasped for air inside the protective suit, condensation forming on the clouded window of the helmet. Embers fell around him from the burning ceiling. He picked his hammer off the floor, and then was yanked off his feet, a grip on his ankle pulling his feet out from under him. He slammed into the ground hard and was dragged out of the shop. His breath was driven out from him again as he was slammed into the packed dirt of the historical village's central road.

The other creature had caught up. He snarled at Arthur as he approached. This one wasn't at the station.

No. He *was* there. It was Jack. Just as ugly as the others.

Arthur pushed himself to his feet, and he swung his

hammer with two hands, thudding off of Jack's hide. Arthur swung again, but Jack caught it in a huge clawed hand and tossed it behind him, out of sight in the smoke.

Jack moved fast, faster than Arthur thought possible, and he was in the air again, Jack picking him up and throwing him into a nearby wooden building. He felt ribs break, and he couldn't breathe as the pain shot through him and he crumpled to the floor.

He struggled to his feet, his strength and size falling out of him. Jack was there, next to him, and Arthur pushed at his leg—with no result. Jack pulled off the protective helmet, and Arthur could smell the smoke again.

Jack grabbed him by the neck, then pulled him off the ground.

"ONLY, HUMAN," said Jack, a deep growl rumbling through him.

"You talk a lot," said Arthur, pulling out the shotgun he had snaked down his pants leg, blasting Jack's side at point-blank range, opening a hole in him. Jack let go, screaming. Arthur fell and landed on his feet, pain jolting through him from his broken ribs.

He pumped the shotgun and fired once more, advancing. The buildings burned around them, and fire filled Arthur's vision. The recoil jolted through his broken ribs, but there was nothing else now. He racked another shot.

Jack put up his arms defensively, covering his face and neck, and Arthur shot him in the same place on his torso, the wound opening further. Jack yowled in pain, backing away.

Enough shots, and Arthur could find his way to Jack's heart.

He fired again. At this range, the shot was tearing Jack apart. Blood misted behind him, turning into steam from the heat. He racked another round.

For Emilia. For Conquest. For Heather.

Arthur fired again, and again, and again, racking shells after each shot, the wound in Jack's torso getting worse and worse. He saw bones chip, shatter, and fly through the air, blood pouring out of the wound. He fired, and fired, and fired again. Jack struggled to stand. He would defend this town, or at least what was left of it. He would defend his daughter.

He pumped the shotgun the final time, and fired. Click. Nothing.

He tried again. Out of shells.

Arthur looked down at the shotgun, and then threw it aside. He was never a fighter, even with all his size, but he squared up anyway. His fists were all he had.

Jack paused, lowering his defenses. Wet gore leaked from the gaping wound in his torso, but Jack ignored it. His huge eyes took in Arthur, and then with an imperceptible burst of quickness, he was on Arthur, both on the ground.

Arthur struggled with everything he had, his hand snaking into the open wound on Jack's torso and squeezing on whatever he could find. Jack yowled again, but then his claws wrapped around Arthur's skull, and he began to squeeze.

Colors danced in Arthur's eyes.

He saw Heather in them.

He saw Emilia.

He would find his way to Jack's heart

He would find his way

Arthur's grip on Jack's insides started to loosen. A second later his skull cracked and shattered.

The historical village burned as Jack fed on him, the wound in his side closing while he ate.

42

Heather and JH watched as the two creatures passed them. The human pair hurried to the exit of the village, and the entrance of the mine.

JH was in front of her. She ran behind, her shotgun ready. They hurried through the smoke, the village burning behind them. The ticket booth and gate were visible. They'd be safe inside.

A shape in the smoke sprung at them, shoulder-checking Heather off of her feet, hundreds of pounds hitting her hard. She landed on her back, the wind driven out of her. Her helmet bounced off the ground and she saw stars, the pain from her ribs ripping through her. She couldn't breathe.

"Sheriff?" asked JH, turning around as the creature whipped by him, snatching the shotgun from his grasp. JH fell backwards, stunned, and began scooting back, sliding himself on the ground and away from the creature. It looked at him, then broke the shotgun in half, metal, plastic, and ammo spilling all over the ground.

"WEAK," it said.

The wave of pain passed and Heather breathed again, a big gasp of smoke-filled air. The shotgun was still in her hands. She pushed off the ground, forced away the pain, and climbed to her feet, pumping a shot into its back. It growled, wheeling on her, forgetting about JH. JH continued to scoot backwards, climbing to his feet before running through the entrance gate and into the smoke.

"Which one are you?" she asked.

It didn't answer, only stared at her with its small, hooded eyes. She racked a shell into the chamber and held the shotgun out, pointing it at the beast. It circled, and she mirrored it, like a boxer.

She studied it as they circled. It was over eight feet tall, and its chest, arms, and shoulders were huge, mass upon mass of muscle and bone. Hard to damage, no soft tissue. Its skull was large as well, the eyes small, difficult to hit but vulnerable. Its legs were lean and sinewy, strong, but with less protection. The lower torso and his stomach made an easy target. But no vitals there. Heart, lungs, brain.

It feinted a lunge, but Heather didn't bite. It was trying to advance on her, and sooner or later she'd have to fire. It was trying to bait her. Regardless of how much bone protected their weak points, a point-blank shotgun blast would kill or cripple. At ten or twenty feet, it would only hurt. These creatures were used to a lot of hurt.

It feinted one more time, and then charged, a hand the

size of a catcher's mitt reaching for her throat. One lucky rake and her throat would be cut. She hip fired the shotgun, then dove out of the way, rolling into a crouch and pumping the riot gun. The creature yelled in pain, holding up a hand that was half gone, only a forefinger and thumb remaining. Broken ribs grated inside her. She gritted her teeth and forced herself to stand.

"BITCH," it growled at her.

"You're gonna have to do better than that," she said. She could feel the blood trickling from her nose, running over her lips and dripping off of her chin. She licked her lips and spit.

It rushed her again and she fired, but missed. She dove the opposite direction at the last second, avoiding his claws. She rolled, her ribs screaming. She was too slow.

It didn't pause, instead cutting back towards her. It was quick, and she fired the shotgun just as the creature grabbed it with its uninjured hand, the blast flying into the air, missing everything but the smoke. The shotgun was pulled from her grasp and he threw it away.

Heather stumbled, off balance, and he grabbed her by the throat with his good hand, lifting her off the ground. She floundered in the air. It was going to rip her throat out. It lowered its jaws, and she stabbed upward through his snout, her knife going all the way through its mouth and nose.

It dropped her, a horrible moaning coming from it. Blood was pouring out of its maw, black gore filling its mouth. It got a hold of the knife and yanked it out, dropping it on the ground.

She pulled out her pistol, the only weapon she had left. She didn't hesitate, firing several rounds into its face, hoping to blind it. The bullets bounced off its skull, leaving bloody pock marks all over its face. She emptied her clip and loaded another, her last.

She fired again, this time aiming for its eyes. It charged, bringing its arms up, the bullets lodging themselves in its forearms. Her gun clicked empty, then the beast hit her, knocking her off her feet again. It was on top of her, its one good hand wrapped around her throat, nearly a metric ton on top of her, crushing her broken ribs.

She couldn't breathe.

She struggled, punching it with everything she had, but its strength was unassailable. Her vision blurred, her strikes weaker and weaker. She would die here.

A cannon went off and it screamed, its grip loosening. Her first gasping breath of smoke felt like heaven. It fell off of her. A second cannon shot went off, and it screamed once more.

Its abdomen was open, a massive chasm exposed by the successive explosions. Its ribs were broken, shattered, gone, and she could see its lungs, obscene organs ballooning as it struggled to breathe. She crawled, getting her breath back. Her ribs ached, a deep pounding pain that would not recede.

She found her knife where it dropped, covered in black blood, viscous like oil, stinking. She grabbed it, then climbed, straddling the enormous beast, ignoring the pain in her ribs, her breath coming in ragged whoops.

It was choking on its own blood, in shock from the massive damage it had received. Its eyes focused on her, and she stared back as she stabbed him in its bare heart. It shook, and died.

Heather climbed off to see Susan Bieter and Alice Ames come out of the fog, Alice holding a massive rifle. Alice looked like she had aged a decade in a day, her eyes hollow and distant. Susan appeared haggard and worn. They were both covered in ash and blood.

Heather coughed and spit, trying to catch her breath. She could feel the bruises raise on her throat, the blood pouring out of her nose.

Sheriff," said Susan. "You made it. Anyone else left?"

Heather thought to Arthur, to James. "JH is in the mine. No one else."

Susan only nodded, her face inscrutable.

Alice threw the elephant gun down next to the remains of Gunner, now back in human form. "Out of ammo."

Heather pulled her knife out of Gunner and wiped the blood off on a pants leg, sheathing it on her belt. She found her shotgun. Conquest burned behind her.

July 4th

43

Heather and Alice waited for what was left of The Pack. They hid in the darkness, the ambush ready.

JH had been in the control room, the door locked and deadbolted. He had opened it when he saw that Susan was among them. He embraced her. Heather looked back, the burning town spread out in front of her. The historical village was burning. Arthur hadn't caught up.

She could feel the pain welling up inside of her, a great hollow ache rolling through her and exploding through her heart. She swallowed it, pushed it down and away because if she let it emerge it would swallow her whole. Then she'd walk back into the fire, and let the smoke envelop her.

They had to finish off The Pack. One or two or three left, it didn't matter. The Pack couldn't leave Conquest, not after what they had done. Heather wouldn't allow it.

The generators hummed, deep inside the mine, the control center filled with monitors, lights, and alarms. It was the base of operations for the mine itself, and for most of the historical village. It was only a few rooms, but it was dug into the rock itself, and was impregnable.

JH and Susan were left in the control center. Alice and Heather would stay outside.

They would come through the mine, hungry, hunting. Heather and Alice, armed, would wait, serving as eyes and ears for JH and Susan. The Pack would come for them both, bloodthirsty, and on cue, JH and Susan would detonate the explosives they had planted at a chokepoint, obliterating the creatures and ending the nightmare. Anything still alive they would finish with the few remaining shotgun shells.

JH didn't argue with the plan. Heather was sure he was fine staying in the hardened control room, while she was out risking her ass. She had expected a complaint, about something, anything, but he had been quiet.

The explosives were left over from the Revitalization Project, when they had blasted additional space into the entrance of the mine and blown open the additional exit down at the pass. They were old, but it should still work. Heather worried that they'd bring the mine down on top of them. None of them were engineers, but JH assured them it was safe. It didn't take long to plant them.

Now they waited, in the darkness.

She sat on one side of the choke point, Alice on the other. They had turned the lights off. Both were armed with flashlights, but they sat in the dark, the sounds of their breath barely audible.

Her whole body ached, but the air was mostly clear inside the mine, a welcome change. She could feel an inch of ash and blood on her face, the skin crusty beneath her nose. Every breath sent a wave of agony through her.

She had toured the mine in high school. They all had, an easy field trip. Almost all of them had snuck into the mine, late at night, to drink, or to have sex. Or both.

She looked down into the darkness of the mine, deeper down the main corridor. She had stumbled down there with her best friend Erica. Erica had *acquired* some cheap vodka from her parent's liquor cabinet, flavored like whipped cream.

They had found a small chamber off the main corridor and sat down in the darkness, their flashlights bouncing off the stone walls. The bottle was half gone in short order, and they were both drunk, talking about school, and college, and boys.

Heather knew then that she didn't like boys, but she played along with Erica anyway. Talking about this boy or that. Erica had a crush on this one, or that one. She wondered how good of a kisser that one was.

They were close, their shoulders touching, and talk of kissing led to a quiet, simple kiss between them. Heather's heart fluttered. It was the first time she had kissed a girl, and a spark of joy lit in her.

They kissed harder, which led to more, and more. They wandered out of the mine in the early morning, before the sun rose, the bottle empty, thrown out in a back-alley dumpster.

They woke up in Erica's house, and she felt an optimism, a hope that she didn't know was absent. But she didn't know how to bring it up, and Erica never mentioned it again. They were still friends, but they never drank together again. Erica soon had a boyfriend, and they saw each other less.

She followed Erica on social media. She moved to Florida with her husband. She had two kids. They were cute. She'd share a picture of Heather and her in high school sometimes, and Heather would always like it. But that was it.

Alice had volunteered to stay out with Heather because she knew the mine well, having done tours for years now. She was familiar with the twists and turns, and could lead them through it in the dark, if need be.

"Why did this have to happen here?" asked Alice. Her voice made Heather jump.

"Any of it?" asked Heather.

"All of it," she said. "The fire, the monsters."

"I don't know," said Heather. "Bad luck."

"It feels like a judgment," said Alice. "Like we're being punished."

"We're still alive," said Heather. "It'll be over soon."

"Will it?" asked Alice. Her question hung in the air, and Heather didn't know how to answer. They heard a noise echoing down the cave. Heather's walkie talkie cracked. "One of them. Coming down." JH's voice.

They could hear the creature. Any noise in the cave echoed back and forth, the sound bouncing off the walls. His breathing, his footfalls became louder and louder as he got closer to them. All they needed to do was sit tight. If he wanted to get to them, he needed to come this way. A few hundred more feet and he'd be caught between the explosives. They'd chew him up.

Heather breathed with purpose, trying to slow her heart rate and remain quiet.

"I CAN, SMELL, YOU, HUNTER," said the creature, his voice rumbling down the cave. "I WILL STILL, WIN THIS."

It was Jack, alone. Even in this form, she could hear the desperation in his voice. He had lost all his brothers. He needed to think that this was still victory.

He continued down into the mine. He was getting close now. She could hear him in the darkness, letting his nose lead his way.

She waited, waited, his footsteps getting closer and closer. Now. She clicked her walkie talkie. "Hit it."

She waited, tensing for the coming explosion, the noise, the heat, the fire, the shockwave that would rip through the mine. She closed her eyes, plugging her ears. Waiting for the blast that would end this nightmare.

It didn't come. She spoke again into her walkie talkie. "NOW." Jack heard her now for sure.

No explosion. Jack was moving past the explosion zone, closer to their position. Still nothing, and he continued, now in the clear, and now close enough to sniff them out and attack. Heather readied her shotgun, her hand touching the knife at her belt. Still there.

She aimed the shotgun at where she thought he would be, hoping Alice would do the same. They could hurt him, knock him off guard. They could maybe still kill him. Her finger rested on the trigger, ready to pull. Then the explosion hit.

It hit her like a punch in the gut and knocked her over. The sound itself had size, the explosives more powerful than they had thought. The mine shook, the sound of long-held supports being blown away and falling rocks filling the area. Her ears rang. She could feel stone and pebbles bombard her as they flew away, down the mine. The only way back to the entrance was now blocked.

They were trapped, the only exit much farther down, at the pass. Trapped with Jack.

She scrambled for her walkie talkie. "The explosion missed him. Turn on the lights. The lights!"

There was no answer. She clicked in again. "Please, hurry! Come in!"

There was another long pause, but finally the walkie talkie cracked. JH's voice. "I told you you would pay."

The walkie talkie went dead in the dark, and another sound filled the darkness as the echo of the explosion dulled and the dust settled. It was deep, from past their position, and repeated over and over. Susan would have been able to place it, but Heather couldn't, not at first.

A dull barking filled the mine, and Heather realized it was Jack. He was laughing.

44

Susan watched as JH betrayed them, another thing falling apart.

"What are you doing?" asked Susan, watching JH as he ignored Heather's transmission.

"I got it in hand," he said.

"Didn't you just hear Sheriff Hill?"

"I have it in control," he said, his eyes glued to the closed circuit monitors that showed scenes throughout the mines and historical village.

"You need to do it now!" she said, trying to push past him to the detonator. He elbowed her, and she fell backwards, landing on the floor of the control room.

Heather called for the explosion again, and JH ignored her, watching the feeds. The walkie talkie sat on the control panel, Heather's requests rejected. Susan sat on the hard floor, staring in disbelief.

JH waited a few moments longer, and then triggered the explosions. Everything rumbled and shook, and the feeds in front of them went out, one by one. The place was falling apart. She put her hands over her head, protecting herself, expecting the lights to go out, and the room to collapse, killing them both.

It didn't. The rumbling stopped, and the mine stopped shaking. The lights stayed on.

"I told you you would pay," he said into the walkie talkie, putting it down.

She studied JH. He was looking from monitor to monitor, his eyes bouncing wildly from feed to feed, most gone, looking for something. His hands clasped and unclasped by his sides.

"You lied to us," said Susan. "You planned this."

The feeds were static, the cameras destroyed by the explosion. His eyes were manic, his breathing heavy, his mouth open.

"Are you listening?" she asked again, picking herself off the floor. "Do you realize what you've done? They're trapped down there with that thing. You've killed them."

JH turned, staring back. His eyes were wide, his cheeks pink.

"This is all her fault, Susan," said JH. "She was responsible for all of this. This was the only way. Now we can move on."

"Her fault?" asked Susan. "She didn't cause the fires. She was out there fighting those things!"

"They tried to bargain, Susan," he said. "You weren't

there. She refused. James tried to set things right, tried to compromise with them, to get them to leave. He's gone Susan. Dead, I'm sure. And it's her fault. It's her fault James is dead. My legacy, gone."

He stared at her, through her. He said it all with such purpose, with such belief.

"Your legacy?" she asked, standing up. "That's what you care about? With all this? Dozens dead, our town gone? Your legacy?"

"All I have is my name," he said.

"You never cared about him," she said. "And now you're killing people, invoking him."

"What did you say?" he asked, staring daggers through his black eye.

"You broke him," she said. "James. And he died. Died for your worthless name."

He punched her, square in the nose. It broke with a snap, and blood began pouring from it. She fell again, hard on her back, groaning with pain.

"Worthless?" he asked. "My name is what pulled this town out of the gutter. My name is what paid for your house. My name gave James everything he had. The best part of him was *my* name, and you're lucky you ever got it."

He turned, leaving her on the ground, bloody, his attention back at the monitors. Her nose hurt like hell, and she could taste blood. She wiped it away with the back of her hand and looked at JH, who had already forgotten about her.

Alice and Heather were down in that hole, and he was going to let them die, trapped in the dark with that creature. She wouldn't allow it. Not after all this.

She stood up, her body aching. She grabbed the fire extinguisher off the wall. It was heavy, probably 30 pounds. She walked up behind him and swung the extinguisher with a grunt, the cold metal thunking off his skull.

He went down with a thud, groaning. She hit him again as he struggled on the ground, the rounded metal edge of the extinguisher dully ringing with every blow, over and over again. He stopped moving, and she stopped, his head a bloody mess.

She dropped the extinguisher. He was dead. She stepped over his body and turned on the lights, and auxiliary lights, hoping something would work. She grabbed the walkie talkie.

"Heather? Come in," she said. There was nothing, no answer. Most of the monitor feeds were down, filled with static or black screens. She grabbed a flashlight.

Rocks filled the area, but it wasn't completely impassable. She could see the dim glow of the auxiliary lights through gaps in the rocks. The old mine was stronger than she thought.

She started digging.

45

Heather stood up, turning on the headlamp on her helmet and holding her shotgun out. Dust was still floating in the air. She looked at the collapsed tunnel. No time to dig through. Alice was next to her, her helmet on. The laughing was close, just a bit farther down the mine. Jack was past them. They'd have to get through him to get out.

They moved together, their lights trained ahead. Jack stopped laughing, stopped making any sound altogether. The tunnel that led out to the pass was deep, almost to the bottom of the mine, another several thousand feet. They had five shotgun shells between them.

They came to a fork. "Right," said Alice. "Left leads to the pool."

The pair went right, still with no sign of Jack.

"Maybe he just ran," said Alice.

"I don't think so," said Heather. "His group's been destroyed. He has nothing else."

There was a skittering noise from down the cave, approaching. They tensed, and then a bat flew past them. "Must have come in from the smoke," said Alice. "The biggest chamber is up soon. It used to be the main staging area for the second phase of the mine. Lots of cover. Be ready."

The cart tracks started here, and they both watched their step. The narrow corridor curved right and down. They couldn't see around the bend.

The mine opened up in front of them, and Alice wasn't lying. The chamber wasn't enormous, but it was much bigger than anything they'd been through before. There were displays lining one wall, along with the various cart tracks laid down along the floor leading through several different tunnels. The chamber wasn't symmetrical, and boulders were strewn throughout the room. They stood five to ten feet high.

A shotgun blast went off, the shot flying up into the ceiling of the room. Heather turned, and Alice had been picked up and pushed backwards. Jack had emerged.

Heather ran after them, but couldn't take the shot, fearing she would hit Alice. Jack drove Alice into the rock wall, and she slumped, the back of her head smashing against the hard stone. Jack dropped her, then darted back around a boulder. Heather turned the corner and he was gone, her light not finding him. She kneeled down next to Alice, checking her pulse. Slow but steady. The back of her head was busted open, but it wasn't deep.

She heard a small noise, and then he was on her. So fast,

faster than any of the others. She pulled the trigger, and the shot grazed him, but her shotgun was gone in an instant, ripped from her grasp and smashed into bits in one quick motion against a nearby boulder. His other hand grabbed her neck, lifting her into the air. She slid her knife from her belt and stabbed him in the hand. He yowled and threw her. Heather flew across the space, landing and then sliding across the cart tracks, the cold metal slicing open her back. She could feel the blood start to flow. Her helmet flew off her head, the headlamp cracking and going out. The pain was excruciating, her broken ribs holding her hostage. Blood was pouring down her back.

"THIS, IS ALL, OURS," he said, the deep rumble surrounding her. "I, WILL SHOW, YOU."

Her knife was still embedded in Jack's hand, and she was lost in the darkness without her headlamp. Sounds bounced around her. Jack was circling her. She struggled to her feet.

He hit her again. She was slammed into the ground, breath driven out of her, no air to scream with. She got her arm up as Jack lunged, and his obscene jaws clamped down on her left forearm, his weight pressing down on her.

His teeth sank deep into her skin, forcing even more blood out of her. She could feel the pressure on her bones. He would bite her arm off. He wanted to punish her. She pushed the pain away.

Her other hand slid through the dirt, onto Jack's arm, that pinned her to the ground. Her knife. She grabbed the handle, and yanked it out. He didn't let go. Heather slid the knife into his mouth, levering his jaw open, the edge cutting into lips and gums, black blood flowing out of his mouth and onto her.

He screamed and let go of his bite, finally. She slid the blade out of his mouth and swiped at his eyes. Heather needed him off. She needed to breathe. She felt contact and he screamed again, and then he was off of her. She scrambled to her feet, bloody breaths filling her lungs.

Her left arm hung limp next to her. Her world was pain and darkness.

She could hear Jack. He was still there. She held out her knife, her only weapon, warding off the darkness.

Alone now. Her father dead, killed by this thing, this shape, that pretended to be man.

He would pounce soon, and rip her apart. No strength left, no breath left. Her body was collapsing, the blood pouring out of her.

Arthur, the town, dead.

Blood dripped off her hanging left arm. Jack circled in the darkness. He was buying time, his eye healing. It was a matter of time.

A heavy noise rang through the area, and a red light filled the cavern as the auxiliary emergency lights kicked on. She could see now, see the space. She held the knife out in front of her, the handle slippery with her blood.

Jack hit her then, from behind, her neck snapping back with the force. Her vision swam, but she maintained consciousness as Jack drove her into the ground, her face scraping against the dirt floor. Her mouth was full of dirt. She spit it out and rolled over, swinging the knife as hard as she could into Jack's eye once she was face to face with him. He screamed, but held her down with a single clawed hand, ripping the knife out of his ruined eye and throwing it across the cavern.

Jack's left eye was bleeding, and he cradled the socket, protecting it. "ENOUGH, OF THIS," he said. "I AM MORE, THAN YOU." He moved, grabbing her throat with both hands. Heather pushed off with all her strength, but it was nothing. He opened his jaws wide, wider than she thought possible, and brought her to his mouth. He was going to crush her in his jaws.

But would you die for it?

A spark of fear and panic rushed through her as she struggled. He was just too strong. Her hand clapped against her belt, and she remembered. She grabbed the flashbang and popped the pin, shoving her arm as deep down his throat as she could, Jack choking as she left it there. He held on to her, and she covered her ears with her hands, closing her eyes.

The flashbang went off, blowing out Jack's throat. He finally dropped her, dark gargling noises coming from his destroyed neck. She coughed, catching her breath, and he clutched his throat, trying to breathe. Jack stumbled, and then fell. Black blood was gushing through his fingers.

She ran over to one of the displays, smashing the glass with a rock. She pulled the replica pick-axe from the display. Jack was struggling to breathe, big wet breaths whistling through his throat. He would heal.

His size meant nothing now, his extended, swollen muscles and bones futile. His eyes were fixed on her, and she saw the look of disbelief. Loss was unfamiliar.

"PLE—" he choked out, and she brought the point of the pick-axe down through his eye. He grunted, but still moved, so she brought it down again, blood in her hands. It broke his skull, and he went still.

She dropped the pick-axe, and went back to Alice. The other woman was still unconscious, but alive. Heather sat next to her. Heather's body was broken. So tired. *Keep your eyes open, Heather. Don't give in now.*

She kept them open, and Alice came around.

"What happened?" she asked. "My head is fucking killing me."

"We won," said Heather. "It's over."

"Thank Christ," said Alice.

A flashlight beam cut through the red light, and Susan was there, her hands battered, her nose bloody.

"Oh my God, you made it," she said. "Where's Jack?"

Heather motioned with her head towards his now-human body. "Dead."

"Where's JH?"

"Dead," said Susan. "He had planned it from the start. He was going to leave you down here to die. I killed him—I didn't—"

"Susan," said Heather, interrupting her. "You did what you had to. I need help."

Susan's beam passed over Heather, and she saw the damage done. "Christ. Let's get you to the control room. There's a medical kit there."

Susan and Alice let Heather lean on them as they made their back up the mine.

"We won," said Heather, with a slim, blood-smeared smile. "We got all the monsters."

"About that," she said. "What are we going to tell everyone? They're going to ask us questions."

Heather's smile remained.

"We'll tell them the truth."

46

Alice knocked on the door in the small suburb of Seattle. She heard footsteps from inside the house, and Kate Yamamoto opened the door.

"Hi, I'm Alice Ames," she said, extending a hand. Kate took it and returned a gentle handshake. Alice had called yesterday to set up the meeting.

Kate was in her mid-50s, with gray and silver streaks in her black hair. Her voice was warm, and her face earnest.

"Come in, Alice," she said. She led her into the living room. "Please, have a seat. Can I get you anything to drink?"

"Maybe some water," said Alice. She had a lot to say.

"Sure," she said. "I'll go get Hiroshi. He's working in the garden. Just give me one second."

"No problem," she said. Kate left the room, and Alice

could hear her walk back into the house and call for her husband.

She looked around their living room. It looked much like her parents' living room. A couch with a matching loveseat, a flatscreen tv mounted on the wall, and a fireplace with pictures and keepsakes on the mantel. Pictures of Kyle were everywhere. Alice got up and looked at them. The pictures tracked his childhood, with Kyle as child, into adulthood. She also found pictures of Kazuko, when she was younger, with young Hiroshi, and a picture of all of them from the fabled lone trip to Japan.

She felt a presence close by, and she looked to see Hiroshi standing next to her, admiring the pictures as well.

"It is the only picture we have of all of us," he said.

"Kazuko told me," she said.

"You speak Japanese?" asked Hiroshi, a little surprised.

"No," she said. "I used the Translate app on my phone. We talked through that."

"Ah, technology," he said. He turned and faced her, extending his hand. "I am Hiroshi. I was—am, Kyle's father."

She grabbed his hand, and he shook it, a firm handshake, businesslike. His hair was white, and his face was lined with wrinkles.

"Would you like to sit? Kate should be in a moment with some water," he said. He sat down on the couch. Alice took the loveseat. Kate appeared with a glass of water, and she sat down next to her husband after handing it to Alice. There was an awkward moment of silence.

"Thank you for seeing me," Alice said. "I know it's a little weird to hear from me, a year after everything."

"You went through a lot," said Kate. "We were surprised,

yesterday, when you called, but if you do have something new to tell us about that weekend, we want to hear it. Even if it may be hard. You said the official story isn't completely true?"

Alice looked over at the couple, on the north side of middle age. Hiroshi had taken Kate's hand. They looked at her with sadness in their eyes.

"You talked to the FBI?" she asked.

"Yes," said Hiroshi. "They told us about their deaths, and helped arrange us picking up the bodies. They were—unhelpful in providing information beyond the bare minimum."

"You deserve to know the truth," she said. "It's going to sound crazy. But I hope the fact that I came all the way out here to tell you in person will help convince you."

She told them everything, starting from the beginning and ending getting rescued and interviewed by the FBI. About The Pack, the fire, about getting knocked out in the mine. They let her speak. Alice wanted to look at them, see their faces, but she was afraid if she did she wouldn't be able to finish.

She stopped, taking a long drink of water. She looked at the Yamamotos, who were still silent. They looked down. They gripped the other's hand tight.

"I know it's hard to believe," she said. "But I wanted you to know. You lost a son and mother, and it wasn't fair. Kyle was a good man. When he died, Kazuko was lost, and I tried to help her, and I tried to protect her from those things, but they got her anyway, and she died in the smoke—"

Alice broke down and started sobbing. Kate got up, grabbing a box of tissues, sitting next to Alice. She put an arm around her, holding her as she sobbed. "I'm sorry," said Alice, through her tears. Kate handed her a tissue, and Alice wiped her eyes and blew her nose.

Hiroshi got up, kneeling in front of Alice, to be at eye level with her. "My mother was a strong woman, and it sounds like she recognized the same thing in you. In the last year, Kate and I have learned that life is brutal. That sometimes you love something, invest your whole heart and life into it, and you lose it without a rhyme or reason. But you cannot let a brutal life turn you into a brute. Do not blame yourself for the actions of men."

Alice hugged him, almost knocking him over. He held her while she cried. She finally let go and collected herself, then blew her nose again.

"Thank you for listening," she said, again.

"We were about to have lunch," said Kate. "Would you like to join us?"

They ate lunch. The Yamamotos asked about her life, and they talked about Seattle. Kate gave Alice her email address, and told her to write at least once a month. "Stay in touch, and call when things get hard," she said.

Alice hugged them again before she left. She had another couple days in Seattle. It was a nice city, but it wasn't home.

•

The sound of hammering woke Heather. Work started at 7 AM every day, workers nailing frames, laying down roofs, putting up siding. Conquest's second rebirth was remarkable.

Heather's new home had been finished a month or two ago, the wood still fresh. It was solid, big enough to grow into. She took her morning coffee on the porch, watching the town wake up, the sun filtering in through the three peaks. She stretched her arms, her left still aching, only just starting to regain the strength it once had.

There was no smoke, no fire, not this summer. They endured it, and they would rebuild. Rebuild bigger, and better, and stronger than before.

"Could they let me sleep in for once?" asked Sam as her arms embraced Heather from behind. Her skin was warm for the cool morning, and Heather relished in it before she sat down across from her, Heather's hair a mess.

It was their house. Heather had committed to Conquest, and Sam had committed to her. She was still gone for weeks at a time for work, but Heather's optimism had convinced her, convinced her to settle down here.

"Is it any worse than your alarm?" asked Heather. "Or your second, or your third, or your fourth alarm?"

"Hey, I choose when they go off," said Sam. She rubbed the sleep from her eyes. "And they don't keep ringing all day long."

"How many rides today?" asked Heather.

"Just one," said Sam. "A private tour with a rich couple. Easy peasy."

"Do you tell them about last summer?" asked Heather.

"Only if they ask," said Sam. "But they all ask. Don't worry, I don't tell them too much about my world-famous girlfriend, sheriff and defender of Conquest. And future mayor."

"I'm not the mayor yet," said Heather.

"You better win, after all you've done," said Sam.

The interim mayor was a councilman, and had done a good job in the wake of the fires, but made no secret about wanting out as soon as an election could be held. Heather would be running, along with a few others, all local businessmen.

"I like my chances," said Heather, looking out over the town.

"You're giving them an awful lot of credit," said Sam.

Heather's relationship with Sam wasn't a secret anymore, not with them buying a house together. She wasn't quite shouting "I'm a lesbian!" from the rooftops, but in Conquest it was close enough. It was a gamble. Despite all she'd done, she knew the town. She knew the people here. Would they vote for a lesbian? She didn't know.

They'd vote for *her*, though.

"It's another step," said Heather. She finished her coffee and started to get ready for work.

Sam's arms wrapped around her again, and she felt her nuzzling into her neck. It was warm and soft and comforting.

"I'll be late," said Heather.

"One time won't hurt," said Sam, and Heather let Sam pull her back into bed.

•

Heather drove through town, patrolling. There was a steady supply of tourists, who were happy to give the rebuilding town their money. Every motel in town had a running discount until construction was finished. The surrounding forest was nothing but burnt remnants, but small green saplings poked through the dirt.

Her windows were down, one hand on the wheel, one arm crooked comfortably out the window, the warm summer breeze whipping over her exposed skin.

She stopped at Susan's house, recently finished. The house smelled like lumber. Heather could feel the hard wood of the new door under her knuckles as she knocked. Susan opened the door, holding her sleeping baby boy. Susan smiled when she saw Heather. She held her finger to her lips, and beckoned her in.

Susan walked into a side room, and Heather walked into the kitchen, sitting down at the table. A laptop was set up with paperwork strewn around it. Susan joined her after a moment, without the baby.

"How's he doing?" asked Heather, trying to keep her voice down.

"Oh, he's great," said Susan, smiling. Her nose had healed a little crooked, but she looked the same otherwise. "He never sleeps and he cries all the time, but—well, he's amazing."

"I don't know how you get any work done," said Heather.

"I just don't sleep," she said. She had a cup of coffee in front of her.

"You getting enough business?" asked Heather.

"The village is still only partially open, so that's hurting things a little, but the mine has never done better, actually. Our little adventure has only enhanced its history," said Susan.

"What do the tour guides tell the tourists about our adventure?" asked Heather.

"The official story," said Susan. "To the letter. The nefarious biker, known only as Jack, brutally murdered JH, but was then killed himself by our own Sheriff Hill."

Heather couldn't help but smile a little at Susan's theatrical version, even though it was the version of events that leaked out to everyone.

They hadn't left the mine that night. Hidden in the control center was a stock of supplies that would last weeks. They'd patched up Heather's back, and her arm, and they'd waited for the cavalry. Heather got in touch with the FBI.

The FBI had gotten the real version of the events. And then they'd fabricated the story that everyone else got, which was that a gang of bikers had tried to take advantage of a fire to rescue one of their own. They had then been stopped by the local sheriff and some responsible citizens. Their bodies were taken by the FBI, and all their human victims cremated. Heather, Susan, and Alice were the only three left, and they all had the same story. Why wouldn't anyone believe them?

Neat and tidy. It was heroic, and sexy, and got press throughout the country. Heather went on four different talk shows.

Conquest had recovered, appointed an interim mayor, and started to rebuild, flush with insurance money. Susan had inherited ownership of the mine, the historical village, and property all around the town. Overnight, she'd become the most powerful person in Conquest.

"How are you?" asked Susan.

"I'm okay," said Heather. "Busy as hell. Still understaffed."

"No I mean, like, are you *okay*?" asked Susan.

"As good as I can be," said Heather. "Being busy helps. I've also, been talking to someone, and I think that's helped."

"If you ever need to talk, and not have to worry about, you know, spilling the beans," said Susan. "I'm here."

"Have you spoken to Alice?" asked Heather.

"When I've had a chance, but between the business, and the baby, and everything," said Susan. "It's hard to find time to be a person. She's out in Seattle now, on vacation."

The baby started crying from the other room, and Susan smiled a patient smile.

"I should get back to work anyway," said Heather. "I'll let you take care of little Andrew."

"I'll try to stay in touch," said Susan. "I promise." Heather left with a wave.

Susan returned to Andrew's side, and comforted him. She held him as he cried.

She studied his face, its familiar shape. It showed no sign of changing.

She held him as he cried.

Acknowledgments

Thank you to Josiah Davis, for his help with the book. To my team of beta readers: Andrew, Matt, Yousef, Megan. To my wife, for the neverending support. And thank you, for reading.

About the Author

Robbie Dorman believes in horror. Conquest is his first novel. When not writing, he's podcasting, playing video games, or petting cats. He lives in Texas with his wife, Kim.

You can follow Robbie on Twitter @robbiedorman

Subscribe to his newsletter at robbiedorman.com/newsletter